"You're the new owner?"

"What's the matter, Becca? Did you think I was always going to be a rodeo bum?"

The scorn in his voice made her shock turn to anger. "Yes. Once a rodeo man, always a rodeo man is what you told me. Was there any reason for me to think otherwise?"

Becca studied him. His eyes were the same bright blue, but in the nine years that had passed since she'd seen him, they'd taken on an expression that should have belonged to an old man.

His eyes softened as he watched her. "You've changed, too, Becca."

"I grew up, Grady," she said, turning to leave.

"I can see that. Where are you going?"

He put his hand on her arm. The touch was shockingly intimate.

She stepped away. She knew she should tell him the truth now. All of it.

Her throat tightened as she thought of her daughter. Her daughter—and Grady's.

Dear Reader,

Summer's in full sizzle, and so are the romances in this month's Intimate Moments selections, starting with *Badge of Honor*, the latest in Justine Davis's TRINITY STREET WEST miniseries. For everyone who's been waiting for Chief Miguel de los Reyes to finally fall in love, I have good news. The wait is over! Hurry out to buy this one—but don't drive so fast you get stopped for speeding. Unless, of course, you're pulled over by an officer like Miguel!

Suzanne Brockmann is continuing her TALL, DARK AND DANGEROUS miniseries—featuring irresistible navy SEALs as heroes—with *Everyday, Average Jones*. Of course, there's nothing everyday about this guy. I only wish there were, because then I might meet a man like him myself. Margaret Watson takes us to CAMERON, UTAH, for a new miniseries, beginning with *Rodeo Man*. The title alone should draw you to this one. And we round out the month with new books by Marcia Evanick, who offers the very moving *A Father's Promise*, and two books bearing some of our new thematic flashes. Ingrid Weaver's *Engaging Sam* is a MEN IN BLUE title, and brand-new author Shelley Cooper's *Major Dad* is a CONVENIENTLY WED book.

Enjoy all six—then come back next month, because we've got some of the best romance around *every* month, right here in Silhouette Intimate Moments.

Yours,

Leslie J. Wainger
Executive Senior Editor

Please address questions and book requests to:
Silhouette Reader Service
U.S.: 3010 Walden Ave., P.O. Box 1325, Buffalo, NY 14269
Canadian: P.O. Box 609, Fort Erie, Ont. L2A 5X3

RODEO MAN

MARGARET WATSON

Silhouette® INTIMATE™ MOMENTS®

Published by Silhouette Books

America's Publisher of Contemporary Romance

SILHOUETTE BOOKS

ISBN 0-373-07873-0

RODEO MAN

Copyright © 1998 by Margaret Watson

Printed in U.S.A.

Books by Margaret Watson

Silhouette Intimate Moments

An Innocent Man #636
An Honorable Man #708
To Save His Child #750
The Dark Side of the Moon #779
*Rodeo Man #873

*Cameron, Utah

MARGARET WATSON

From the time she learned to read, Margaret could usually be found with her nose in a book. Her lifelong passion for reading led to her interest in writing, and now she's happily writing exactly the kind of stories she likes to read. Margaret is a veterinarian who lives in the Chicago suburbs with her husband and their three daughters. In her spare time she enjoys in-line skating, birding and spending time with her family. Readers can write to Margaret at P.O. Box 2333, Naperville, IL, 60567-2333.

For Karen. Thanks for a lifetime of friendship and sharing. I can't wait to see what we do with the next thirty-five years, but I'm counting on your sense of adventure!

Thanks to Kathy Lechner for her help with the horses.

Prologue

"There's someone else, Grady."

Becca Johnson gripped the phone more tightly in her hand, praying that Grady would see through her lie. Praying that he would say the words she needed to hear, *I'm coming home.*

But all she heard on the other end of the telephone line was a heavy silence. A silence that vibrated through the fabric of her lie, until she opened her mouth to tell him the truth.

Before she could speak, Grady said, "That's too bad, honey. I'm gonna miss you. But it's probably for the best. You don't need any rodeo man sniffing around you once every three or four months. You need someone you can count on, someone to be there for you every day."

You could be there for me. I want to count on you, she wanted to cry. But she didn't. Holding the phone so tightly she thought she might break it, she said, "I'm glad you understand. No hard feelings, right?"

She heard his swallow in the silence. "Right. No hard feelings. You take care, now."

The careful click as he hung up the phone seemed to fill

the room around her as it echoed in her head. Why had he just accepted what she'd said? Didn't Grady Farrell know she needed *him*? Couldn't he see that she loved him, no matter what she said?

Staring at the receiver still gripped in her hand, Becca felt her stomach twist and tighten. She had made a mistake. She shouldn't have lied, shouldn't have played such a stupid trick to make Grady come home. She should have known it would blow up in her face.

Replacing the receiver carefully in its cradle, she sank down into a chair. It would be all right, she told herself. Grady would call again in a few months, like he always did, and she could apologize to him then. It wouldn't matter that she'd be away at college. Her parents would give him her phone number. And if they wouldn't, she could track him down herself. She had a schedule of the rodeo circuit. She could figure out where he'd be and when. She would just keep making phone calls until she found him.

Her stomach churned again, and Becca took a deep breath and willed the nausea away. It must be the tension of not knowing where she stood with Grady, she thought wearily as she pressed a hand to her abdomen. This was the second time in as many days that she'd felt sick to her stomach.

Or maybe it was just thinking about Grady and wondering what he was going to do. Closing her eyes, she swallowed around the lump in her throat. That was enough to make any-one sick.

Becca flopped more deeply into the chair. It was the first of September, and she would be starting her second year of college soon. Things would work out with Grady, she told herself bravely. He'd call in a couple of months like nothing had happened, and she'd tell him then that she'd lied. That there never would be anyone else but him.

Things would work out. They had to.

Chapter 1

Dr. Rebecca Johnson leaned against the side of the stall and waited for the fresh-faced young man to slip a halter over the head of the horse.

"The new owner is supposed to be here sometime this week." The ranch hand tossed her a grin over his shoulder as he buckled the strap behind the horse's ears. "He won the ranch playing poker, you know."

"That was the rumor," Becca replied. "But you know how rumors get started. Sy probably just sold the place."

"He didn't." The young man shook his head earnestly. "One of the guys heard him and the ranch manager talking. Yelling, really." He gave her another grin. "Sy said he lost the ranch playing poker, and there wasn't anything he could do about it since there were witnesses. Pretty cool, huh?"

"Yeah, pretty cool."

Becca moved to the horse's head and expertly opened its mouth. This ranch hand was only a few years younger than she was, but she felt ancient in comparison. To throw away a piece of land, a business that wasn't just a home but represented security and stability, on the turn of a deck of cards, seemed like the utmost in folly to her.

Pulling a long instrument out of the back pocket of her jeans, she inserted it into the horse's mouth and began filing its teeth. All the horses on the Flying W Ranch were due to have their teeth floated this month. It wasn't the most exciting part of being a veterinarian, but it was necessary. Becca worked methodically as she listened to the ranch hand assigned to assist her.

The young man chattered as she worked, and much of what he said echoed of the speculation that had been circulating around Cameron, Utah, since the rumors had started. No one knew who the new owner was or the details of how he'd come to own the Flying W. But the poker-game story had been one of the most popular.

Stepping back from the bay horse in front of her, Becca watched as the animal shook his head and flattened his ears as he snorted at her. Smiling, she reached out a hand and scratched his nose. "You go ahead and tell me about it, fella. I know you're a tough guy."

Her assistant ran his hand down the horse's neck. "Beau here is a sweetie. He's one of my favorites."

"Mine, too," Becca admitted, letting her hand linger on Beau's head. "That's why I started with him."

She bent down and picked up her bag, placing the long file in a disinfectant solution. "Let's get the next one done."

Two hours later she dropped the file back into her bag, then straightened. "Thanks for your help, Randy."

The young hand smiled shyly at her. "You're welcome, Doc. I liked helping. You have a nice way with the horses."

"I like working with them." Stepping out of the stall, she bent to pick up the stack of records piled on the floor. "You go ahead and get back to work. I know you have a lot of things to do, and I'm just going to make sure there's nothing else that needs to be done today."

Becca watched the young man walk out of the barn into

the sunlight, then slid onto the floor and stretched her legs out in front of her. It would take a little time to record what she'd done on all the charts, and she wasn't likely to be disturbed here in the barn. Picking up the first record, she began writing.

She'd been working for a while when the sound of voices in the distance drifted into the barn. The voices got closer, and she wrote a little faster on the last chart as she recognized the voice of the ranch foreman. She needed to get back to town on time this afternoon, and if the foreman caught her in the barn, he'd probably think of several other things the horses needed.

Flipping the last chart closed, she scraped the stack of them into her arms and stood up, grabbing her bag. But as she moved down the center aisle of the barn, she realized she was too late. The foreman and whoever he was talking to were at the door already.

Becca plastered a smile on her face as she walked a little faster. If she simply said hello and kept moving, she could be in her truck before the foreman realized she was leaving.

"Hi, Doc." The foreman tipped his hat as he walked into the barn, then turned to the other man and said, "This is Doc Johnson. She's our vet."

Becca opened her mouth to say hello, then the other man stepped into the barn and out of the bright sunlight that had obscured his face. The files tumbled out of her suddenly nerveless hands as she stared at him.

"Becca?" the man whispered. Shock filled his eyes.

"Grady?" Horrified, she stared at the face that had haunted her dreams, day and night, for the past nine years. "What are you doing here?" she blurted out.

"What am I doing here?" His gaze traveled down her body, then back to her face. His eyes hardened. "I own this ranch."

"*You're* the new owner?"

"What's the matter, Becca? Did you think I was going to be a rodeo bum for the rest of my life?"

The scorn in his voice was enough to turn her shock to anger. "Yes, that's exactly what I thought. Once a rodeo man, always a rodeo man is what you told me." She gripped her bag more tightly and straightened her back, fighting down a wave of emotion. "Was there any reason for me to think otherwise?"

Grady opened his mouth to answer, then seemed to remember they weren't alone. Turning to the man standing next to him, he said, "Get lost, Tucker. I'll talk to you later."

Shooting her a speculative look, Tucker turned and headed toward one of the other buildings. Becca watched him until he was out of earshot, then slowly turned back to face Grady.

His eyes were the same bright blue, and his hair was just as black as she remembered. The only difference was that now it was cut short instead of hanging over his collar. But the nine years that had passed since she'd seen him had carved their mark on his face. The lines in his face were now deep creases scoring his cheeks. There were lines around his mouth, too. But his eyes looked like they'd aged far more than nine years. Grady had always been a lot more than two years older than her, in every way that counted. Now his eyes held an expression that should have belonged to an old man.

His eyes softened as he watched her. "You've changed, too, Becca."

She didn't care that he'd caught her staring. "I grew up, Grady."

"I can see that you did."

His gaze moved down her body again, lingering at the lush curves that weren't quite hidden by her T-shirt and denim jeans. Suddenly his eyes weren't soft anymore. They blazed with a fire she remembered all too well. It was the fire that had kept her awake more nights than she could count. Forcing herself not to cross her arms over her chest, she waited until his eyes returned to her face. "And my name isn't 'Becca' anymore. I go by 'Rebecca' now. Or 'Doc.'"

"So you're the vet for the Flying W. I had no idea you wanted to be a vet."

"You never had any idea what I wanted. You never asked."

The fire in his eyes went out, replaced by a flicker of pain. It was quickly extinguished. "I made some mistakes. You were one of them."

She thought she had made herself immune to pain from Grady Farrell. She was wrong. Bending down to pick up the files she'd dropped, she bit her lip to keep from answering. Nothing good could come of rehashing the past with Grady. It had taken her too long to get over him. She wasn't about to give him another chance to crush her heart.

As she moved past him, he put his hand on her arm. "Where are you going?"

Becca stared down at his hand. His fingers curled around her arm, holding her lightly, but she was unable to move. The touch of his hand on her bare skin was shockingly intimate. Each of his fingers burned into her, imprinting on her the strength in his hand, the heat that flowed from it. And the way her heart fluttered in her chest at his touch.

Swallowing hard, ignoring the heat that rushed through her, she stepped away from him. As his hand fell away, she had a moment of illogical hope that he wouldn't let her go. *Right, Becca,* she said to herself acidly. *Just like he wouldn't let you go nine years ago.*

"I'm leaving," she replied, her voice surprisingly level. "I finished my job here and I have other things to do."

"It's been nine years, Becca. Surely you can spare a few minutes."

He spoke quietly, all the mockery gone from his voice.

The edge of longing she saw in his eyes took the bite out of her anger. It also made her back up another step. She didn't want to feel anything but anger for Grady Farrell. She couldn't afford to.

"For what? To reminisce?" She tried to keep the anguish out of her voice. "You know I'm a vet, and I know you just won the Flying W in a poker game. Doesn't that about sum it up?"

"How do you know how I got this ranch?" he asked sharply.

"Cameron, Utah, is a small town," she replied. "You of all people should know how small towns are. Nothing is a secret."

"Did Sy Ames tell you that?" Grady leaned closer, pinning her to the spot with an intense look.

"I don't talk to Sy." Her answer came out more clipped than she intended, and she tried to soften it. "I don't have to. The foreman, Jimmy Tucker, lets me know what has to be done."

"Is Tucker saying that Sy lost the Flying W in a poker game?"

"I have no idea what he's saying about the ranch. I don't gossip with him."

"Then who do you gossip with?"

Becca felt her face coloring. "I'm just repeating what everyone in Cameron is saying. Why is it such a big deal, anyway?"

"I guess it isn't." He spoke easily, but she saw that his eyes were guarded and careful. "What were you doing here today?"

"Floating teeth." She nodded down the aisle of the barn. "All the horses were due."

He leaned back against a stall and folded his arms across his chest. "So you became a vet. Why aren't you back home, practicing in Trinity?"

Becca fought down the spurt of fear and willed her face into unreadable lines. "Why aren't you back home running your father's ranch in Trinity?"

His face darkened, but after a moment reluctant admiration filled his eyes. "You've grown up in more ways than one, Becca."

"That happens." She shifted the charts in her arms and moved toward the door, desperate to get away. Seeing Grady again was bringing back all sorts of feelings she wanted to forget. And it was bringing back the guilt she thought she'd successfully buried.

"I'm sure I'll see you around." She paused, and in spite of herself her voice softened. "I'm happy for you, Grady. Happy that you have this ranch, that you can settle down."

"I never thought this would be what I wanted. I'm still not sure. I never wanted any obligations, any restrictions." He watched her steadily as he spoke. "You know me. I believe in traveling light."

Grady had never wanted to be tied down, by anyone or anything. An ache of regret moved through her again, a dull, familiar, nine-year-old wound. "I'm happy that you at least have a chance to see what restrictions feel like."

As she turned to go, Grady touched her arm again. "Are you, Becca?" His low voice seemed to bore deep inside her, to find that place that always responded to him, and to no one but him. "Are you really? What would have happened nine years ago if I'd had this ranch?"

Pain tore through her, a pain composed of regret, yearning and bitterness. But it was a pain she couldn't share with him. Not now, maybe not ever. "Don't ask me that, Grady. It doesn't make any difference. I can't go back and change the past, and neither can you."

Her arms trembled, and one of the charts slipped to the floor. She bent to pick it up, but Grady was there before her. But instead of picking up the chart, he stared at her left hand, then reached out and took it in his.

All she could think of was that his hand still felt the same. Hard and callused, but warm and full of life. And when his fingers curled over hers, she couldn't stop the trip of her heart or the flutter of her pulse.

Still holding her hand, Grady stared at it for a long time before he looked up at her. "Did you marry him, Becca?" His voice was almost a whisper in the quiet barn.

"Who?" She couldn't draw air into her lungs. She couldn't feel anything but the way his skin felt on hers, the way her hand ached to curl around his and hang on.

"The 'someone else.' The last time I called, you told me there was someone else."

She stared at their joined hands, remembering every word of her foolish lie and the consequences of it. She'd been such a child back then. Her lie had changed her life and Grady's forever. And she knew she should tell him the truth. All of it.

Swallowing hard, she drew her hand away and stood up. She couldn't. At least not today. Someday, she promised herself. He had a right to know, and someday she would tell him. But not today.

She might have been a child nine years ago, but now she was an adult. She'd chosen her path then and she would deal with the consequences now.

"I'm not married, Grady." She wanted to touch him again, to take his hand and lose herself in his strength and warmth. But she tightened her grip on her charts and her bag instead. No matter what her body was telling her, Grady Farrell would be nothing but trouble. "And now I do have to get back to town."

"It's been a long time, Becca. If there's no one waiting for you, what's the rush?" Heat filled his eyes as he watched her.

She closed her eyes, knowing he would see the pain in them, and fought down the need to tell him the truth. That someone *was* waiting for her.

It wasn't just her own life she was playing with, she reminded herself. And opened her eyes. "I do have other clients," she said, striving for a businesslike tone.

"Of course." Grady watched her coolly, the heat gone from his eyes. "I understand." He rose slowly and reached out to pluck the stack of files from her arms as they headed toward the door of the barn. "Do you own the practice?"

"I own part of it," she said, glancing sideways at him, wondering at the sudden change in his sudden coolness. "I have two partners."

"Do all of you come here to the Flying W?"

She hesitated, but realized he could find out the truth easily. "No, I'm the Flying W's vet. Unless there's an emergency at night."

"I suppose you take turns with that."

She didn't, but she wasn't about to tell him that. She didn't want to get into the reason she didn't do emergency calls.

"How often are you out here?"

"It depends on what needs to be done." Before she could describe her usual schedule, she realized what he might be getting at. "If you'd prefer that another one of the vets come out here from now on, I'm sure we can work it out," she added stiffly.

Grady stopped in his tracks and turned to face her. "That's not what I meant. I'm sure you're a damn good vet. I was just trying to make conversation."

She glanced at his face, at the hard angles and deep lines scored into his cheeks, at the hidden depths of his eyes. Grady Farrell looked like a man comfortable with silence. He didn't look like the kind of man who ever felt the need to make conversation. "What is it that you want, Grady?"

He stared at her for a long time. Nine years ago she had been able to read every expression on his face, every nuance of what he was thinking. Now his face was that of a stranger, closed and hard.

Finally he turned and headed for her truck. He walked slowly as he said, "Just passing the time, that's all." He gave her a humorless smile. "I'm finding out all sorts of interesting things about my new town today, aren't I?"

When they got to her truck, she loaded her bag into the back, then reached for the stack of charts Grady carried. After a momentary hesitation, he handed them to her. After she replaced them in her portable file, she took a deep breath before she turned to him.

"Goodbye, Grady."

Instead of answering her, he leaned against the side of her truck and crossed his arms over his chest. "Tell me why you came to Cameron."

She raised her eyebrows as she stared back at him, hoping to hide the surge of fear at his words. She couldn't tell him the real reason. Not unless she was willing to tell him all of the truth. "The veterinary practice here was looking for an associate," she said lightly. "I liked the area, so I applied for the job. I bought into the practice a year later."

"There was another reason, wasn't there?"

Becca stared at him, appalled. Had he read her mind? "What do you mean?"

"When Sy mentioned that his ranch was in Cameron, the name sounded familiar. As if I'd heard it before. Didn't you talk about Cameron once, a long time ago?"

"I doubt it, Grady." Her hands gripped the edge of the truck behind her back, steadying her. Reminding her what was at stake. She would have to give him part of the truth. "I visited my friend Laura Weston here in Cameron while I was in college, but I doubt if I told you. There's probably a lot I've forgotten."

The lie came out easily, and she dragged in a breath. "Maybe you were in a rodeo once in Cameron."

"I would have remembered that."

His words lanced through her, and the pain gave her the strength she'd been reaching for. "Of course you would have. God forbid something should be more important than a rodeo. That's one thing I haven't forgotten."

"You always did see things in black and white, didn't you?"

Not anymore, she wanted to say. Instead, she replied stiffly, "There's nothing wrong with that."

Instead of answering, he reached out and touched her short hair. "You cut your hair."

She resisted the impulse to run her hand through her curls. "It's more practical to keep it short." She would never tell him how she'd cried as she cut her hair, and how its loss had pierced her heart.

"I suppose it would be easier."

He fell silent, and she wondered if his thoughts were anything like hers. She wondered if he was remembering the times he'd buried his face in her long waves, telling her he could spend the rest of his life just breathing in the fragrance of her hair. Or the times her hair had wrapped itself around both of them, binding them together more tightly than any vow or promise.

Deliberately she let go of the truck and rubbed her hands along the legs of her jeans. "You look good, Grady."

A self-mocking smile flickered over his face, then disappeared. "Thanks, Becca."

"I told you, I go by 'Rebecca' now." Every time he called her 'Becca' was another small stab at her soul.

"Surely old friends are allowed a little leeway?"

She turned abruptly and climbed into her truck. "If you'd rather, you can call me 'Doc' like everyone else on the Flying W. I'll be seeing you, Grady. I have to get going."

Before he could answer, she slammed the door and turned on the ignition. Revving the engine, she turned the truck and headed down the driveway, skidding on the gravel under her tires.

Take it easy, she warned herself as she eased her foot off the accelerator. The last thing she needed was for Grady to think she was running away from him.

Even though that was exactly what she was doing.

She didn't look in her rearview mirror until she was at the end of the driveway. Just before she turned onto the highway, she glanced back toward the barn. Grady was still standing where she'd left him, staring toward her truck. As she accelerated onto the road, a cloud of dust billowed up around her, and when it had cleared, Grady was gone.

The drive back to Cameron seemed endless. Her thoughts chased themselves in her head like squirrels in a cage, each one more desperate than the last. One of her partners could come out to the Flying W from now on. She wouldn't have to see Grady again.

That's stupid, she told herself fiercely. Cameron was a small town. She'd run into him every time she turned around. Panic filled her at the thought, and her mind raced ahead. She would have to leave Cameron and find a job somewhere else. A veterinarian could always find work.

As she approached the edge of the small town, she gripped the steering wheel more tightly. The first thing she had to do was calm down. She couldn't go to Laura's house in this state of mind, even though they'd been friends since their freshman year in college. Forcing herself to take deep breaths, she put Grady out of her mind as she pulled up to the curb of the small blue house.

Becca took one last breath as she deliberately uncurled her hands from the steering wheel, then she got out of the truck. Plastering a smile on her face, she headed up the sidewalk.

Before she was halfway to the door, it flew open and a girl came running down the walk. Her two black braids flopped wildly on her back as she threw herself into Becca's arms.

"Mommy! Laura said you might be late, but I knew you would be here on time."

Becca's arms closed around the girl as she held her in a fierce embrace. "Of course I'm here on time. You know I'll always be here for you, sweetheart."

And she would be. Cassie would be the most secure, most loved child in the world. Becca hadn't been able to give her everything, but she could give her that. She'd made the vow the day Cassie was born and hadn't broken it yet. Becca felt her throat swell as she hugged her daughter more tightly. Her daughter and Grady's.

Chapter 2

Grady watched the dust swirl around Becca's truck as she sped down the driveway. The truck skidded once, then righted itself, and he felt his mouth curl in a grim smile. She was in a hell of a hurry to get to that next client.

Becca. The bitterness and anger he'd thought he'd banished once and for all bubbled up inside him like molten lava, scorching every part of him. He'd thought they shared something special, something unique. Something that would last forever. And then she'd thrown it away with her casual words.

There's someone else, Grady.

He'd hated her for a long time. Hated her with a heat and a fervor that equaled the passion he used to feel for her. And like a stubborn child he'd refused to call her again. Then he'd had the accident five years ago. He'd been in a hospital for months, his leg broken and all the ligaments in his knee ripped to shreds. He'd known it was the end of his rodeo career, and nothing mattered anymore. Becca became just a distant memory, like his father's ranch and the rodeo and everything else that used to matter to him.

Until today.

Until he'd walked into a barn and seen her walking out. And the fire that ignited inside him when he'd looked at her had nothing to do with hatred.

Turning abruptly, he headed back to the house. He'd been burned before and had no intention of playing with fire again. "Tucker," he called as the screen door banged behind him. "Where are you?"

The foreman emerged from the office. "Right here, Mr. Farrell."

"Let's finish that tour," Grady said.

They were heading toward the barn again before the foreman spoke. "So you know Doc Johnson?"

The tone was casual, but Grady wasn't fooled. Everyone on the ranch would hear about his encounter with Becca before the day was out. "We grew up in the same town."

His tone didn't encourage conversation, but Tucker wasn't deterred. "What a coincidence. Did you know she was the vet here in Cameron?"

Grady shrugged, forcing himself to act nonchalant. "I had no idea."

The foreman glanced over at him. "Sounded like you both were real surprised. Doc Johnson's a good vet. Sy always made sure we asked for her when we needed a doc. Always made it a point to be here when she came out, too."

Grady thought about Sy Ames and felt his mouth tighten. Could Becca be involved with him? The thought disturbed him. Remembering the curious blankness of Sy's eyes and the hatred that raged in them when he thought no one was watching, Grady wondered what Becca saw in the man.

It didn't matter, he told himself. He wasn't responsible for Becca.

"'Course, everyone in Cameron likes Doc Johnson," the foreman continued, apparently oblivious to Grady's ominous silence. "She and her—"

"That's enough, Tucker." Grady cut him off with a slashing motion through the air. "I want to hear about my ranch, not Dr. Johnson."

Tucker threw him an injured look. "I thought you'd be interested in her, since you grew up together and all."

"I'm perfectly capable of finding out all I need to know about her myself. Why don't you tell me about the cattle, instead?"

A few hours later, Grady leaned against the fence of one of the corrals and looked out over the pasture tucked into the curve of low green hills. *His pasture.* The thought of being tied down to a piece of land didn't stir panic as it would have a few years ago. Now it felt good. Hell, it felt more than good. It felt right.

He looked at the red cliffs in the distance towering over his pastures, the soft rock eroded by the wind and rain into a thousand different, fantastic shapes. Their contrast with the green pastures and the stands of pine and aspen trees that bordered them made this a magical place, one of awesome natural beauty. The thought flashed into his mind that he was only missing one thing. An image of Becca danced in front of his eyes, but he crushed it without a second thought. He didn't need the complications of a relationship. He wasn't missing a thing. Life was damn near perfect just the way it was.

Grady slowed his truck as he drove past the sign in front of the small building on the outskirts of town. Cameron Veterinary Hospital was painted in white letters on a black piece of wood. Even though the building was small, everything about it was scrupulously neat and clean. Spotting Becca's truck parked to the side of the building, he impulsively swung into the parking lot and killed the engine.

It had been five days since he'd seen Becca at the Flying W. Not that he was counting, he reminded himself. But in order to get the ranch up to speed as soon as possible, he needed to discuss the health of his cattle herd with the ranch's vet. And now was as good a time as any.

Walking in the front door, he nodded to the receptionist. "I need to see Dr. Johnson."

The woman gave him a perky smile. "Did you have an appointment?"

"No." He looked around the empty room. "Is that going to be a problem?"

"I'm sure Dr. Johnson will be able to work you in. Is this concerning one of your animals?"

"It's concerning my herd. I'm Grady Farrell, the new owner of the Flying W."

The woman's eyes lit with interest. "Why, how nice to meet you, Mr. Farrell. We've all been wondering about you."

He had no doubt of that. He remembered life in a small town too well. "I need to know how my herd is doing before I can make any decisions." He smiled at the woman. "You know how it is with a new property."

She fluttered back at him. "You must be terribly busy getting settled, but everyone in Cameron would love to meet you. There's going to be a rodeo and fair on the Fourth of July in a couple of weeks. You should join us. Practically the whole town will be there."

Grady froze at the word *rodeo,* but long practice kept his face impassive. "Thanks," he said, forcing himself to give the receptionist another lazy grin. "I'll put it on my calendar."

He took a seat and picked up a magazine. He could feel the receptionist's eyes on him, but he didn't look up. After a while the woman turned away and pulled out a file drawer.

From around the corner he heard Becca's voice. It was muffled, but there was no mistaking it. Then a door must have opened, because her words became much louder.

"I'm sorry, Mr. Ames, but you obviously have the wrong impression." The chill in her voice would have put frost on the walls.

"I don't think so, Rebecca. I can call you 'Rebecca,' can't I?"

"You can call me 'Dr. Johnson,' just like the rest of my clients."

"But I'm no longer a client. I don't own the Flying W anymore."

Even from the waiting room Grady could hear the venom in Sy Ames's voice.

If Becca heard it, she chose to ignore it. "Then we don't really have anything to discuss, do we?" She walked around the corner, and Grady saw the tension and anger in her face. "You can settle up your account with Stella, Mr. Ames. Good luck to you in your future endeavors."

She pushed past him and disappeared into the back. Ames stood staring after her for a long time, then turned to the receptionist. The hatred that Grady had noticed once before flashed in the stocky man's eyes for a moment, then his face was carefully blank again.

Stella greeted Ames with another perky smile, but it faltered after a moment. When the printer finally finished his bill and she handed it to him, Grady saw her hand shaking. Ames took the piece of paper and slammed out the door.

The receptionist took a deep breath and turned to Grady, her eyes troubled. "I'll go and see if Dr. Johnson can talk to you now."

Grady nodded once, the knot of tension in his gut slowly easing. He hadn't known that Sy Ames was back in town. He twisted around to look out the window at the parking lot, but Sy was gone. When he turned back to the room, the receptionist was behind the front desk again.

"You can talk to Dr. Johnson now."

He followed the receptionist into a small room, and she shut the door behind him. He supposed it was a typical veterinary examination room, and he let his gaze wander over the instruments on the counter. They were neatly arranged and spotless, just like the rest of the clinic.

The door opened, and Becca slipped into the room. "What do you want, Grady?"

Her voice was filled with tension, and she didn't meet his eyes. Instead, she stared down at the file in front of her.

"I wanted to talk to you about my herd. Find out if it's healthy, what kinds of problems it's had. What needs to be done."

She continued to stare down at the file, and he studied the crown of her head. Her short blond hair was streaked from the sun and curled around her face. He wondered if it still felt like silk, and he had to stop himself from reaching out to find out. Clenching his hands into fists, he stepped back from the table so he could see her face.

Slowly she looked up at him. Her gray eyes were huge in her face, full of an emotion he couldn't identify. Finally she said, "Why are you here, Grady?"

"Just like I told you. I need to discuss my animals with you."

"That's not a spur-of-the-moment discussion. I need to get a lot of paperwork and files together, then we need to sit down together for a while."

"I'm free right now."

"I'm not." She didn't glance at her watch, but when she picked up the chart, he saw her hand tremble. "Why don't we make an appointment for another time?"

"Was it Ames?" he asked bluntly.

"What do you mean?"

"He upset you, didn't he?"

"It's the nature of the business," she said carefully. "Not every client is going to be happy every time."

"He wasn't here on business, was he?"

Her eyes darkened. "How do you know that?"

"It's pretty obvious, Becca. He doesn't own the Flying W anymore. He doesn't have any animals, so why would he need a vet?"

"Maybe he was here to settle up his account."

Grady allowed himself a thin smile. "You've forgotten that I know Sy Ames. Voluntarily paying a bill is the last thing he would do."

He watched her gather herself. "It doesn't matter why he was here. He's gone now, and I don't expect him to be back."

"Come have some lunch with me," he found himself saying. "We can share horror stories about Sy Ames."

She gave him a shaky smile, but shook her head. "I can't. I'm on call over lunch. I have to stay here."

"Fine. I'll be right back."

Without waiting for her to answer, he opened the door to the exam room and walked out of the clinic. It didn't bother him that Becca was upset, he told himself, but he wanted to discuss his animals with her. He ignored the fact that he hadn't even thought about discussing his herd until he'd seen the sign for her clinic on the way into town. Suddenly, discussing his cattle was at the top of his list of things to do.

Fifteen minutes later he was back, carrying a large bag and two containers of soda. The door was locked, but when he knocked the receptionist opened the door.

"I'm sorry, Mr. Farrell. The clinic is closed until one-thirty."

"I brought lunch for Dr. Johnson. I thought it would make our discussion a little more pleasant. And besides, she seemed like she needed a break."

Stella studied him for a moment, then opened the door. "You're right. I don't care for that Mr. Ames." She hesitated as if she was going to say more, then turned away. "She's in her office. You go right on back."

Grady paused in the door of Becca's office and watched her. The desk was covered with charts and notes scribbled on scraps of paper, and she was deep in thought as she wrote on one of the charts. A flannel shirt hung on the back of her chair, and the T-shirt she wore clung to her curves. Curves she certainly hadn't had nine years ago. He let his gaze linger on her as she wrote, and he felt himself stirring. Nine years ago, when she was nineteen, she had been slim as a boy with small breasts and slender hips. She was still slender, but she had the body of a woman now. His hands ached to feel the weight of her breasts and trace the curve of her hips.

Would her skin be as soft, as warm as he remembered? And would her hair have the same scent, the scent that had haunted his dreams for years?

He wasn't going to find out, he reminded himself harshly. He might be curious about Becca, but that was all it was. He wasn't interested in her. Not after what she'd done to him. And even if he was interested, he didn't have time to get involved with anyone right now.

He must have moved because she looked up with a start. "Grady," she gasped. "What are you doing here?"

"I told you I'd bring lunch." He held up the bag.

"I don't have time to eat."

"That's not the Becca I remember," he teased. "You used to eat anything that wasn't nailed down."

A shadow passed over her face, and she pushed her chair farther away from him. "Things change, Grady. I'm not hungry and I have a lot to do today."

"You can spare a few minutes for lunch."

She sighed as she threw her pencil onto her desk. "You're still as stubborn as a Missouri mule, aren't you?"

"Nope," he said, pulling a chair away from one of the other desks and sitting down. "I'm worse. Now, are you going to eat?"

Her mouth curved briefly in a reluctant smile, and she reached for the bag. "It depends on what's in here."

Grady stilled as she pulled the sandwich and chips out of the bag, suddenly realizing what he had done. He wanted to snatch the bag away from her, but it was too late.

She stared at the roast-beef-and-cheese sandwich for a long time, and when she looked up at him her eyes had softened. "You remembered what kind of sandwich I like."

He shrugged, trying to act nonchalant. "Amazing what you can pull out of your subconscious, isn't it?"

Becca didn't answer. Her gaze was fixed on the bag of chips. "And the chips, too," she whispered.

He had chosen her favorite brand of barbecue corn chips. "They didn't have a very big selection at the restaurant," he muttered.

She reached out and touched the bag that contained the chips. As he watched her fingers linger on the foil, unbidden memories of picnics they had shared in the past came surging back. Of Becca touching him, her fingers skimming over his skin with a touch that burned all the way down to his soul.

When her eyes met his, he realized that she was thinking about the same thing. Her gray eyes were hot and dark, full of memories he wanted only to forget.

"So tell me about Ames," he said, his voice harsh and too loud.

"Ames?" Becca's voice was low and throaty in the silence of the office. He heard the confusion in her tone, then watched as she realized what he'd said. She looked down for a moment, and when she looked back at him the heat had disappeared from her eyes, leaving them cool and closed. "What about him?"

"Are you seeing him?"

"What?" Her shock was clear, and he found himself relaxing back into his chair, unclenching hands he hadn't even realized he'd fisted.

"You know, dating him."

"Not that it's any of your business who I'm dating, but no. I avoid Sy Ames whenever possible."

"That's not what I heard."

She stared at him for a moment, then said, "You should know better than to listen to gossip, Grady."

He ignored the relief that flooded him. "Then is he bothering you?"

"I imagine Sy will be leaving Cameron now that he doesn't own the Flying W."

"I don't give a damn about his travel plans. I asked if he was bothering you."

"There's no need for you to be concerned about what happens between me and Sy Ames."

Her eyes flashed at him, but he ignored their warning. "I bought the Flying W from him. I have a right to know if there's going to be trouble."

"So you didn't win the ranch from him in a poker game."

He scowled at her. "Don't change the subject, Becca. Is Sy bothering you?"

She leaned back in her chair and watched him. "I fail to see how anything that happens between me and Sy is going to affect the Flying W."

"Damn it, Becca, don't dance around the question. Tell me what's going on between the two of you."

"I know more about most of the people in Cameron than I know about you, Grady," she said gently. "Why should I confide in you?"

He sighed and shoved his hand through his hair, feeling a twist of pain at her words. "You're right. But when I saw him in the clinic earlier, I wanted to tear his throat out. I don't like the idea of him harassing you."

Her eyes softened again. "Thank you for being concerned, Grady. But you have enough going on right now, and Sy will be leaving. It's nothing you have to worry about."

But he was going to worry about it anyway. "I'll tell you what. We'll have a swap of information. I'll tell you what you want to know about the ranch, and you tell me about Sy Ames."

She hesitated for a moment, then nodded. "That sounds fair. You go first."

A reluctant smile curved his mouth. "No way. You tell me about Sy first. He's the problem, not the ranch."

Studying his face, she finally smiled back. "You always were a better negotiator than me. All right. Sy it is."

Her smile faded, and she crossed her arms over her chest. He didn't miss the gesture, even though he was pretty sure it was an unconscious one. It told him all he needed to know about Sy Ames.

"Shoot," he said, his voice too curt.

"I didn't notice anything at first," she began, her gaze fixed on something in her mind. "I was flattered when he requested that I do all the veterinary work at the ranch, and I didn't pay attention to the fact that he was always around when I went out to the Flying W." She looked at him then and shrugged. "I guess I was pretty naive. One day there was no one else in the stable, and he tried to corner me in a stall. I told him in no uncertain terms to back off, and that was the last time he tried to touch me. But he was always there when I was treating one of his animals, watching. He gave me the creeps," she said frankly. "But as far as I know, being creepy isn't illegal."

"Do you really think he's going to leave Cameron?" Grady struggled to keep his voice level, to control the killing rage that welled up inside him.

"I don't know why he would stay. He didn't grow up here. He bought the Flying W about five years ago, and now that he doesn't have it anymore, what would hold him here?"

You. He didn't want to voice the thought. "Why did he come by here today?" he asked.

"He was asking me out," she replied, not meeting his eyes. "It doesn't matter since he's gone."

It mattered, Grady thought grimly, but he didn't say anything to Becca. Instead he shrugged, reaching for his sandwich.

"You owe me some information before you start eating," she reminded him.

He forced himself to flash her a grin. "I was hoping you'd forget."

"Not a chance, Farrell."

He set the sandwich down with a show of reluctance, delighted that she seemed to have put Ames out of her mind. "There is some truth to the rumor about the poker game."

"What happened?"

"I was in a poker game with Sy and a few other guys down near Las Vegas. I'd been doing some work for one of them, but I'd never met Sy. It was down to Sy and I, and the pot was pretty big. He was pretty confident that he was a winner, so he'd thrown in some IOUs. When I won, he couldn't cover them."

He wouldn't tell her that one of the other men had caught Sy cheating. Just like he wouldn't tell her about the hatred that had poured from Sy as he'd laid his cards on the table.

"So that's how you got the Flying W?"

"Not quite. I bought the ranch from him, fair and square. The money he owed me from the poker game made a nice down payment. But I kicked in more of my own money, and I took over a hefty mortgage."

"So Sy has nothing to complain about."

"Not a thing," he said flatly. "He got a good price for the ranch. Hell, I did him a favor. He would have lost the place completely in a couple of years."

"What do you mean?"

"I haven't had a chance to go over all the books, but he wasn't managing the Flying W very well. It should be making a lot more money than it has been."

"So Sy has no reason to hold a grudge against you."

"That's never stopped anyone in the past." He stood up from the chair, suddenly anxious to leave. He had been sitting here, talking to her like the past had never happened. For a moment she had been the Becca of nine years ago, a woman who would never lie to him, who always told him exactly what she thought. In another minute he would have been asking her advice. "Be careful of Sy, Becca. For as long as he's around."

Carefully she brushed the crumbs of the sandwich into a napkin. "I will. Thanks for telling me what happened with the ranch."

She leaned over to throw the napkin in a wastebasket, and the T-shirt pulled taut against her chest, outlining her breasts and the slender curve of her waist. Grady closed his eyes as a wave of desire crashed over him. *Forget it, buddy,* he told himself. Becca was the last woman on earth he intended to get involved with. And she had made it clear she felt the same way about him.

"Thanks for having lunch with me," he said as he was halfway out the door. "Let me know when we can discuss my herd."

"Goodbye, Grady." He heard her words as the door of the clinic clicked shut behind him. He was sure he only imagined the sadness in them.

Becca stood at the window and watched Grady leave, even though she told herself to get back to work. He had only stopped in to talk business with her, and that was the way she wanted it. Although they hadn't ended up talking about his herd at all.

Forcing herself to look away before his red truck pulled out of the parking lot, she sat down at her desk and pulled one of the patient files toward her. But the file swam in front of her eyes, and she finally shoved it away and left the clinic.

She had actually been enjoying spending time with Grady. For the brief time they'd been together, she had allowed herself to think only of Grady. There had even been a moment when desire for him had stirred inside her. Appalled with herself, guilty, shaken, she gripped the steering wheel more tightly and abruptly turned the truck down a side street.

Easing her foot off the accelerator, she automatically slowed down when she neared the park. Laura brought the kids here about this time every day during the summer, and Becca looked for Cassie's dark head as she drove slowly by.

Cassie was playing a game with several other girls and boys, and Becca smiled as she watched them run and yell. In spite of the long hours she'd had to work both in vet school and afterward, her daughter was a happy, well-adjusted child. Becca vowed fiercely to herself that nothing would change that.

What would happen when Cassie found out that her father was now living in Cameron? The panic that had been hovering over Becca all week enveloped her again, making her heart race and her hands tremble. How could she do that to Cassie? What would Grady say when she told him? Grady had always wanted to ''travel light'' through life. He'd told her so again just a few days ago. How would he feel about having a child? Would he be mad? Indifferent? Would his fury spill over and hurt Cassie, even accidentally?

Her thoughts tumbled over one another as she sped away from the park and headed out of town. Should she leave, sell her interest in the practice back to her partners and move? Should she tell Grady the truth? Should she lie, tell him that Cassie was someone else's child?

Grady had a right to know, her conscience reminded her. But whose rights were more important, Grady's or Cassie's? Swallowing a sob, she pulled off the road and buried her face in her hands.

Chapter 3

The next morning Becca stumbled into the clinic, her head aching and her eyes gritty from lack of sleep. She'd spent the night tossing and turning, and was still no closer to an answer.

"Good morning, Dr. Johnson," Stella chirped at her.

"Hi, Stella." Becca took a gulp from the cup of coffee she held and picked up her messages from the counter. Her eyes zeroed in on the paper that said "Flying W."

Scanning the message, which just said she needed to go out to the ranch right away, she laid it down as her heart began to pound. "What's going on at the Flying W?" she asked, trying to keep her voice steady.

"Dr. O'Connor has been out there most of the night," the receptionist answered. "One of their horses has colic."

"What happened?" she asked sharply.

Stella shrugged. "I have no idea. Dr. O'Connor just called and asked that you relieve him as soon as possible."

Becca shuffled through the rest of her messages and found nothing urgent. "Call him and tell him I'm on my way. Then you can call the rest of these people and tell them I had an emergency.''

Hurrying out to her truck, she drove carefully through the outskirts of town, then pressed the accelerator to the floor. When she got to the ranch, she jumped out of the truck almost before it had stopped and rushed into the barn.

Her partner stood in front of a stall, his arms resting on the top of the door. "Hi, Pat," she called, and he turned.

"Hi yourself, Rebecca." He gave her a smile, although his face was gray with fatigue. "I think he's going to be all right."

She looked at the horse who was standing quietly, his head hanging down, and realized with a pang that it was Beau. "What happened?"

Pat O'Connor shrugged. "Who knows? It was colic, but we couldn't figure out why." He detailed the medication the horse had been given, then stepped away from the stall. "He's your baby now. I'm going home to get some sleep."

The other vet moved out of the barn as someone else entered, and she knew without looking that it was Grady. She wouldn't allow herself to turn around and look at him. She was too afraid of what he would see in her eyes.

"We missed you last night," he said, his voice gravelly from lack of sleep.

She did turn around then. "I don't take emergencies at night."

"So Dr. O'Connor said. How come, Becca?"

"Because that's what it says in my partnership agreement."

He let his gaze linger on her for a moment, and she struggled to keep her eyes steady. She refused to let him see the fear his words stirred. As she watched him, she realized that his face was shadowed with a day's growth of beard, and the bright blue of his eyes was smudged with fatigue. She had no doubt he'd been here all night with Pat O'Connor, and something stirred inside her that wasn't fear.

"I thought all vets handled emergency calls," he finally said.

"I don't." She stepped into the stall, as much to get away from Grady as to examine the horse.

She listened to Beau's heart and examined his eyes, then gently palpated his abdomen. Everything seemed to have settled down. "Let's get him moving," she said, snapping a lead onto the horse's halter.

Grady moved away as she led the animal out of his stall, then fell in beside her as she led Beau out into the sunlight. "Is he going to be all right?" His voice was quiet, but she heard the concern in it.

"Pat thinks so," she said, glancing over at him. He was watching the horse with worry in his eyes, and she felt her heart soften just a little.

"What do you think?"

He was walking next to her, and his hand brushed against her arm as they left the barn. Heat swept through her and settled in her chest. It was only the sun, she assured herself. It was unusually warm, even for early summer.

"What do you think, Becca?"

His voice jerked her back to reality. "I'm sorry. What did you say?"

"I asked if you thought Beau was going to be all right."

"I think so," she said, forcing herself to concentrate on the animal. "He's past the crisis point, anyway. Once we get the results of the blood tests and ultrasound that Pat did, we'll have a better idea."

"The horses were restless last night," Grady said finally as they walked.

She looked over at him, surprised. "What do you mean?"

"I heard them out in the barn, snuffling and moving around. I went out to check, but I didn't see anything wrong."

Grady reached over to pat Beau's face, and his hand accidentally brushed her arm. Heat seared her, and she jerked away from him.

''Maybe they sensed Beau was getting sick,'' she finally said.

''Maybe.''

They walked in silence for a while. Grady stayed next to her, and with every casual brush of his hand her temperature crept higher. Walking next to him was like walking beside an electrical field. She felt like she was being pulled into it against her will. Shifting the rope to her other hand, she ducked under the horse's head and moved his other side.

Grady glanced over at her, and she could see an echo of her awareness in his eyes. *No, I won't allow it,* she told herself frantically. She *wasn't* attracted to him, and she wasn't going to get involved with him.

''You don't have to walk with me,'' she said, struggling to keep her voice even. ''I'm going to walk him for a while, and I'm sure you must have other things to do.''

''Not a thing,'' he replied, reaching up to touch the horse. ''My new ranch manager arrived today, and he's fully capable of running the place without me for one day.''

''So you're just going to follow me around all morning?'' She couldn't keep the sharpness out of her voice.

''I trust you, Becca. But Beau is my horse. I want to be here.''

His words didn't really surprise her. From the time he was very young, Grady had taken great pains to watch over any animals in his care. His mother, who had died when he was ten years old, had been the same way. Becca remembered the incident she had witnessed when he was only fifteen. He had beaten a ranch hand on his father's ranch because the man had mistreated a horse. Her mouth tightened as she also remembered that the incident had ended with Grady's father beating him.

Shifting her hand on the rope again, she stopped and examined Beau's abdomen again. He stood quietly while she worked, docile from the tranquilizer he'd been given. When she folded her stethoscope into her pocket, she looked up to see Grady watching her.

Forcing herself to smile, she said, "It sounds good. I do think he's going to recover."

Grady nodded, but she saw his face relax. She turned away so she wouldn't have to see the caring on his face. He'd always cared about his animals, she reminded herself. It was the people in his life that he'd had a problem with.

As they walked in the sun, she saw a man approaching them from her side. When he was ten yards away, she stopped abruptly.

"What's wrong?" Grady turned to look at her.

"I think someone is looking for you."

As the man approached, Becca's chest tightened and her fingers curled around the rope. She'd never imagined she'd see Ron Perkins again.

"Hey, Ron," Grady called, moving away from the horse. "What's up?"

"I need to talk to you for a minute."

"No problem," he answered easily. "But as long as you're here, you might as well meet our vet."

No, Grady, she prayed, but it was too late.

"Becca, this is Ron Perkins. He's an old friend of mine and now he's the ranch manager of the Flying W. Ron, this is Becca Johnson, also known as Doc."

Becca extended a nerveless hand to Ron, and as he took it he looked at her for the first time. Shock bloomed in his eyes, a shock she was sure was reflected in hers. "Doc," he said briefly. He watched her carefully, waiting, no doubt, to see if she would tell Grady that they'd met before.

That was something she had no intention of doing. She would not reveal how she'd humiliated herself to Ron Perkins, begging him to contact Grady for her. She couldn't bear to relive the desperation that had driven her to Ron, or the despair that had followed his refusal to lead her to Grady.

"Mr. Perkins." Her voice was equally short. He hesitated

for a minute, his eyes darkening as he watched her, then he turned to Grady. Becca slowly let out her breath when Ron didn't look at her again. It seemed he was no more anxious than she was to explain their past dealings to Grady.

As the roar of blood pounding through her veins receded, she heard Ron talking to Grady about what needed to be done today. They talked as if they'd known each other for years. And they had, she reminded herself bitterly. They were close enough friends that Ron hadn't hesitated to turn away a pregnant woman begging him to tell her where to find Grady. She'd wondered if Grady had ever even mentioned her to Ron. The thought had only made her pain worse.

Swallowing once, she tugged at the rope and led the horse away from the two men. Just before she turned the corner to the barn, she glanced back over her shoulder. Ron was still listening to Grady, but he was watching her. As he caught her eye, the expression on his face hardened.

What could she do? she thought frantically as she stumbled over a stone in the dirt. She would have to leave. She had no other choice. Ron knew she'd been pregnant. She'd told him the baby was Grady's. All it would take was one slip of his tongue, and Grady would know.

Didn't he have a right to know? The small voice inside her piped up again, refusing to be stilled. She'd wrestled with that voice all night and still hadn't decided what to do. Grady's rights versus Cassie's. On paper there was no contest. Cassie would always be first. But was it fair to Cassie to keep her father away from her?

Shaking her head, she forced herself to put it out of her mind. She couldn't decide right now. And today her first responsibility was to Beau. Once she was sure he was all right, she could worry about Grady.

An hour later, after managing to avoid Grady, she slipped back into the barn and put Beau in his stall. His intestinal sounds were close to normal, and he appeared to be pain free. When he snuffled over his empty food bucket and looked annoyed, she felt herself relax. If he was hungry, he was well on the road to recovery.

Gathering up her equipment and the charts that Pat had left behind, she headed for her truck. She had everything stowed in its proper place and was getting ready to leave when Grady appeared.

"Are you leaving?" he asked.

She nodded. "Beau is much better. I'll be back to check him once more late in the afternoon, but I think he's going to be fine."

She started to open the truck door, but Grady put his hand on the door to stop her. "We need to talk, Becca. Can you come into the house for a few minutes?"

Her throat constricted as she studied his face. Had Ron said something to him about what had happened nine years ago? Did he already know about Cassie? It wouldn't take much for him to find out she had an eight-year-old daughter. "I have a lot of work waiting for me back at the clinic," she said, edging toward the truck. "I hurried out here and left a lot of things hanging."

"You can call and find out if there's anything urgent, can't you?"

She nodded reluctantly. "I suppose so."

She hesitated for another moment, then followed him to the house. Grady held the door for her, and she was forced to pass too close to him. His heat seemed to reach out and caress her, a heat laced with his scent. It slammed into her, bringing back too vividly all the nights she'd dreamed about him, tossing restlessly in her too hot bed, consumed with wanting him.

She didn't want him when she was awake and rational, she reminded herself. All she wanted now was a way out of her dilemma.

"What is it, Grady?"

"Didn't you need to call your clinic?" He raised one eyebrow at her, an expression that was haunting in its familiarity.

She drew in a deep, shaky breath. "Yes, I did. Where's the phone?"

He pointed to a telephone hanging on the wall, and as she headed for it she tried to calm herself. She would make it through this talk. She had made it through everything else that had happened in the past decade.

"Stella?" she said when the receptionist answered the phone.

Grady watched Becca speaking to her clinic and wondered why he'd asked her to come into the house and talk to him. He didn't have anything to say to her. Or at least nothing that couldn't be said as they stood next to her truck. His only concern with Becca Johnson was professional, he reminded himself. The only thing he wanted from her was good care of his animals.

The hell it was. His gaze drifted down her body, again covered in denim and cotton, and his muscles tightened. The soft material couldn't hide the lush curves beneath it. She was even more desirable than she'd been nine years ago, and his hormones hadn't forgotten a thing.

Neither had his mind. He moved abruptly away from her as he forced himself to remember their last conversation. She had played him for a fool, and he wouldn't quickly forget that. He'd been faithful to her during the long months on the rodeo circuit, dreaming of their future together, and all that time she'd been with "someone else."

She hung up the phone and turned to face him. For a moment he thought he saw wariness in her eyes, then she blinked and her face was merely tired. "Everything appears to be under control," she said, and her voice sounded forced. "So what was it you wanted to discuss?"

Her chin tilted into the air as if preparing for a blow, and he wondered why. As she watched him, the hint of vulnerability he saw in her eyes made him lean back against the wall and cross his arms in front of his chest. He had no intention of getting involved with her again.

Sure, he wanted her. She was a desirable woman. And he was still breathing, after all. As he studied her, she stared back at him. Abruptly he turned away, afraid that if he watched her for another moment he would do something really stupid. Trying to quell his wayward body, he said gruffly, "This is probably as awkward for you as it is for me."

There was no sound behind him for a moment, as if she was holding her breath. Finally she said, "Meeting each other again after all this time, you mean?" Her voice sounded cautious.

"What else would I mean?" He swung around to face her. "Is there something else I should feel awkward about?"

She shook her head, too rapidly. Her curls flew around her face. "Of course not." She shrugged, but the movement looked awkward and forced. "I've just never been in this situation before."

He studied her face. She didn't quite look him in the eye, and he wondered why. Becca never had been able to lie worth a damn. And she'd never once lied to him. "What's going on, Becca?" he asked.

Fear flashed in her eyes, but she gathered herself as he watched. Straightening her back, she swallowed once, then looked him in the eye. "What do you think is going on, Grady? I never imagined I would see you again. Now you're one of my clients, and we're both in an uncomfortable situation. If I continue as the Flying W's vet, we're going to be seeing a lot of each other. Can you handle that? I'm not sure I can."

"Why not, Becca?" Without thinking, he took a step closer to her. "It was over between us nine years ago. Wasn't it?"

He moved another step closer, and her scent drifted around him. It was the scent burned into his memory, the same one that surrounded him at night when he woke from dreams, his body hard and aching. A fire ignited deep inside him and spread to every part of his body. "There's nothing between us, is there?"

"Of course not. But we never had any kind of closure to our relationship. That's making things awkward for both of us." She spoke too quickly, her voice breathless. He watched her chest rise and fall beneath the T-shirt, and the flames licked at his belly.

"Define *awkward*, Becca."

Slowly, reluctantly she lifted her gaze to his. As their eyes met and held, the soft gray of her irises darkened until all he could think about was the way her body would feel pressed against his, the way her mouth would taste. He moved closer, so that every breath he drew was filled with her essence.

"This is awkward," she whispered.

"You're right," he said, moving closer and bending down so that his mouth was inches from hers. "It's damn awkward."

"Grady, no," she murmured, her gaze locked with his. But she didn't move away.

Her breath fanned against his mouth, stirring the need inside him even higher. He watched her for another moment, then lowered his lips to hers.

Her taste exploded in his mouth, its familiarity a bitter taste on his tongue. Reaching out, he pulled her against him with hands that were anything but gentle. Desire swirled with anger and pain inside him, and he wanted only to punish her. He wanted to make her suffer, to lie awake at night and remember. He wanted her to wake from dreams aching with need, despising herself for her weakness.

He wanted her pain to equal his.

She murmured something incoherent against his lips, and he tightened his hold on her. Finally, through the red haze of his desire and anger, he felt her struggling against him. Disgusted with his lack of control, appalled at his behavior, he let her go. But when he would have moved away from her, she slid her hands up to his shoulders. Her fingers gripped him lightly, tentatively, but he was powerless to move.

Her mouth was unsure as it clung to his, and slowly he

wrapped his arms around her again. The rush of passion that swept over him at the touch of her mouth consumed his anger. There was room for nothing but her, and his anger and pain disappeared as his desire blazed out of control.

His hands moved over her back, touching, remembering, savoring the changes. His fingers caressed the curve and swell of her hip, pulling her against him more tightly until every part of their bodies were touching. He heard her breath catch in her throat as he feathered his hand over her hip once more.

He was on fire for her. Her breasts pressed against his chest, making his groin tighten to the point of pain. Sweeping his hand roughly up her back, he tangled his fingers in her hair to hold her head steady for his kiss. Her mouth moved under his, clinging to his lips with a desperation that matched his own.

Her hands still gripped his shoulders, but now her fingers were digging in, holding on as if she would never let go. Grady groaned as he backed her up against the wall. She twined herself even more tightly around him as her mouth opened beneath his.

His hips moved against hers as his tongue swept into her mouth, tasting and possessing. Sliding his hands down to her hips, he pulled her more tightly against him so that her soft core rested against the hard length of him. Her gasp feathered into his mouth, and he shuddered against her, helpless against the need that consumed him.

She reached up to pull him closer, and her fingers slid into his hair. It was a familiar gesture, one that she'd done a thousand times before, one that he'd dreamed about a million times since. But that had been in another lifetime. One that he'd tried hard to forget.

Slowly he lifted his mouth from hers and looked down at her. Becca's eyes were closed, her lids heavy with desire and her face tight with passion. Color suffused her cheeks, and he knew some of it was due to the friction of his whiskers against her delicate skin. Need spasmed inside him again, and he took his hands off her and moved away.

Her eyes slowly opened and focused on him. He saw the exact instant that realization hit her. Hot color flooded her face, sweeping away the delicate tint of passion. The softness in her eyes vanished, replaced by mortification.

She recovered her voice first. "I'm sorry, Grady. That should never have happened."

"Still hot for me, Becca?" He wasn't sure the harsh words completely hid his panic.

But he had miscalculated—she didn't turn and run. "I don't believe I was the one who initiated that kiss."

He looked at her face, the face that had lived in his dreams for too long, and anger flared inside him again. "But you didn't fight it very hard, did you?"

"I'm sorry," she said again. She stood up straight and slid her palms down the sides of her legs, almost as if she was wiping them off.

"It's not that easy to wipe away what happened, you know."

"Isn't it?" She gave him a cool look. "I've already forgotten."

His entire body throbbed with anger, but he forced himself to lean back against the wall and crossed his arms over his chest. He'd be damned if he'd let her see how that kiss had affected him. "A few minutes ago it didn't feel like you would be forgetting anything soon."

For a moment her composure slipped, and he saw a vulnerable woman in her eyes. A woman who was unsure of herself and shaken by a passion she didn't want to feel. Then she gathered herself again and moved away from the wall. "A few minutes ago I forgot I had other obligations. That was all. I'll see you some other time, Grady."

He had to admire her poise. If he hadn't noticed her hands shaking, he would almost have believed her. Almost. Because she couldn't have been faking the kiss they had shared.

"Sure, Becca. I'll see you around." But he didn't move aside for her to leave. If she wanted to pass him, she would have to brush against him. The voice of his conscience roused from somewhere deep inside him. It told him he was being a first-class jerk, but he suppressed it easily.

Her chest rose as she drew a shaky breath, but before she could speak, Tucker stuck his head in the room. The foreman looked past Grady and relaxed when he saw Becca standing near the wall.

"Hey, Doc, I'm glad you're still here. Laura called. She's been trying to get you on the car phone. She needs you to call her back right away."

Grady watched the color disappear from Becca's face as she took a step forward. "Is something wrong?"

Tucker shrugged. "Laura didn't say. But she sounded pretty frazzled."

"Who's Laura?" Grady asked.

Ignoring his question, Becca slid past him and hurried out to her truck. Grady watched her through the window for a moment and saw her hand shaking as she stood near the truck and held the phone. As she talked, the tense expression drained from her face and she nodded once. When she replaced the phone, he could almost hear her sigh of relief.

Grady pushed past Tucker and strode out to the yard. Ignoring the churning in his stomach, he laid one hand on Becca's arm, stopping her from getting into her truck. "What's wrong?" he asked.

"Nothing." She tried to smile but failed miserably. He could see the remnants of frantic worry in her eyes. "Only a small crisis, easily handled."

"What is it, Becca?" he asked quietly. "Something sure as hell is wrong."

"It's nothing, Grady." Her voice was stronger as she pulled her arm away from him and got in the truck. "Just something that I needed to know about."

Tucker moved behind him. Grady hadn't realized that the

foreman had followed him out of the house. "Everything okay with Cassie, Doc?"

Becca went utterly still. Her face drained of color, and her hands tightened around the steering wheel until her knuckles gleamed white. Finally, without taking her shocked eyes off the foreman's face, she whispered, "She's fine, Tucker."

The foreman let out a sigh. "I was worried when Laura said she'd been trying to get hold of you. Kids can have accidents, especially little scamps like Cassie."

"Who's Cassie?" Grady asked, staring at Becca. It felt like a hole had opened up in his stomach.

Slowly Becca turned her head to look at him. Her eyes were huge and dark, and she reminded him of a trapped animal. She licked her lips once and said quietly, "Cassie is my daughter."

"Your daughter?" His voice sounded as incredulous as he felt. Then another thought stabbed at him. "How old is she?" Grady leaned closer to Becca, his heart pounding.

"She's eight."

"Eight." Even after all these years, the pain of her betrayal surprised him. It slammed into his chest with the force of a hammer, and he curled his fingers around the door of her truck to stop himself from falling backward. She had been pregnant with someone else's child when she'd told him to get lost. "I guess when you said there was someone else, you weren't kidding, were you, Becca?"

He saw the shock bloom in her eyes and didn't wait for more. Pulling his hands away from the door of her truck as if they were burned, he turned and walked away. The barn was almost within reach when he heard the sound of her truck starting. Stopping, refusing to turn around and watch her leave, he let the waves of pain wash over him as he listened to the sound of her engine fade into the distance.

Chapter 4

Becca drove blindly, her eyes fixed on the dusty road but her mind still numb with shock. *Grady thought Cassie was someone else's child.* She wasn't sure whether to laugh or cry. It was her salvation, her way out, but her conscience wouldn't let her take it.

She couldn't do that to Grady. He *was* Cassie's father, and he had a right to know. But not right now. Not until she knew him better. Becca swallowed hard, shifting her grip on the steering wheel. This might give her the breathing space she needed. She could ease into the subject with Cassie, getting her used to the idea of a father, and she could also get reacquainted with Grady. The more she knew about him, the easier it would be to figure out how to tell him. Maybe he had no interest in being a father. He still wanted to travel light. Maybe he would want nothing to do with Cassie.

Maybe he wouldn't believe her when she told him the truth.

If he didn't, it would be no more than she deserved, she reminded herself bitterly. She'd had her chance, a few minutes ago, to tell him he was Cassie's father, and like a coward she'd let it slip through her fingers. Why would Grady believe her when she did tell him?

And maybe, after today, Grady would want nothing further to do with her. He thought she'd betrayed him in the most despicable way possible. Any interest he'd had in rekindling their relationship must have died in the dust of his yard.

And he had been interested. She had tasted it in his kiss. Even now, thinking about the way his mouth had moved over hers made her tremble. When she bit down on her lip, she tasted Grady there, and longing shot through her.

Grady. He had lived in her dreams for the past nine years, and now he was living in her town. She allowed herself to remember the way he had tasted and felt, and then she stored the memories away in her heart. They were likely to be the last ones she had, she reminded herself as Laura's house came into view. Cassie was her priority, and nothing could change that.

The truck had barely stopped moving before she was out and running up the walk. A harried-looking Laura met her at the door, a toddler cradled in her arms.

"Thank goodness you were able to come so quickly," she said as she opened the screen door. "I'd hate it if Cassie got sick, too."

Becca brushed her hand gently over the child's head, finding him hot and damp with sweat. "How is he?"

"He's not too bad. Jenny is the one who's really sick."

Becca hurried toward the living room, where Laura's six-year-old daughter lay on the couch. Her eyes were too bright in her flushed face.

"How are you feeling, honey?" Becca asked, squatting next to her.

"My tummy hurts," Jenny replied. "My head, too."

Becca picked up the washcloth that had fallen onto the couch and replaced it on the child's head. "Is that better?"

The child nodded mutely, and Becca smoothed her hair away from her face before standing up again. "Is there anything I can do before Cassie and I leave?'' she asked Laura, who had followed her into the room.

Laura shook her head. "Thanks, but I have an appointment at the doctor's office in a little while. We'll be fine until then."

Becca looked around. "Where's Cassie? We'll get out of here and leave you alone."

"She's upstairs watching television in my room. I didn't want her spending any more time than was necessary around Jenny and Todd."

Becca called up to Cassie, then turned to Laura. "Thanks for calling me to come get her. I wouldn't want you to have to worry about her while you were taking care of your own kids."

"I didn't want her to get sick," Laura answered. "I hope it wasn't a problem for you, calling you like that."

Becca hesitated. She had never told Laura who Cassie's father was. Laura had guessed, but Becca had been too upset at the time to confide in her. Now she needed advice, and there was no one she trusted more than her longtime friend. But Laura had enough to worry about at the moment. The truth would have to wait.

"Not at all," she finally said. "I was just finishing up at the Flying W. That's why I got here so fast."

She turned away from Laura as Cassie came running down the stairs. "Hi, honey," she said softly as Cassie hugged her. "Get your stuff together so we can leave. Jenny and Todd are sick, and Laura has to take them to the doctor."

"Jenny puked on the floor. It was gross." Cassie wrinkled her nose.

"She doesn't feel good, sweetheart," Becca replied. "And we need to leave so you don't get sick, too." She spied Cassie's things in a neat pile by the door and scooped them up.

Pushing open the screen door, she turned to Laura. "I'll call you tonight. You let me know if you need anything."

Laura nodded once, but didn't say anything. "I mean it,

Laura.'' Becca stopped, her hand on the door. ''Being a single mother is hard enough when everything's going well. When your kids are sick, you need all the help you can get. Lord knows you've done enough for Cassie and me. If you don't promise me you'll call, I'll be back here at seven tonight.''

At that, Laura turned to look at her, and for a moment her eyes were full of anguish. Her husband had walked out on her the year before, when Todd was less than a year old. Becca knew how hard Laura had worked to make things as normal as possible for Jenny and Todd. Then Laura straightened, and Becca watched her friend wrap herself in the amazing strength that usually sustained her.

''You know I'll call you, Becca. I always do, don't I?''

Becca smiled at her friend. ''Just so you don't forget. I'll talk to you later.''

Cassie was already sitting in the truck, playing with one of her plastic horses. Becca smiled as she hurried to join her. Thank goodness her daughter was so adaptable.

''What are you playing, honey?'' she asked as she slid into the driver's seat of the truck.

''Horses,'' Cassie answered, and continued with her game.

''Which horse is that?'' She nodded at the one in Cassie's hands.

''That's my horse, Mr. Bojangles.'' She moved him around her, making him gallop across the seat, the dashboard and the window. ''We're famous rodeo stars. We used to be barrel racers, and now he's my calf-roping horse.''

Becca felt her throat tighten as she watched her daughter's absorbed play. Cassie had always been fascinated by horses and rodeo events, and Becca had told herself it was only because she lived in a ranching town. But as her daughter had grown older, Becca had been forced to admit that her interest seemed to be growing stronger. She devoured books about the rodeo and watched any rodeo that was on television. She'd tried to ignore it, telling herself that Cassie's obsession with the rodeo would pass, but now all she could think about was Grady, and the way his eyes used to light up when he talked about the rodeo.

"I don't think you're old enough to rope calves, honey," she said as she smoothed her hand down Cassie's shiny black hair.

"I know." Cassie grinned up at her. "But when I am old enough, I'm going to be the best."

Becca turned away so Cassie wouldn't see the tears filling her eyes. She imagined Grady had said something very similar when he was eight years old. The competitive fires burned as fiercely in Cassie as they had in her father.

Before Becca could start the truck, Cassie glanced over at her. "What's a single mother?"

"What?" She stared at her daughter, unsure of what to say.

"You said Laura was a single mother. What's that?"

Becca searched for the right words to say. "A single mother is when there's no daddy living with the mommy and children," she answered slowly.

Cassie cocked her head as she examined her mother. "Kind of like you and me, right?"

"Just like you and me," she said, reaching out to hug her daughter.

"How come Laura and Jenny and Todd don't have a daddy?"

"Their daddy couldn't stay with them, just like yours. But he still loves Jenny and Todd a whole bunch."

"Does my daddy love me?"

Cassie's voice was almost a whisper, and Becca almost shuddered with the pain. "I'm sure he does, honey." But she wasn't sure, not really, and Becca clutched Cassie to her a little more tightly. There was no way she would take a chance on hurting her baby. If she didn't think Grady would love and cherish his daughter as much as she did, there was no way in hell she would tell him about Cassie.

She knew what it felt like to be rejected by parents. And Cassie would never know that kind of pain.

She needed to change the subject before Cassie noticed that her hands were shaking and her eyes were full of tears. "How would you like to come with me to finish up my rounds?" she asked, trying to make her voice light.

"Can I, Mommy? Really?" Cassie leaned away from her, her small face glowing. Her love of horses and ranching lodged in Becca's chest with another tiny dagger of pain.

"Yes, you can come with me. But remember the rules."

"I know. Stay in the truck, and don't interrupt you unless it's a real emergency," Cassie recited. "But I can see a lot from the truck. Sometimes the cowboys ride their horses over to the window, and they let me pet the horse's nose." Cassie's eyes glowed, her questions about her father seemingly forgotten.

Becca smiled and tugged on one of Cassie's pigtails. "Just be sure they don't think your fingers are sugar cubes and try to swallow them."

Cassie giggled. "You're silly, Mommy."

She tried to be silly for the rest of the afternoon, keeping Cassie giggling and happy beside her. The last thing she wanted was for Cassie to notice her worry. By the time she turned into the Flying W driveway at the end of the day, Becca had almost managed to keep smiling for the whole afternoon.

Almost. When she saw the familiar barns and house of the Flying W in front of her, her heart began an erratic thumping in her chest. It was only anxiety, she told herself. It had nothing to do with whether Grady would be around. Anyone would be anxious after what had happened between her and Grady earlier in the day.

Instead of the kiss they'd shared, she tried to focus on Grady's face at the instant she'd told him she had a daughter. His shock, and the anguish that had followed it, were something she would never forget.

But she wouldn't forget that kiss, either. Touching him, tasting him, feeling the long, hard length of his body pressed close to hers had stirred feelings she'd long ago suppressed. If she closed her eyes, she could recall every plane and curve of his chest and back. Her hands tingled with the feel of his hair, springy and soft beneath her fingers. And her mouth burned with his remembered taste.

"We haven't been to this ranch in a long time, Mommy." Cassie bounced in the seat, her face pressed against the glass of the window. "This is a big ranch. Look at all the new horses they have."

Becca tried to wrench her mind away from the images of Grady. "There's a new owner, pumpkin, and he has a lot of horses. There's a lot going on here, so it's very important that you stay in the truck. I wouldn't want you to get hurt."

Please, please don't let Grady be around, she prayed. She wasn't sure she could handle another encounter, especially after Cassie's questions about her father. Her soul felt stripped bare and raw, and she honestly didn't know what she would say or do if she ran into Grady.

"I'll stay in the car," Cassie promised, already rolling down the window. "Look at that horse over there," she said, her voice rising with excitement, pointing toward a corral. "That's the prettiest horse I've ever seen."

Cassie gestured at a paint pony. His blotchy white-and-dark-red coloring gleamed in the sunlight, and as they watched he tossed his head and snorted at the man standing in the corral with him. Becca pressed a quick kiss on her forehead and slid out of the car. "That's a great horse, honey. Why don't you watch and see what they're doing with him while I check on my patient?"

Cassie nodded, already absorbed by the horse and trainer working in the corral. Once again Becca was reminded of Grady's single-mindedness and determination when it came to the rodeo, and once again pain squeezed her heart.

Making sure both the windows were rolled down for Cassie, she grabbed her bag from the back of the truck and hurried to the barn that sheltered Beau. If she was lucky, Beau would be in good shape and she could check him and leave before she saw Grady or Ron Perkins or Tucker.

But as she approached Beau's stall, she knew her luck hadn't held. Someone was in the stall with Beau, and before she saw him she knew it was Grady. His low voice was murmuring to the horse, and for a moment she stood outside the stall and watched him stroking Beau's nose.

Grady's head was bent close to the horse's ear, although Becca couldn't hear what he was saying. She didn't really need to hear, though. His concern for his horse was stamped on his face. For just a moment she wondered if she'd ever see the same kind of concern on his face for her, then pushed the thought away. This wasn't about her and Grady. Right now it wasn't even about the fact that Grady had a daughter he was unaware of. She was here as the Flying W's veterinarian, and she had better remember that.

Shifting her bag in her hand so it made a jangling noise, she waited for Grady to look up and see her. Immediately his face closed down and became unreadable. His eyes hardened and he straightened, holding on to Beau's halter.

"How is he doing?" Becca forced herself to ask.

Grady didn't answer for a moment. His gaze raked her, and she saw the anger and scorn in his eyes before he carefully shuttered them. "He seems to be doing much better," he said, his voice flat and distant.

If she had to deal with Grady right now, she much preferred him distant, Becca told herself. It was easier to handle than the scorn she'd just seen in his eyes.

Slipping into Beau's stall, she examined the horse carefully, listening for intestinal sounds and finally palpating him. Grady stood and watched her, not saying anything, his gaze inscrutable. His presence seemed to shrink the stall down to a tiny box, scarcely big enough for her and the horse, let along Grady. As she bent over Beau, Grady's shoulders blocked the light from the window high in the wall, and for a moment the shadows in the stall slid over Grady's face, hiding his expression. It was just as well, Becca tried to tell herself, but instead she shifted so she could see his eyes again. They were still carefully blank.

Striving to appear as unaffected and professional as she could, Becca nodded toward Beau's food box. "Has he eaten anything?"

"We gave him a little hay about an hour ago. He ate it right away."

"Has he shown any signs of discomfort?"

Grady shook his head. "I've been with him since he ate the hay. Everything seems fine."

"Good," she murmured, backing out of the stall. Grady's dedication to his animals was almost painful to watch. If only he'd shown a similar dedication to the people in his life. "I'll come back tomorrow to check on him again, but I'd say he's out of danger." She paused by the door of the stall. "You were very lucky to find him right away. It could have been a lot worse."

"*Lucky* is a relative term," Grady said, moving toward her.

She almost backed away, but managed to hold her ground. "What do you mean?"

Grady stopped on the other side of the stall door. Thick slats of wood separated them, but his scent filled her head and her skin tingled as if the air was full of static electricity.

"Someone deliberately overfed Beau to give him colic." His voice was hard.

"What?" Becca stared at him, unsure she'd heard him correctly.

Jerking his head toward the feed room, Grady said, "He got an extra helping of corn and oats last night, after the barn had been checked for the last time. That's what gave him colic."

"How do you know? And who would do something like that to a horse?"

"I don't know who would do it. But someone did. Tucker found the feed scoop in the wrong place, and dirty. He'd washed it and put it away the last time he came through the barn. There were traces of grain in Beau's feed box, again after it had been washed out. That's why the horses were restless last night, moving around and making too much noise." His mouth pressed together in a grim line. "Just like they would have been if there was someone in the barn."

"Why?" she burst out. "Why do that to Beau?"

"I have no idea. But I intend to find out."

Becca stared at him, aghast. "That's horrible."

Grady's eyes softened momentarily. "I guess we agree on one thing, then, Becca."

Becca felt herself leaning closer, absorbing the softness in Grady's blue eyes. Then she reminded herself harshly that there was far more that she and Grady disagreed about, and she abruptly drew back. How could she forget that Cassie, Grady's daughter, was sitting in her truck, just outside the barn?

Bending down to gather her equipment, she was glad her face was hidden from Grady's perceptive eyes. "What are you going to do?"

There was a pause, then Grady moved away. "Keep a damn close eye on everything around here," he said, his voice harsh again. It was hard to believe that there had been even a brief softening of his anger. "If someone is trying to cause trouble, he'll try again eventually. And then we'll catch him."

And he would regret what he'd done, Becca thought to herself. She'd seen for herself what happened when someone abused one of Grady's animals, and it wasn't a pretty picture.

Trying to act businesslike, she stood and gripped her bag in her hand. "Beau should be fine tonight, but if you have a problem, give the clinic a call."

"But not you, right, Becca?" The scorn was back in his face.

"No, not me," she answered quietly. "I don't take emergency calls because I can't leave Cassie alone at night."

"Doesn't Cassie have a father?" he asked, slamming the stall door with unnecessary force.

"He's not in the picture," she managed to say. The dust motes in the air quivered from the slamming of the stall door. She focused on them, rather than on Grady's face.

"So the someone else didn't last, either."

She couldn't answer. Now wasn't the time or place to tell him the truth, and she wasn't sure when there would be a right time or place. Until she knew him better, until she knew what his reaction would be, she couldn't tell Grady anything about Cassie. It might not be fair to him, but it was the best thing for Cassie. And right now that was all that mattered.

"I'll be here tomorrow," Becca repeated, and she started for the barn door.

She could feel Grady standing behind her, could feel his gaze burning into her back between her shoulder blades. But he made no effort to follow her, and she took a deep, shuddering breath of relief. After everything that had happened today, she couldn't face dealing with his first sight of Cassie. He would meet Cassie eventually. In a small town like Cameron that was inevitable, but she wanted to choose the time and place.

By the time she reached the truck, her legs were rubbery and her whole body was shaking. Throwing her bag in the back, she hurried to the cab and climbed in, wanting nothing more than to drive away from the Flying W without a backward glance.

But Cassie was half out the window on her side of the truck, blissfully rubbing the ears of the paint pony she'd been watching in the corral. Jim Tucker sat on the horse and watched her with a huge grin on his face.

When he spotted Becca, he tipped his hat back and nodded at Cassie. "This little gal has an uncommon way with horses, Doc. We're just starting to train Pete, here. He's been as wiggly as a snake and twice as feisty. But he's standing here for Cassie like a big old puppy dog.''

Becca watched the blissful expression on the horse's face and felt another spurt of fear. But she forced her face into a bland smile. "I'm glad she likes animals," she replied, easing Cassie back into the truck. "Being the daughter of a vet, she's going to be around a lot of them."

She buckled Cassie's seat belt, then started the engine of the truck. But Tucker shook his head and answered before she could get away. "It's more than that, Doc. There's a bond between Cassie and this horse that don't make any sense. Why ain't he as skittish around her as he is around other people?" Tucker spit a stream of tobacco juice into the red dust. "Some things you just can't explain," he said as he drew the horse away from the truck.

As she drove away, Becca saw Grady standing in the doorway of the barn. He leaned against the wall in a casual pose, but she wasn't fooled. Even from a distance she felt the anger in him, felt the waves of tension that flowed from him. She looked over at Cassie, who had her face pressed against the window of the truck as she watched the paint pony getting smaller and smaller.

She didn't know how much longer she could bear this. Grady had to know the truth, had to be told. But once again she remembered his remarks about traveling light, about not being tied down. How did she reconcile his rights with Cassie's needs? It wouldn't be fair to either of them to force the situation. As she turned onto the road that led back to Cameron, she vowed to spend enough time with Grady to find out how he felt about children, to judge how he would react to hearing that he was a father. It would be painful for her, and harder than anything she'd ever had to do, but she could do it for Cassie. She could do it for Grady's daughter.

At nine o'clock that evening Becca heard the quiet knock at the door and put down her book with a sigh. All she wanted to do was crawl into bed and sleep for the next ten hours, but she couldn't do that yet. Grabbing her purse and keys, she opened the door to let her teenage neighbor into the house.

"Hi, Amy," she said, forcing herself to smile. "I shouldn't be too long tonight. There are only a few animals to check at the clinic."

"Take your time, Doc," Amy Morgan answered with a smile. She nodded at the pile of books in her arms. "I have plenty of homework to keep me busy."

"Cassie's asleep," Becca said as she paused at the door. "She had a long day, so she shouldn't wake up."

"No problem." Amy flopped into a chair and opened one of her textbooks. "If she does, Cass and I both know the drill."

Becca sighed as she climbed into her truck. Going back to the clinic at night to check on her patients wasn't her favorite part of her job. But it had to be done, and she was thankful that Amy was willing to watch Cassie while she did it. As she drove the few blocks to the clinic, she pushed her weariness out of her mind and concentrated on the animals in the clinic.

Twenty minutes later she was almost finished treating her last patient, a cat with a urinary problem, when she heard a noise that made her pause. It sounded like someone had jiggled the back door.

"It's just the wind," she said out loud, the words echoing in the silent building. But she stroked the cat on the table to keep him quiet while she listened more intently.

The noise echoed through the kennel again, louder and more distinct. It sounded like someone had turned the doorknob. Becca lifted her patient off the table and put him back in his cage, then wiped her suddenly sweating hands down the sides of her jeans. She glanced at the telephone, then told herself not to be ridiculous. No one could possibly be trying to break into the clinic.

It was obvious that she was in the building. Her truck was

parked in front, and lights blazed out of all the windows. Who could possibly be foolish enough to attempt a break-in while she was here? If someone wanted to burglarize the clinic, why wouldn't he wait until she'd left?

A chill rippled up her spine. Everyone in Cameron knew she checked on her patients in the evening. Maybe that's why someone was trying to get in.

Closing her eyes, Becca told herself she was being stupid and forced the fear out of her mind. If someone was trying to get in, it was because he had an animal that needed help. That's all there was to it.

Hurrying toward the reception area, she glanced out into the parking lot. The only vehicle there was her truck. She turned and started toward the rear of the clinic and the back door, but as she walked into the darkened kennel, she heard the doorknob jiggling again. The hair rose on the back of her neck, and she slowly backed up.

Why would someone with an injured or sick animal go to the back door? And why not just knock? Maybe she was overreacting, but she reached for the telephone on the reception desk. She'd feel a lot better if Sheriff McAllister came over to take a look.

As her hand closed around the telephone, someone began pounding on the front door. Her heart leaped in her chest as she tried to punch in the numbers for the sheriff's office. When her fingers slipped and she hit the wrong button, she quickly depressed the button and began dialing again.

"Becca, are you in there? It's me, Grady," a voice called from the other side of the door.

Becca froze at the sound of his voice. Had it been Grady at the back door? No. She knew immediately that it hadn't been him. Grady didn't sneak around, didn't try to break into buildings. That wasn't his way. If he had something to say, he'd say it to her face. At least he always had in the past. And she knew instinctively that hadn't changed.

Dropping the telephone back into its cradle, she walked to the door. "Grady?" she said, hating the way her voice wobbled. "Are you still there?"

"I'm here. What the hell is going on, Becca?"

Chapter 5

Grady waited impatiently as Becca opened the locks on the front door. As soon as she pulled the door open, he stepped inside.

"What the hell is going on here?"

A look of confusion passed over her face. "What do you mean?"

"What are you doing here at almost ten o'clock at night? I thought you didn't do emergencies."

Becca's face relaxed, but only a little. She was sheet white. "There isn't an emergency. I always come over here around this time to check on any animals that are in the clinic."

Grady felt some of the anger he had felt draining away. When he'd seen her truck outside the clinic, a confusing combination of anger and concern had swirled up in him. She'd told him she didn't do emergencies. Had she lied to him? And if she hadn't, what had induced her to come to the clinic so late?

He said the first thing that came to mind. "Where's your daughter? Is she here with you this late?"

He thought her face became even whiter. "She's at home, with a baby-sitter."

For the first time he noticed that her hands were shaking, and his anger disappeared completely. "What's wrong?"

She stared at him for a moment. "Were you trying to get in the back door just a few minutes ago?"

"Of course not. I saw your truck, stopped and knocked on the door. Why would I go to the back of the building?"

"I don't know. But I heard something or someone at the back door, then you were pounding at the front door a few moments later."

Fear curled in his belly, and he took a step closer to her. His first instinct was to grab her, to make sure she was all right. He stuck his hands in his pockets instead. "I wasn't at the back door. Show me where it is."

Her eyes huge in her pale face, Becca watched him for a moment, then nodded. "Back here."

He noticed that she threw on all the lights in every room they walked through. Nothing like letting a prowler know they were coming, he thought, but he didn't say anything. If there had been someone at the door, he would be long gone by now.

Finally she pointed at a door that stood in the back wall. "It goes to a kennel area, but the fence would be easy enough to climb," she said. As she stared at the door her face tightened again, and a wave of anger swept over Grady once more.

"Go call the sheriff," he said gruffly. "I'll take a look outside."

"Maybe you should wait, Grady," she said in a small voice.

Had she noticed the stiffness in his walk? "I can handle the kind of coward who tries to sneak into a back door." His voice was ice cold.

"I know you can, but we don't know who's out there. I don't want you to get hurt."

She was worried about him. He couldn't stop the treacherous pleasure that seeped through him, although he tried to ignore it. "I won't get hurt, Becca."

She watched as he unlocked the door. Even though she was behind him, he was too aware of her presence. "Go call the sheriff," he repeated. As she turned and headed toward the front of the clinic, the back kennel room suddenly felt lonely and empty.

When he heard her voice murmuring into the telephone, he eased the door open and looked into the kennel area. The runs looked ghostly in the dim light, the wire of the fencing leaving distorted shadows on the concrete floor. Nothing moved.

He stepped into the shadows, cursing once again the injury that had left his leg stiff and less than completely mobile. Moving slowly down the walk in front of the dog runs, he waited for a flash of movement, for some sign that the intruder was still on the clinic grounds.

But nothing stirred in the silence. When he reached the last run and peered into the shadows, he turned and headed toward the back door. Whoever had been trying to get into the clinic was long gone.

Becca was waiting for him just inside the door. "Sheriff McAllister is on his way," she said, searching his face. "Did you see anything?"

"He's gone."

Her shoulders slumped, and for the first time he noticed the weariness etched on her face. "There *was* someone at the door." Her voice sounded almost defensive.

"I believe you, Becca. I just didn't see any sign of him." He wanted to reach out and smooth away the worry lines on her forehead. Hell, he wanted to do a whole lot more than that.

Cursing the need surging through his blood, he stepped through the open door and carefully moved away from her. As she swung the door shut, he noticed odd marks on the paint of the door and reached out to stop her. He was aiming for the doorknob, but instead his hand touched her arm.

Becca froze, staring at his fingers as they curled around her arm. He couldn't stop himself. He needed to touch her, to feel the warm smoothness of her skin. Her pulse bounded beneath his fingers, and his hand tightened on her.

He was angry with her, he reminded himself. She had betrayed him, and he wasn't interested in Becca Johnson anymore. He hated her, in fact. But his body called him a liar as her subtle, clean scent surrounded him.

He leaned toward her, his treacherous hormones remembering how she'd tasted and felt that morning. Remembering that no one else had ever had the power to move him the way Becca did.

Closing his eyes, he skimmed his hand up her arm, feeling her shiver in response. His fingers glided over her skin, every touch evoking a memory of another time, long ago, when Becca welcomed his touch and he craved hers. He lingered on her neck, her short curls feathering against his fingers. The touch of her hair brought back another wave of memories, of her long hair tangled around both of them. Nothing on earth could have stopped him from sliding his fingers into her mass of curls. Her hair was as soft, as silky as it had been nine years ago. Lost in the sensation, helpless against the memories that crashed through him, he leaned closer and glided his mouth over hers.

Becca trembled in his arms, her hands against his chest. He thought she was pushing him away, but when he moved, he realized that her hands were clenched in his shirt. Groaning, he pulled her closer and gave himself up to the sensations crashing through him.

Her body was firm and supple against him. The swell of her breasts and the curve of her hips burned into him, stirring old memories and creating new ones. Becca fit him perfectly, the way she did in his dreams. Slowly her arms crept around him, until she was holding him as tightly as he held her.

Her mouth shifted under his lips, then she was kissing him with a desperation that mirrored his. All thought, all restraint disappeared as he tasted her again, and his control slipped away from him. The past and the present fused together, and suddenly it was as if the past nine years didn't exist.

She made a small sound in the back of her throat, and Grady opened his eyes to realize that he'd pushed her against the wall of the clinic. He'd lifted her into the notch between his thighs, and her soft core was snug against his swollen erection. Becca's eyes were closed, and her face was flushed with passion. Her swollen lips were parted and moist, and as he stared at her, her eyes fluttered open.

They were filled with desire and longing, and a spear of almost unbearable need lanced through him. Lowering his mouth to hers, he kissed her again, his mouth and tongue moving to the throbbing rhythm that his body demanded.

He felt the instant that she tensed. The distance between them was suddenly far more than the few inches that separated them.

"What's wrong?" he said, pulling her back toward him.

She looked up at him, her eyes still full of desire and the flush of passion staining her cheeks. "Sheriff McAllister is here. Didn't you hear his car pull up?" she whispered.

A car door slammed outside the building, and Grady stepped away from Becca, swearing beneath his breath. All the ugly words he knew came spilling out, fueled by frustrated desire. Becca stared back at him, her hair disheveled and her lips swollen and still wet from his kisses, and he swore again. The sheriff would take one look at them and know exactly what they'd been doing.

"Go get yourself together. I can talk to the sheriff."

She stood straighter. "Thanks, but this is my clinic. I'll talk to him."

"Becca," he began, but he was interrupted by knocking on the front door of the clinic.

She hesitated for a moment before turning to go. No longer was she the vulnerable woman he'd held in his arms just moments before. Now she looked cool and professional. But she wasn't completely composed. The bloom of passion was fading from her face, and her gaze was once more focused and clear. But her hands weren't quite steady as she straightened her shirt and finger-combed her hair. And deep in her eyes he saw the desire she was trying so hard to hide.

"I'm sorry, Grady," she said quietly. "It was wrong of me to let that go so far. I was scared and—" her eyes dropped "—it was reaction, I guess. I wasn't thinking. It won't happen again."

The pain that was never far away found him again, reminding him of all that Becca stood for. Betrayal, anger and hurt swirled through him, replacing the need he'd felt just minutes ago.

"No, it won't." His voice was harsh. She flinched, then turned and hurried toward the front door. He watched as she walked away. When he realized that his gaze lingered on the sway of her hips as she vanished through the door, he turned away with a muttered oath and slammed the back door to the clinic shut.

The sound echoed through the building in a satisfying way, but he sighed and leaned against the wall. His leg ached with a familiar throbbing, reminding him he needed to sit down. Instead, Grady walked slowly through the back kennel room, looking at the windows and noticing how easy it would be to break into the building.

He was scowling a few minutes later when Becca walked back into the room with a tall, golden-haired man wearing jeans and a khaki shirt with a badge pinned above the pocket.

"I didn't see anything, and I didn't hear anything once we came back here," she was saying. The tall man listened carefully as he leaned over her. In Grady's opinion he was standing much too close. When the sheriff touched her arm, Grady pushed himself away from the wall and moved to stand in front of Becca.

She looked up at him, startled, but he only saw her out of the corner of his eye. He was staring at the other man.

The sheriff let his gaze wander over Grady, but he didn't back up. Instead, he pocketed the small pad of paper he was using to take notes and hooked his fingers in his gun belt. "And you would be...?"

Grady hesitated for an instant, then he stuck out his hand. "Grady Farrell. I'm the new owner of the Flying W."

"Devlin McAllister." The sheriff shook his hand with a firm, no-nonsense grip. "What are you doing here, Mr. Farrell?"

"I saw Becca's car parked out front and stopped. I wanted to make sure she was all right. When she let me in, she told me she had heard someone knocking at the back door."

The sheriff watched him carefully, his gray eyes giving nothing away. "That wouldn't have been you, would it?"

Grady looked at the sheriff standing next to Becca and felt the wall between them. Becca and McAllister were on one side; he was on the other. He wanted to grab Becca and pull her over to his side, to break down that wall. But instead, he took a step backward.

"No, Sheriff, it wasn't me. I don't think Becca believes it was me, either."

McAllister glanced over at Becca. "Doc?"

She shook her head. "It wasn't Grady, Sheriff. That's not his style."

The sheriff rocked back on his heels, never taking his eyes off Grady. "I thought you said you were the new owner of the Flying W, Farrell. How well can Doc Johnson know you?"

"I know Grady from a long time ago, Sheriff. We grew up together." Becca's voice was low-pitched but firm. "He said he wasn't at the back door, and I believe him."

Becca's words warmed him, and for a moment he wanted to step through that wall and pull her to him. But he dodged the temptation, forcing himself to remember all that stood between him and Becca. A few stolen moments of passion were one thing. He and Becca had always fit together perfectly in that department, but life wasn't made up of moments of passion. It was made up of what went on outside of the bedroom, and in that department he and Becca were miserable failures.

"You might want to take a look at the door," he said to the sheriff. Without waiting to see if the other man followed him, he headed toward the door.

The marks he'd noticed on the door in the moment before he'd kissed Becca were still there. Raw and fresh, they radiated out from the lock like a spiderweb. Becca gasped when she saw them.

"Those marks weren't there this morning," she said.

McAllister glanced up at her. "You sure?"

"Positive. We would have noticed them. It looks like someone was trying to break the lock."

That was exactly what it looked like, and Grady saw that the sheriff thought so, too. After another look, he stepped away and spoke quietly into his radio. Then he turned to Becca.

"I'm getting our deputy that handles evidence over here. He'll try to lift some fingerprints. We'll look around for any other evidence, but chances are slim." The sheriff gave Becca a look filled with regret. "Since he didn't actually get into the clinic, he probably didn't leave much behind for us to find."

"Thanks, Sheriff." Grady saw Becca glance surreptitiously at her watch. "Do you have any idea how long it'll take?"

"Could be a couple of hours, maybe longer if he finds anything."

Grady grasped Becca's elbow and drew her away from the sheriff. Her skin was warm and smooth beneath his hand, but he did his best to ignore the longing that swept through him. Once they were alone, he dropped her arm like he'd been burned. Two mistakes in one day were more than enough.

"Why are you so worried about the time?" he asked.

She drew a deep breath and ran her fingers through her

hair. It made her curls spring away from her head, and he imagined her hair would look like that when she got out of bed in the morning. Gritting his teeth, he resisted the desire that threatened to crash down on him again.

"My baby-sitter expected me back a while ago," she finally admitted. "She has to go to school tomorrow. It's not fair to expect her to stay up and wait for me."

"Is there someone else you can call?"

She chewed on her lip as she thought, and Grady remembered what her mouth had tasted like. It seemed like hours ago, but his body reminded him it had really been only minutes. He needed to get away from Becca, to let his head clear and remember all the reasons he didn't want anything to do with her.

"Do you want me to relieve your baby-sitter?" he asked.

"No!" Panic flashed in her eyes for a moment, and he watched her struggle to control it. "No, Grady, but thank you." The words sounded forced. "If Cassie woke up and found a stranger in the house, she'd be scared."

He nodded at the truth in her words, even as he wondered at the panic behind them. "I hadn't thought of that. Do you want me to stay here, then, while you go home?"

She shook her head, the panic fading from her eyes. "I can't do that. I'm part owner of this clinic, and I'm responsible for what happens here. I'll think of something."

"You can't be in two places at once," he argued, not sure why he was pressing her. He wanted nothing to do with Becca or her problems.

"Believe me, I know that." She closed her eyes for a moment and rubbed her forehead. With a flash of insight Grady realized that her dilemma was nothing new. As a single parent, she had to face these choices all the time.

But thinking about Becca's daughter also reminded him of all she stood for. Stifling the urge to comfort Becca, to reassure her, he stepped back and waited. Finally she raised her head. There was a weary resignation in her face.

"I'll call Amy's mother and explain the situation. She'll probably be able to sit with Cassie until I can get home."

"Why don't you call Cassie's father? Couldn't he stay with her?" He knew it wasn't the time or place to discuss this with Becca, but the subject of her daughter was like a sore, throbbing tooth in his mouth. He couldn't keep himself from probing at it.

Becca's face closed up. "That's not an option." She pushed past him and headed toward the front of the clinic.

A few moments later he heard her voice, murmuring on the telephone. Guilt stirred inside him. She was having a rough night, and he wasn't making it any easier. He went toward the sound of her voice, moving more slowly than he wanted to. Gritting his teeth, he tried to ignore the pain stabbing at his leg as he headed for her office.

She was just walking out the door by the time he reached it. "I'm sorry, Becca," he said. "I was out of line."

She watched him steadily, her eyes impossible to read. He stirred uneasily. In the past he'd been able to read every thought on Becca's mobile, expressive face. Now it was like staring at windows with the curtains tightly drawn.

"I appreciate your help here tonight, Grady." Her voice was cool. "Thank you for stopping. But I don't want to keep you any longer. I'm sure you hadn't planned on spending so much time here tonight."

He listened in amazement. "Are you telling me to get lost?"

"I'm telling you that I can handle it from here, but I'm grateful that you stopped."

"I don't want your gratitude, Becca," he muttered.

"Then what do you want?"

Her question stopped him cold. He wanted her hunger, he thought. Her need. He wanted her to want him the way he wanted her. But that was a lie, because as much as his body might crave her, his mind knew better.

"The hell if I know," he muttered.

Becca's face softened in the dim light, and for a moment he thought he saw the gleam of tears in her eyes. But the next moment they were gone. "Maybe we need to start over, Grady," she said softly. "We were friends once. Maybe we can at least be friends again."

He looked at her, standing only inches away from him, but separated from him by a huge gulf. They *had* been friends once. "That was a long time ago," he said quietly.

"Yes, it was. But we can't change all that's happened since then. All we can do is go forward. We're both living in the same town, and I'm going to be at your ranch on a regular basis. It'll be much easier for both of us if we can at least be civil and polite."

"Is that your definition of friendship?" he asked, something bleak and cold twisting inside him. "Polite and civil?"

"No, it's not. But it's a place to start."

"What about this?" he asked, reaching out to skim a finger down her face. He felt her tremor of response, and an answering jolt of desire shook him. "Is this part of being friends?"

He cupped his hand against her neck and felt her pulse race, but she didn't move away. "We're both adults, Grady. We're capable of controlling ourselves. I don't jump into bed with every man I'm attracted to."

He pulled his hand away from her neck, refusing to think about how good her skin had felt against his fingers. "I just wanted to get the ground rules straight, *buddy*."

"Don't make this more difficult than it has to be, Grady. This is a small town, and there's no way we can avoid each other. Surely we can both be adults."

"I've been an adult for a long time," he said, and her eyes softened.

"I know you have. It was one of the things that I loved about you. You did what you had to do and made the most out of it. You lived your life the way you wanted to live it."

"But I lost you. So I guess I didn't do everything right."

Her face closed up again. "We all make mistakes, Grady. As you said a few days ago, I was one of yours. It was a long time ago."

"Becca, I didn't—"

Before he could finish, the sheriff walked around the corner. "We're almost finished here, Doc. We couldn't find any prints, which makes me suspicious. There should have been some from the people who use that door every day. It looks like your prowler wiped down the door."

Grady thought Becca's face paled. "Any ideas who it could be?"

The sheriff shrugged. "My guess is that it was kids. Probably doing it on a dare, especially since they could see you there." His face darkened. "Or maybe looking for drugs. That's supposed to be a big-city problem, but we've got our share. Get better locks, and be sure you have a few loud dogs in your kennel every night. That'll scare off the kids."

"Thanks, Devlin." Becca held out her hand, and the tall man shook it as his face softened.

"I'll have my men patrol by here more frequently for the next couple of weeks. We'll keep an eye on the place. In the meantime make sure all your abusable drugs are locked up."

"We already do that. Thanks again, Dev."

McAllister tipped his hat, then walked out the front door. Grady noticed that he checked it once it was closed to make sure it was locked.

Becca turned and headed for the back of the building. "I'm going to make sure the door is locked and all the lights are off," she said, her words echoing in the now empty building. A few minutes later she walked back into the front, snapping off the lights behind her.

She hesitated, then held out her hand to him. "Thanks again, Grady. I'm very glad you stopped when you did."

Curling his fingers around hers, satisfaction coursed through him when he felt her hand tremble. "It was my pleasure," he said, his voice husky.

Instead of letting her go, he pulled her toward him and brushed his mouth over hers. When he stepped back, he thought she looked disappointed.

Recovering quickly, she grabbed her purse and keys off the counter and headed for the door. Once they were in the small parking lot, she opened the door to her truck and stood behind it. He wondered if it was supposed to protect her from him. "Good night, Grady."

He stopped on his way to his truck. "I'm following you home," he said. "I want to make sure you get inside safely, then I'll walk your baby-sitter home."

"That's very thoughtful of you, but I don't live far. And Amy lives right next door."

He watched her in the moonlight. In the pearly light, her hair looked almost white and her face was pale. But the dark circles under her eyes were clearly visible. "The more you argue with me about it, the longer it's going to take for you to get home. Your baby-sitter is waiting for you, remember?"

Becca opened her mouth to argue with him, but she must have seen the determination on his face because she turned and got into the truck. As he followed her down Cameron's quiet streets, he wondered what he was doing. He'd planned to stay as far away from Becca Johnson as he could. But the first time he saw her truck, late at night, he stopped to find out why.

He was just being neighborly, he told himself. That was all. When you lived in a small town, you were expected to be neighborly. He'd wanted to make sure Becca was all right. There was nothing more to it.

He had no intention of getting involved with Becca Johnson again. Not in this lifetime.

Chapter 6

Becca glanced into her rearview mirror one more time. Grady's truck was still behind her, and she leaned back against the seat with resignation. She knew him well enough to know that he wouldn't leave until he'd made sure she was inside her house and Amy's mother was home safely.

What capricious fate had made him drive by her clinic tonight, just when she was there? And why had he stopped? Shivering again as she thought about the moments of terror when she'd heard the prowler at the back door, she acknowledged that she was very glad Grady had come by when he had.

She tried to ignore what had happened between them in the kennel afterward, but the desire he'd stirred in her was almost impossible to banish completely. It hovered under her skin, making her jumpy and restless. And far too aware of Grady.

When she pulled into the driveway of her small home, he pulled in right behind her. And before she was completely out of her truck, he was standing beside it. As they walked toward her stairs, she noticed that he was limping. It was very slight, so slight that most people wouldn't have noticed, but she knew Grady too well. She was too aware of his body.

"Did you hurt yourself out in the kennel tonight?" she asked as she watched him pull himself up the porch using the handrail.

"No. Why do you ask?" He looked up at her.

"You look like you're limping."

He stopped on the stairs. "It's your imagination." His voice was flat.

She shrugged. "I didn't want to think you'd hurt yourself while you were helping me."

"Don't worry, I'm not going to sue the clinic." His words were sharp, but she thought she heard pain beneath them.

"I didn't think you were, Grady. I was concerned."

"Don't be," he muttered. "There's nothing wrong with me."

She saw his struggle to walk normally, but she didn't say anything. How could she accuse him of keeping secrets from her when she was keeping an enormous secret from him? He was right—it was none of her business. The thought made her sad, but she pushed the feeling away. Grady didn't want her sympathy, or her prying. She wasn't a part of his life.

With her hand on the doorknob, she turned to him. "Do you want to come in while Amy's mom gets ready to go?"

"Thanks, but I'll wait outside. I'll look around a little, make sure no one's been here."

Becca couldn't prevent the wave of relief that crashed over her. It would have been churlish and ungrateful not to invite him in, but she didn't want Grady in her house. There were enough ghosts of him there already. It would have been more than she could bear, to picture him in her living room and feel his presence each time she walked into the house.

"Fine. We'll be right out."

She slipped into the house and let the door close quietly behind her. It was an odd feeling, knowing Cassie's father was on the porch of her house. But she couldn't deal with that feeling right now. She had to send Shelly home and make sure Grady left, too. Then she could think about what had happened tonight.

In a few minutes she was standing on the porch, watching Grady walk her next-door neighbor home. Shelly had been thrilled to meet Grady. By now the whole town knew that Grady Farrell, the rodeo star, had bought the Flying W. Becca knew that within the next few days, everyone in the neighborhood would hear how he'd escorted Becca home from the clinic.

She didn't care, she thought wearily as she leaned against the door. She'd been gossiped about before, and it hadn't destroyed her. And if she started to spend more time with Grady, there would be plenty more for people to gossip about. That's what happened in small towns.

It was the only way she could decide how to tell him about Cassie, she told herself. She had to get to know Grady better, and the only way she was going to do that was spend time with him. She thought about the passion that had flared between them at the clinic, and her hand tightened on the doorknob. That couldn't happen again. She had to keep Cassie and her needs in the front of her mind, not her own reaction to Grady. He might be the only man who'd ever stirred her that way, but that didn't tell her what kind of father he would be. It didn't tell her how he would take the news that he was a father. And that's all she could be interested in right now.

She'd had her chance to make a life with Grady, and she'd ruined it. Now she had to think about Cassie, and only Cassie.

Grady appeared again, heading for the porch. She wanted to run inside and hide from him, but she straightened up instead.

"Thanks for seeing Shelly home," she said.

He looked up at her as he started climbing the stairs, and to her surprise a small smile curved his lips. "That woman is something else," he said.

"What do you mean?"

"If I'd let her, she would have had my whole life story out of me in the time it took to walk her next door. She's good."

Becca surprised herself by smiling back at him. "I should have warned you. Since you bought the Flying W, the whole town has been buzzing about the rodeo star in our midst. Everyone in Cameron follows the rodeo, and they all know you're a world-champion bull rider. I'm sure Shelly was thrilled to meet you."

"Are you going to fill her in on all the details tomorrow?" he asked.

The smile faded from her mouth. "I would never gossip about you, Grady. You should know that."

He watched her steadily. "There's a lot I don't know about you anymore."

"Some things don't change."

"I know," he whispered, his eyes gleaming in the darkness.

He reached out and cupped her cheek, and Becca felt herself flush at his reminder of what had passed between them. An ember of the desire that had burned so brightly just a little while ago flared up inside her. She longed to lean into his touch, to let his hand warm her. She'd been cold for so long.

Instead, she moved away, breaking the contact. "Thanks again, Grady, for all you did tonight." She hesitated. "I'm not sure what I would have done without you," she finally admitted.

He shoved his hands into his pockets, but he didn't take his eyes off her face. "You would have been fine, Becca. You would have called the sheriff and done what you had to do to protect your business. I saw your strength tonight. You take care of what's important to you."

His eyes softened and his mouth relaxed. She remembered the taste of his mouth all too well, and the touch of his hands seemed to be imprinted on her skin. She swayed toward him, unable to take her eyes off his.

"You've grown up, Becca."

His whispered words glided past her ear and brushed her cheek. But they also reminded her of Cassie, asleep upstairs. She reached for the image of her child as Grady's presence on her moonlight-drenched porch tempted her to forget her responsibilities, forget what she needed to do. He was too close. All she needed to do was reach out and she could touch him. One touch, and he would be kissing her again. And this time she wasn't sure she could summon the will to stop.

Closing her eyes, she whispered, "Good night, Grady," as she fumbled with the door behind her.

He watched her for a moment, then brushed his finger over the corner of her mouth and turned away. As he started down the steps, he turned to her and said, "Sweet dreams, Becca."

She didn't move until his truck disappeared around the corner of her street. Trying to will away the empty feeling, telling herself that she did the smart thing, she listened until she couldn't hear his truck anymore, then went into the house. Making sure all the doors and windows were locked, she finally headed up the stairs to bed.

Before she went into her room, she went into Cassie's, just like she did every night. The last thing she did before she slept was check her daughter.

Cassie sprawled in the center of her bed, her blankets sliding onto the floor. She was a restless sleeper, and Becca picked up the blanket and covered her again before she pressed a kiss to her daughter's sweet-smelling hair.

"I won't let him hurt you," she whispered into Cassie's hair. "No matter what happens, you won't be hurt. I promise."

Smoothing her hand down the silk of Cassie's hair, Becca kissed her once more, then backed out of the room. Cassie was a wonderful child, happy and well-adjusted. Nothing was going to change that, she vowed.

* * *

Two days later Becca woke up in the morning to hear Cassie whimpering. Running into the other bedroom, she found her curled up in a ball in the center of her bed. Her blankets were on the floor, as usual, and Cassie was shivering.

"What's the matter, honey?" Becca asked.

"My tummy hurts," Cassie cried. "And my head. I don't feel good, Mommy."

Becca touched her daughter's head and found it burning hot. "You have a fever, sweetheart," she said. Pulling the blanket over her daughter, she added, "You probably have what Jenny and Todd had."

"I don't want to throw up," Cassie whimpered. "That's yucky."

"Maybe you won't." She smoothed her hand down Cassie's hair, brushing it behind her ear. "Stay here in bed while I call the clinic."

Cassie looked at her, panic in her eyes. "I don't have to go to Laura's today, do I?"

"Of course not. I'll stay home with you."

Cassie burrowed into her pillow. "That's good, Mommy. I want you to be with me when I don't feel good."

Becca hurried down to the phone and called the clinic. After talking with Stella, she walked slowly back up the stairs, mentally rearranging her calls for the next day. According to Laura, Jenny and Todd had been fine within twenty-four hours. If Cassie was lucky, she'd be feeling better by tomorrow.

"We're all set, honey," she said as she walked into the room. "I don't have to go to work today," she began, but she stopped when she saw that Cassie had fallen back to sleep. Drawing the sheet up to cover the small form in the bed, she hurried out of the room. She made herself coffee, then brought the coffee and newspaper up to Cassie's room, along with some work she'd brought home from the clinic.

Settling into the chair next to Cassie's bed, she read the paper as she waited for her daughter to wake up.

Several hours later, as she was reading Cassie a story, Becca heard a knock on her door. Leaning over, she kissed Cassie on the top of her head and handed her the book.

"There's someone at the door, honey. It's probably Laura. I called her to tell her you weren't coming today."

"Can I come downstairs and see her?" Cassie asked.

Becca pressed her cheek against Cassie's head, then smiled at her. "You stay in bed, honey. I'll be right back, and you'll see Laura soon enough."

As she hurried down the stairs, Becca felt her smile lingering. She should have known Laura would turn up after she'd told her that Cassie was sick. Laura was that kind of friend.

Pulling the door open, Becca began to say, "Hi, Laura. Thanks…"

Her voice trailed off when she saw Grady standing on her porch. Her first, automatic reaction was pleasure at the sight of him. Pushing that away, trying to hide it, she said, "Grady! What are you doing here?"

He shrugged, looking uncomfortable. "I called the clinic because we needed to have you come out to the ranch, and they told me you weren't in today because your daughter was sick. I had to come into town anyway, so I thought I'd stop by and see if there was anything you needed."

A treacherous pleasure seeped into her, overriding the caution she had imposed on herself after their last encounter. "Thank you, Grady. That was very thoughtful of you."

A dark red flush stained his cheeks. "It's no big deal, Becca. I just thought you might need something. One of my friends on the rodeo circuit had a wife and kid, and he told me more than once about how his wife complained when the kid was sick. He wasn't home, so she couldn't leave the house if she needed something."

This time she had to ask him into the house. Bracing herself, Becca stepped aside. "Come in, Grady."

But he shook his head. "You don't need company today, Becca. I just stopped by to see if there was anything I could pick up for you."

She couldn't help murmuring a silent prayer of thanks. Today, of all days, she didn't want Grady to see Cassie. If Cassie heard someone in the house, she'd come downstairs, sick or not. And all it would take was one look at Cassie for Grady to see the truth. Cassie was the mirror image of her father.

"She has been asking for her favorite soda," Becca finally said. "If you're going to the grocery store, I'd appreciate if you'd pick some up."

"No problem. What kind is it?"

Becca smiled. "You've probably never heard of it. It's called Lemon Fizz."

Grady gave her a sharp look. "Really? Lemon Fizz is my favorite soda, too."

Becca felt as if she'd been doused with cold water. Finally she said, weakly, "What a coincidence. At least you'll know what to look for."

"Yeah." He walked down the porch steps, and once again Becca noticed how he seemed to lean his weight on the handrail, the careful way he moved down the steps. "I'll be back in a little while, Becca," he said over his shoulder, and she noticed that he wasn't smiling any longer. She watched his truck pull out of her driveway, and didn't go back into the house until he was no longer in sight.

This whole charade was becoming more and more complicated, she thought wearily. She was going to have to force herself to spend more time with Grady. Once she knew more about the man he had become, she would be able to judge how to tell him about Cassie.

And it looked like the man he had become was far different from the boy she had known. The Grady she'd known would never have thought to stop to ask her if she needed anything.

She closed the door, but leaned against it for a long time, thinking about Grady.

Grady swerved his truck into the grocery-store parking lot and swore to himself for the hundredth time since leaving Becca. What in the hell had possessed him to stop by her house this morning? He'd told himself he was just being neighborly. That's what you were supposed to do when you lived in a small town. He'd told himself that he would do the same for anyone else, but the truth laughed at him.

He'd done it because he wanted to see Becca. It had been two days since the incident at her clinic. Two lousy days, and he was so desperate to see her that he stopped by her house with a flimsy excuse that anyone with half a brain could see through.

What was the matter with him? He didn't want to get involved with Becca again. He'd told himself that over and over, and he'd told Becca the same thing. And he'd meant it. She had betrayed him and broke his heart, and he wanted to stay as far away from her as possible.

But that's not what his body was telling him. His body was saying that it wanted to be as close to Becca as a man could get to a woman. His body remembered how she'd felt, how she'd tasted, how she'd reacted to him. And his body didn't give one good damn about the way she'd cut him loose all those years ago.

Climbing out of the truck, he winced as his bad leg hit the pavement, then swore and slammed the door shut. That was another thing. He didn't want anything to do with a woman who pitied him. Becca had noticed his limp the other night. If he told her what happened, she'd feel sorry for him. He knew Becca. She wouldn't be able to help herself. She could feel sorry for a mean, mangy, snake-in-the-grass range bull if she thought he'd gotten a raw deal.

He didn't allow himself to limp as he walked into the grocery store and grabbed a carton of Lemon Fizz. He noticed the curious stares as he waited to pay for the soda, but he didn't look around. He wasn't in the mood for social pleasantries.

Then why had he stopped at Becca's? Scowling, he paid the cashier and stomped out of the store with the soda. He knew why he'd stopped at Becca's, and he didn't like the answer one bit.

The bottles of soda clanked in their carton as he drove slowly back to Becca's, and he wondered about the child who would drink the soda. Becca's daughter. If things had worked out differently, she might be his daughter, too.

The thought should throw terror into his wandering soul. Instead, he felt a fleeting sense of loss, as if something precious had slipped through his grasp, never to return.

He turned into Becca's driveway, disgusted with himself. My God, what was the matter with him? He must be getting old. That was the only thing that could explain his sudden weakness and sentimentality.

Becca must have heard him drive up, because she opened the door before he had a chance to knock. She gave him a tight smile when she saw the carton of soda in his hand. "You found it. Thank you, Grady. Cassie will be so happy."

"Glad I could help," he muttered. He wanted to dash away, but instead he asked, "Is there anything else you need?"

Becca shook her head. "No, thanks. We're going to the doctor this afternoon, but I'm sure it's just a virus. I'm hoping that she'll be fine tomorrow." She studied him for a moment. "Why were you calling the clinic this morning? Is something wrong out at the ranch?"

"Nothing that can't wait. I was looking at the books and I noticed that some of the horses are due for vaccines. We'll set it up when your daughter is feeling better."

She nodded. "I should be back at work tomorrow or the next day. Tell Stella to put you on the schedule."

"She already did." He stood on her porch and cursed himself for the inane conversation they were having, but he didn't want to leave.

Finally Becca shifted from one foot to the other. "I'd ask you to come in, but I don't want you to get sick."

"That's all right. I have to get back to the ranch." He paused before he turned around. "Are you sure there's nothing else you need?"

"Positive." The tension in her face seemed to dissipate as her mouth curved up. "Thanks again for stopping, Grady. I can't tell you how much it means to me."

"It wasn't a big deal," he muttered. "I'd do the same for anyone."

This time she gave him a full smile. "I have a feeling that you would, Grady. Even though it might surprise you." She opened the door and stepped inside her house. "I'll see you in a day or two."

She closed the door gently behind her, and he stared at it for a moment before turning to leave. What the hell was that supposed to mean? He'd stopped by her house because he had the hots for her. That was all there was to it. It didn't mean more than that.

As he drove away, he said aloud, "You're reading this wrong, Becca. There's no complicated reason why I stopped at your house. The reason is about as basic and fundamental as you can get."

It didn't mean more than that. It couldn't. He wouldn't let it.

Four days later Becca turned down the driveway toward Flying W ranch. Cassie had been sick the next day, too, and after missing two days of work, she had a lot of catching up to do. This was the earliest Stella could get the ranch into her schedule.

Becca felt her palms sweat as she got closer to the barns and the house. Would Grady be around? Would she see him? How would he react?

She had no idea, but she vowed to be as professional as possible. She couldn't allow herself to think about the passion they'd shared in her clinic, or about Grady's unexpected, thoughtful visit to the house when Cassie was sick. She was here today to vaccinate his horses. Period.

Parking next to the barn, she pulled three boxes of vaccines out of the cooler and grabbed a handful of syringes. Then she went in search of Tucker.

"Grady left all the horses that needed vaccines in the barn today," the foreman told her as he led her into the dim, cool barn. "There they are."

Becca flipped her chart to a checklist of the ranch's horses. "Tell me exactly which horses need which vaccines, and I'll mark them off."

Tucker reached into the rear pocket of his jeans and pulled out a grubby list. "This here's what Grady gave me." He handed it to her.

Becca looked at the list, her chest tightening at the sight of Grady's familiar, slanting handwriting. She hadn't seen it for years. Not since the last letter she'd gotten from him, the one that said he wasn't coming home again for four more months. That was the letter that had triggered her foolish, ill-fated phone call.

Swallowing around the lump in her throat, she nodded at Tucker. "This looks fine. I'll take it from here."

"They're all yours, Doc," Tucker said cheerfully as he headed out of the barn.

Becca studied the list, forcing herself to concentrate on the horses and the vaccines they needed, forcing herself to put Grady out of her mind. All the horses needed rabies and Potomac Fever vaccines, and a few needed a flu rhino booster. Grabbing two syringes and two vials of vaccine for the first horse on the list, she slipped into his stall and began to murmur nonsense words to him in a low voice.

The horse pricked up his ears and turned around to find the source of the noise. Rubbing his ears, Becca slipped her hand down his neck, slapped him lightly twice then injected the first vaccine. The animal snorted and tossed his head, but calmed down when Becca continued to talk to him. She administered the second vaccine, spent a few more moments talking to the horse, then slipped out of the stall to repeat the process on the next horse.

"That was pretty smooth."

Grady's voice came out of the shadows to the left of the stall, and Becca spun around to face him. "I didn't know you were here."

"Tucker told me you'd started on the horses. Why didn't you ask for someone to help you?"

"I wasn't sure anyone was around, and it wasn't a big deal. I've vaccinated plenty of horses by myself."

Grady frowned. "What if one of them decided they didn't like the needle? You should have someone holding them for you."

"That's not always an option," she explained as she filled the next syringe. "I'm used to doing it by myself."

"I'll hold them for you."

She couldn't tell him she'd prefer to work alone, that she dreaded being in the close confines of the stalls with him. After all, they were his horses. Nodding abruptly, she tapped the bubbles of air out of the syringe, then stepped into the next stall.

Grady moved to the other side of the horse, holding his halter and rubbing his nose. When she slapped the animal's neck and injected the vaccine, the horse barely flinched.

"Thank you," she said, almost grudgingly, as they closed the stall door behind them. "That was a big help."

"I aim to please, Becca."

Grady's words were low and intimate in the dimly lit, isolated barn. His bright blue eyes glowed with awareness, and the sounds of activity outside the barn faded away. Becca knew the ranch was bustling with activity, full of men and women with jobs to do, but suddenly it seemed as if she and

Grady were the only people within miles. Memories of the last time they were alone together washed over her with a rush of desire.

It couldn't happen again. Breaking eye contact with Grady, she bent over her bag and dropped the used syringes and vials into a container. Grabbing what she would need for the next horse, she straightened as she filled the syringes. Without meeting Grady's eyes, she moved to the next stall.

Neither of them said much as she moved down the row of stalls, methodically vaccinating the ranch's horses. But each time they stepped into a stall, Becca felt his presence more acutely. When their arms brushed, Grady left a trail of fire behind. Every time he crooned to one of the horses, the soft, musical words fluttered in her chest, making it tighter. When she had to lean close to him, his masculine scent surrounded her, sharpening her longing.

"You don't have to help me with the rest of them," she finally said, a ring of desperation in her voice. "I really am used to doing this myself."

"It's not a problem, Becca. It's going faster this way, isn't it?"

She wanted to scream *no*. It was taking forever to finish. But he was right. Having his help made the job more efficient.

"You must have a lot of other things to do," she said, barely managing not to grit her teeth.

"I do," he admitted. "But they can all wait. I wanted to talk to you about what happened the other night at your clinic."

Chapter 7

"What is there to talk about?" she asked, stiffening her shoulders. "We're both adults, and we got carried away. End of story."

"You think so, Becca?" His voice was very soft. When he reached out a finger and twirled one of her curls around it, her toes curled at his touch. "I don't think we've finished this story yet."

She batted his hand away. "Call it a weak moment, Grady. I was scared. It was nothing more than adrenaline and nerves."

His mouth curled into a smile. "You're good, Becca. Very good. Any other woman, I might have believed her. But I know you too well."

"You don't know me from diddly," she retorted, reaching for another vaccine. "The girl you know ceased to exist nine years ago."

The smile disappeared from his face. "I know." He let his eyes linger on her face for another moment, and she thought she saw pain, hidden deep in their blue depths. "But that wasn't the part of the other night I wanted to talk about."

She jerked her head up to glare at him. "Then why did you let me think it was?"

"I didn't let you think anything. You jumped to that conclusion all by yourself." A devil glittered in his eyes. "But I'm happy to know that it was memorable for you."

"About as memorable as a rash," she muttered.

"I was as close to you as a rash," he agreed, his eyes twinkling.

"I'm happy you're enjoying this conversation," she snapped. "But I do have work to do here. What exactly did you want to talk about?"

"The person who was at your back door." All traces of playfulness disappeared. His eyes turned cold and hard as they stared back at her, and Becca shivered. He would be a formidable opponent.

"I have no idea who that was," she said, turning away to reach for another syringe. She didn't want Grady to know how much it still bothered her. "And there's been no sign of a prowler around the clinic since then. It was probably kids, like Sheriff McAllister said."

"Maybe it was someone who knows you go to the clinic every evening."

Her hand tightened on the syringe. "That's ridiculous. I know everyone in Cameron and on most of the ranches around town. No one would want to hurt me."

"You'd be surprised at what people will do," Grady answered, his voice cynical.

Becca looked at Grady, mourning the hardness in his eyes, knowing she was responsible for at least some of his bitterness. "No, I wouldn't," she said quietly. "But I've lived here for four years and I've never had any problems. I can't believe it was personal."

"And I can't believe that whoever was at the back door

didn't see your truck at the front door," he retorted. "But if you're satisfied, Becca, then I'll drop it."

She wasn't satisfied and she hadn't been able to forget it, but she didn't want to reveal her fears to Grady. Without meeting his eyes, she stepped into the next stall and reached for the horse. "There's nothing to worry about," she muttered as she tapped the horse on the neck, then injected the vaccine.

Grady held the horse steady. "Fine." His hand absently caressed the horse's mane, inches from hers, and for a moment she wanted to let her hand slide under his, to feel his strength as his fingers curled around hers.

Clenching her fist around the used syringe, she backed out of the stall and dropped the used syringe into the disposal container. Without looking at Grady, she pulled the list of horses out of her pocket and studied it.

"It looks as though they're all vaccinated," she finally said. As she looked up at Grady, she couldn't squash the flutter of disappointment. There was no excuse to stay any longer. She only wanted to stay for Cassie's sake, she reminded herself firmly. To get to know Grady again. But a part of her knew better. A part of her knew she wanted to stay for herself, and that part was appalled.

"Not quite." Grady eased the stall door shut and nodded his head toward the far end of the stable. "I have a few of my own horses here. You don't have records for them, but they'll need vaccines in a few weeks. You might as well take care of it while you're here."

"Do you have records? Do you know what they need?"

He nodded. "I got copies from their last vet. Hold on and I'll get them."

Grady hurried out of the barn, and Becca wandered down to the other end of the barn. There were three horses in roomy box stalls, and she recognized one almost immediately. It was Duke, Grady's horse from his rodeo days. Duke and Grady Farrell had been on the cover of virtually every rodeo publication several years ago. They had been world-champion calf ropers, their skill almost unprecedented. The fact that Grady had also been a champion bull rider had made him a myth in rodeo circles.

"Hey, Duke," she said softly, and the huge bay horse snuffled at her and wandered over. He stared dreamily at her while she rubbed his head, then nibbled delicately at the pocket of her T-shirt. She pushed his head away with a grin.

"I see that Grady has you good and spoiled. There aren't any treats in there."

Duke snorted and moved away, and Becca looked in the next stall. A compact gray quarter horse stood at the feed box, but Becca didn't recognize him. Like any horse of Grady's, though, he was in good condition and well cared for.

When she stopped in front of the last box, the largest, she saw an older horse, her back slightly swayed and her joints puffy. Becca murmured to her, and when the mare turned around, Becca stilled.

It was one of the horses from Grady's father's ranch. She knew Diane, because Grady had made the horse his special project. The two had developed a bond unlike any she'd ever seen. Diane was the horse that he had rescued from a beating when he was a teen, a rescue that had resulted in him being beaten by his father. The horse he'd been forced to leave behind when he'd left home.

As Becca stood staring at the mare, she heard Grady behind her. "She's almost twenty-three now. Most of her piss and vinegar has disappeared, but watch yourself around her. She can still nip with the best of them."

"I didn't know you had her."

Grady stepped up to the stall door, and the old mare immediately walked over to him. She dipped her head as Grady scratched her ears, and Becca felt a lump swell in her throat. The bond between Grady and Diane was as strong as ever.

"I've had her for almost eight years now. My father

wanted to erase any trace of me after I left so he put her up for sale, but his foreman let me know what he was doing. My father didn't realize he was selling her to me.''

''Where did you keep her while you traveled the rodeo circuit?''

''I took her with me.''

Becca glanced over at him, but he was looking at the horse. ''That couldn't have been easy.''

He shrugged. ''It was what I wanted. Diane was too cranky to get along with most other people. And I didn't want anyone else taking care of her.''

''So you trailered her from show to show.''

He gave Diane a final pat on the neck and moved away. ''I sure as hell didn't ride her from show to show.''

Grady might not want to discuss Diane and his commitment to her, but Becca was moved by his obvious devotion to the horse. ''That had to be expensive, Grady.''

He gave her his cocky grin. ''When I won, we all ate well. When I didn't, we starved together.''

Becca watched Diane amble over to her feed trough and sample it. Before she could ask any more questions, Grady pulled a computer printout out of his back pocket and handed it to her. ''Here are the records I got from their last vet.''

She scanned the papers and saw that Grady had been right. Their vaccines were indeed due in a few weeks. She nodded at the gray horse in the middle stall. ''Is that another of your roping horses?''

''That's Ron's horse,'' he said. ''His records are there, too.''

''Does Ron want me to vaccinate him, too?''

Grady looked over at her, puzzled. ''Why wouldn't he?''

''Just wondered,'' she muttered.

She scooped up syringes and vaccines and said, ''Who's first?''

''Might as well start with Diane and get it over with. She doesn't like needles,'' he warned.

"If I remember correctly, Diane doesn't like much of anything," Becca sighed as she stepped into the roomy stall with Grady.

The horse flattened her ears as Becca approached her, but Grady grabbed her halter and spoke to her in a soothing voice. Her ears pricked up, but she turned to look as Becca approached her left side.

Dropping the syringes and vials into the apron she wore, Becca held out her hand for Diane to inspect. The horse snuffled and bared her teeth, but Becca didn't flinch. Finally the horse gave a snort and turned back to Grady.

"Congratulations," he said, a hint of laughter in his voice. "She approves of you."

"I don't know how you can tell," she replied as she reached for the first syringe.

"She didn't bite you." This time he grinned at her, and the creases in his cheeks turned into dimples. Becca's heart sped up. "Consider that a major success."

"I can see that Diane has been a favorite of vets over the years," Becca said dryly.

Deliberately not looking at Grady and ignoring her racing heart, Becca tapped Diane's neck and injected the first vaccine. The horse threw her head back and danced sideways, but Grady calmed her with a few words. She repeated the performance for the second vaccine, and when Grady released her, she stamped her foot and moved sideways into the place Becca had been standing.

Becca was already out of the stall. "That was quite a performance for a twenty-three-year-old."

"You should have seen her back in her wild youth."

"I did see her then, and I feel sorry for old Doc Post. He must have had quite a time with her."

"It was always an adventure." Grady spoke lightly, but his hand lingered on the old mare's back. Then, with a final slap on the rump, he moved out of the stall and latched the door. "The other two will be fine."

It only took a few minutes to vaccinate the other two horses. When they were finished, Grady unhooked the lead rope from Duke's halter and waited while Becca disposed of the vaccine vials and syringes. As they headed back toward the barn door, he ducked into the tack room to hang up the rope.

"I have to ask you something," he called from the tack room.

She walked into the dimly lit room. The one window high in the wall let in a stream of sunlight that filtered down toward the floor, and Grady hadn't turned on the bare overhead light-bulb. The room smelled of leather and horses, a pleasant, familiar scent. Grady hung the rope neatly next to several others, then turned to her.

"Can you get one of the other vets to go to the clinic at night?" he said abruptly.

"Are you still worried about the prowler? I thought we'd already discussed it."

"You said you weren't worried. I never said I was satisfied."

"There's nothing I can do about it, Grady."

"Maybe you shouldn't go to the clinic alone at night for a while."

All of her fears came rushing back to her, and she straightened her spine. "Taking care of the animals in the clinic at night is my job. I do it because I don't take emergencies. It wouldn't be fair to ask one of my partners to take that on, too."

"Then don't keep animals in the hospital overnight. If there weren't any animals there, you wouldn't have to go and check them."

"I can't do that. If an animal is sick, they have to be cared for. We don't live in a big city that has an after-hours emergency clinic. We're the only clinic for miles."

Grady leaned against the wall. "Then what are you going to do?"

"I told you, Grady, that I'm going to keep doing exactly what I am doing. Some nights there won't be any animals in the clinic, so I won't have to go. But when there's an animal recovering from surgery, or a sick animal, I'll be there."

"And everyone in Cameron knows that."

"Anyone who's had an animal in the clinic does. I don't put a sign in front of the clinic saying 'Dr. Johnson will be in the clinic every evening between nine-thirty and ten o'clock. All muggers and burglars please make a note of these hours'."

"You never used to have such a smart mouth," he said softly.

The intimate tones of his voice echoed in the quiet, dimly lit room. "I never used to be a lot of things, Grady, including your responsibility. Why are you so concerned about what happens at the clinic?"

He slowly met her eyes, and time seemed to stretch out between them like a rubber band, becoming more and more taut. "Maybe I don't like something like this happening in my town," he finally said.

He pushed away from the wall and moved closer. "Maybe I'd be just as concerned about anyone in your position. Maybe it's not personal at all."

She felt an irrational surge of disappointment. "That's very commendable, Grady," she managed to say. "I'm glad to see you're so civic-minded."

Reaching out, he skimmed one hand down her hair. He never touched her scalp, but she still tingled. "Is it so incomprehensible that I don't want you to get hurt?" he murmured.

"I don't know what you want, Grady. I'm not sure I ever did."

"I don't want this," he muttered. He cupped the back of her head and drew her slowly closer. When she could feel the heat of his body, feel the need that pulsed from him, he lowered his mouth to hers.

Heat speared through her, sizzling along her nerves and

settling low in her abdomen. In spite of his words, Grady
pulled her closer, molding her body to his. She reveled in the
differences between them, in the hard maleness of his body.
They fit together perfectly, in spite of Grady's height. They
always had. As she tried to move closer, she couldn't banish
the thought.

Becca told herself to stop, to move away, but instead she
wrapped her arms around Grady's neck. This wasn't the way
to get to know Grady better. But it felt so right. It felt like
she had come home. This was what she had craved for so
many years; this was what she had dreamed about. One more
kiss from Grady couldn't be wrong.

Grady tasted her surrender, felt her softening as she melted
into him. With a groan he tightened his hold on her, then slid
his hands down her back to cup her hips. He ached to touch
her skin, to let his fingers slide down her spine and smooth
over the soft roundness of her. When she murmured his name
into his mouth, he groaned again.

Pressing her against the wall, he brought shaking hands up
between them and slowly tugged her T-shirt out of the waistband of her jeans. Her hands stilled on his chest, but she
didn't push him away. Instead, her lips trembled under his,
then she tentatively opened her mouth to him.

Every inch of him throbbing with need, he swept his tongue
into her mouth and tasted the velvet sweetness of her. When
she touched her tongue to his, a spasm of need so intense it
was painful swept over him. He had to touch her. Sliding
under her shirt, he splayed his hands on her belly, and her
skin jumped under his fingers.

He couldn't wait another moment. Moving slowly, savoring every inch of her, he cupped her breasts in his hands.
They were heavier than when she was a girl, and they filled
his palms. Fumbling with the catch on her bra, he finally
managed to open it, and he peeled it away as the satiny weight
of her breasts slid into his hands.

Grady wasn't sure if he was trembling, or if Becca was.

When he touched her nipples with his thumbs, she cried out and he swallowed the sound into his mouth. He brushed his fingers over her nipples again, and another spasm rippled through her.

Lost in sensation, knowing that if he didn't regain some control over himself he was going to explode, he smoothed his hands down her sides. Her skin was every bit as satiny as he remembered. And as warm. Her skin burned under his touch, heating as he moved from her breasts to her back. He roamed over her back, letting his fingers linger on the bumps of her spine, on the slight dimple low on her back. The waistband of her jeans was too tight, so he reached around and loosened the button with fingers that fumbled. She stood very still while he slowly lowered the zipper, but she didn't move away.

Her buttocks were smooth and firm, and as he caressed her, he pressed his hips into hers. She moaned then, a small sound in the back of her throat that he drank in with his mouth. His hand drifted lower, toward her heat and the dampness he could already feel, and she swayed toward him. She wanted him, he knew, and he needed her with a ferocity and a fever that he'd never felt before. He had to have her, here and now.

When he unbuckled his belt, she reached to fumble with the button on his jeans. Her fingers brushed the rock-hard length of his erection, and he jerked uncontrollably. He wanted to feel her hands on him, feel her stroking his hardness, feel himself sinking into the hot, wet depths of her.

The button on his jeans came loose, and she slowly pulled the zipper down. It was exquisite torture, and he knew he couldn't bear it for much longer. Closing his eyes, he stood before her, trembling, as she freed him from the white briefs he wore.

When her hand closed around him, he felt his knees buckle. Throwing a blanket over the bales of hay that stood in the corner, he pressed her back onto it, then swept her jeans down her legs. He cupped her through her peach silk panties, feeling

her shiver, sinking into her heat and moisture. Finding her
mouth again, he tasted her longing, her need and her passion,
and knew that it matched his own.

His fingers were tangled in the waistband of her delicate
panties when he heard his name called, faintly and as though
from far away. Becca must have heard it, too, because she
froze beneath him, one leg tangled with his. They lay perfectly still, listening to the person come closer to the barn.

It was Ron Perkins, he realized, and he was heading for
the horse barn. He and Becca didn't move, but he felt her
heart pounding beneath his.

Ron paused at the door to the barn. "Grady?" he called,
and Grady heard the puzzlement in his voice. He was supposed to be in the barn, and Becca's truck was still parked
in front of the barn. He held his breath, willing his friend to
go away. Willing him to disappear off the face of the earth.

After a moment that seemed like eternity, Ron's footsteps
retreated and finally faded away. Grady and Becca still lay
perfectly still on the bales of hay, a tableau of wanton, illicit
behavior. Her shirt was pushed up to her breasts, and her
jeans were shoved down to her knees. And he was just as
bad. He lay half on top of her, his jeans and briefs almost
discarded.

Her eyes were closed, and her face was pale and tight. The
passion that had filled it moments ago was fading, replaced
by an appalled realization of what they'd almost done. Slowly
he lifted himself off her, then took her hand and pulled her
to her feet.

"Damn Ron Perkins to the farthest circle of hell," he said
bitterly. "I'm sorry, Becca. Sorry I started this here, and sorry
you were in a position to have Ron find us like this."

"We seem to be experts at bad timing, don't we?" she
answered, pulling up her jeans and fastening her bra. She
didn't look at him. "All the way around."

He buckled his belt and waited for her to finish pulling
herself together. Her face was now flushed and her T-shirt

was wrinkled, but they wouldn't be embarrassed by anyone stumbling into the tack room.

"Becca, I..."

"Please don't say you're sorry again," she interrupted. "I was as willing a participant as you were, and we both know it." She took a deep, trembling breath and looked him in the eyes. "Grady, we have to talk. Not here, but soon. There's too much between us to just fall into bed together. I don't want to have casual sex with you. I think more of myself than that, and more of you, too."

There wouldn't be anything casual about any lovemaking they did. The thought sneaked into Grady's mind, and he immediately pushed it away. That was all he wanted from Becca, wasn't it? Relief for the need that had filled him since the first time he'd seen her at his ranch. Just a scratch for the itch that had been plaguing him.

"We can talk anytime." He shrugged. "I'm perfectly willing to do a little reminiscing."

Her eyes didn't light up with fury, as he'd hoped. Instead, she watched him with an all too knowing look on her face. "What I really want is to get to know you a little better. To find out who you are now."

"That's easy, Becca. I'm a washed-up rodeo man who somehow ended up on a ranch in Utah. I never planned on being here, never planned on letting myself get tied down this way. But life doesn't always give us a choice."

He winced at the bitterness in his voice and wished he could snatch back the words he'd just spoken. He'd revealed too much of himself, too much that he didn't want Becca, or anyone else, to know. But it was too late. Becca was too damn perceptive. She always had been. And now she'd take his hasty words and run with them.

But she didn't. She looked at him, her eyes troubled. "I'm sorry, Grady," she said, and he didn't understand the regret in her voice. "Sorry that you feel that way, sorry your life didn't end up the way you wanted it to. Sorry you can't appreciate Cameron. Why don't you sell the Flying W and go back to the rodeo circuit?''

"I can't do that,'' he said, his voice flat. "What is it that you wanted to talk about, anyway?''

Slowly she shook her head. "This isn't the time or place to talk. And maybe it doesn't matter now. I think you just answered some of my questions.''

She bent down to brush some hay off her jeans, and he saw that her hand was shaking. When she stood up again, her eyes shimmered like she was about to cry.

"For God's sake, Becca, what's the matter?''

"Nothing.'' She shook her head. "But I have to be going.''

"You're just going to take off, after what happened here?''

"Are you suggesting that we do a replay? Maybe we could invite Tucker and some of the hands this time.'' Her voice was tart.

"Come into the house. You wanted to talk. We could have a glass of tea.''

"No, thanks, Grady. I have to go. I have other clients I need to visit, and other responsibilities at the clinic.''

"Maybe we could go out sometime. To dinner, or something.'' He was willing to get to know her better, as she'd said. Only to find out what it was she wanted from him. Because there was something; he knew that for damn sure.

"Maybe we could.'' She didn't look at him as she bent to pick up her bag.

"Name the time.''

"I'll have to check with my baby-sitters and see when they could watch Cassie for me. I'll let you know.''

He knew when someone was giving him the brush-off. "What's going on, Becca? A few minutes ago you were hot to get to know me again. Now you're acting like I have bad breath, dandruff and pimples.''

A brief smile flitted across her face. "Maybe it would be easier if you did, Grady. I do still want to get to know you.

But it's not that easy for a single mother to go out on a date. I don't have the freedom to pick up and go whenever I want.''

The mention of her daughter was a small stab in his heart that he tried to ignore. ''Fine. You're not giving me a brush-off. Then tell me when you can go.''

She looked at him like a deer caught in the headlights of his truck. ''How about next Saturday?'' she finally said. ''I'll see if Amy can watch Cassie.''

''Great.'' He watched her bend over to pick up the container of used syringes, and his body stirred at the way her jeans and T-shirt outlined her body. Now he knew exactly how she felt and tasted, and it would be a hell of a lot harder to tell himself he didn't want anything to do with her. There were a lot of things he could imagine doing with her, every one of them more tantalizing than the previous.

As he followed her out of the barn, his leg throbbed with pain. He wasn't used to lying all over bales of hay, and his leg was reminding him. The pain reminded him of what Becca could do to him if he let her get close to him again. Forcing himself to forget about his leg, he listed all the reasons why he wanted nothing to do with Becca Johnson. But he was forced to admit that he was lying to himself. He very much wanted to get to know her better, as she had suggested. But only for one reason.

His body burned for her. He wanted her so badly that he could taste the need, feel it in his mouth, filling his senses. He lay awake at night, hard and aching for her. When he finally fell asleep, it was only to dream of Becca.

He wanted her so he could forget about her. Once he'd had her, once he'd satisfied the need that was an aching pain inside him, he could forget about Becca and get on with his life. The way she'd done with him.

That was the only reason he'd agreed to get to know her better. Because he already knew everything he needed to know about her. He'd learned it the first time around.

He watched her truck pull onto the long driveway, and far

in the distance he followed its progress back toward town until it was out of sight. He didn't turn away until it had turned the final curve on the road into Cameron, and all that was left was a cloud of dust.

Becca was no longer a part of his life. There was no room for her in his heart, he told himself. She'd destroyed that part of him nine long years ago. And as he walked back to the barn, he hoped that he was telling himself the truth.

Chapter 8

Becca leaned back against the seat of the truck, deliberately unclenching her hands from the steering wheel and forcing herself to relax. As she'd driven away, she'd seen Ron Perkins, standing by the edge of the house. The look on his face could only be described as one of hatred, and her heart started pounding again as she thought about how close she and Grady had come to being discovered. She had been incredibly stupid, but being caught with Grady by Ron was unthinkable. It would only give Ron another excuse for the hatred he seemed to feel for her.

Why did he think she was a threat to him? Was he afraid she would tell Grady what he'd done nine years ago? Was he afraid he would lose his job because of it?

She didn't know, but suddenly she wondered if Ron might have been her prowler the other night. There was no one else in Cameron who had any reason to hate her, she thought. Sy Ames's face flashed in front of her eyes, and she pushed it uneasily aside. Sy had always frightened her, but she hadn't seen him since the day he'd come into the clinic. Everyone

had assumed he'd left Cameron, and she knew she would
have heard if anyone else had seen him. She shifted on the
truck seat, uneasy about the possibility that Ron was the
prowler. She didn't want it to be anyone involved with Grady.

Grady. What on earth had she been thinking about, she
asked herself? She tried to ignore her still aroused body. They
had almost been caught by Grady's manager, a man who
hated her. Shifting in the seat again, she told herself that she
had learned her lesson.

She hoped.

She was supposed to be working, she reminded herself
fiercely. She had a job to do, and people counted on her.
Ranchers were probably waiting for her right now, with sick
and injured animals that needed her care. Instead of helping
them, she'd been rolling around on a bale of hay with Grady
Farrell.

But in spite of her harsh words to herself, when she thought
about Grady a shimmering of the desire she'd felt earlier rippled through her. It is only physical, she told herself firmly.
That was all it was. And it wasn't very surprising, after all.
She hadn't been involved with anyone since she'd said goodbye to Grady. Nine years was a long time.

And it was going to get even longer. She stared grimly out
the windshield, trying to concentrate on the drive back to
town along the winding road. Until Grady knew the truth, all
of it, she had no business getting involved with him in any
way. And once he knew the truth, he'd probably run as fast
and as far as he could. His words to her today left little doubt
of that.

She had no doubt now that he wouldn't be happy when
she told him Cassie was his daughter, but that made no difference. He had a right to know. When they went on their
"date" next Saturday, she'd suggest that they park somewhere out in the country, somewhere they wouldn't be overheard, and she'd tell him everything.

It was the right thing to do. Selfishly, a part of her wanted to wait. A small voice whispered that maybe she didn't know Grady well enough yet, but she ruthlessly ignored it. She knew enough. And it didn't matter how right she felt in his arms. Her feelings weren't the issue here. She had to tell Grady before she did something terrible, like succumb to her need for him, to make love with him again.

And it wouldn't be casual sex, as she'd told him. At least not on her part. But that didn't matter. She couldn't be intimate with him, share herself that way, when there was something so important she hadn't told him. She would be careful to stay away from him in the meantime, so what had happened in the barn today couldn't happen again.

She refused to think about what would happen after she told Grady about Cassie. She didn't want to think about it. Grady would be angry, and he had a right to be angry. All that was important to her was protecting Cassie. She didn't have to know that her father was living in Cameron. And if she thought Grady would hurt her in any way, Cassie would never know.

The houses on the edge of Cameron came into view, and Becca slowed down. She pulled into the parking lot of the clinic and started to jump out of the truck, then had second thoughts. Pulling the rearview mirror around so she could look into it, she examined her appearance. Did she look like she'd been romping with a client just a few minutes ago?

She straightened her shirt, finger-combed her hair and pulled out a stray wisp of straw. Then, assured that she looked as close to normal as possible, she jumped out of the truck, grabbed the container of used syringes and hurried into the clinic.

"Hi, Doc," Stella greeted her as she walked in the door.

"Hi, yourself," she replied, glancing around the waiting room. Not too many people waiting, she thought, and drew a relieved breath. "What's going on?"

"We've got a couple of calls for you," Stella said, handing her a few files with sticky notes attached. "Nothing critical, though.'' The receptionist gave her a curious look. "I thought you only had to vaccinate some horses out at the Flying W. What took so long?"

Becca fought to keep the heat from creeping up her neck. "There were a few more horses there than I had planned. Mr. Farrell had some of his own that needed vaccines, so I waited while he found their records, then vaccinated them, too." As an excuse, it sounded pretty lame.

But Stella apparently didn't think so. "Good idea. It'll save you a trip back there." She nodded decisively. "Dr. O'Connor has the clients here in the office covered. Go get some lunch, and then take these calls."

Becca couldn't eat if her life depended on it. She reached for the files, studied the notes for a moment, then went into the surgery area to get the supplies she thought she would need. On her way out of the clinic, she said, "It should take two or three hours to get these calls. I'll see you later in the afternoon."

Several evenings later Becca sat at her kitchen table, her hand wrapped around a mug of tea, as she looked over the accounts from the clinic. There were no animals in the clinic tonight, and she thought about her bed upstairs with drowsy longing. Cassie was already asleep, and as soon as she checked her entries in the accounts log, she was going up to bed, too.

A piece of gravel skittered down the driveway and bounced off the wall of her house. Becca raised her head, listening, but when it wasn't repeated, she gave her attention to the accounts once more. Some animal wandering around the house, she thought sleepily.

When she heard the scraping noise coming from the garage behind the house, her hand flinched on the mug of tea, slopping a small puddle onto her fingers. Silently she pushed away from the table, sucking on her burned hand as she stared in the direction of the garage. That was no animal. It sounded as if something hard had brushed up against the aluminum siding.

She couldn't see anything outside. The kitchen lights prevented it. Her hand hovered over the light switch, but she slowly pulled it back. If someone was outside her house, she didn't want to alert him.

Edging into the dark dining room, she stood next to a window and slowly pushed the curtain aside. The hardy bushes and desert flowers she'd planted stood like sentinels in the darkness. For a while she couldn't see beyond them, then her eyes began adjusting to the lack of light.

Her plants left grotesque shadows covering her yard in the faint moonlight. Nothing moved except the bushes swaying in the wind. She stood there for a long time, her eyes straining, but didn't see anything out of place.

Just as she took a deep breath and chastised herself for being foolish, there was a movement in the shadows that wasn't the swaying of one of her bushes. It was a deeper black than the shadows that surrounded the house, and as she stared at it, she realized it was an arm and a leg. The wind blew again, and the figure was once more obscured by the undergrowth.

Fear rose in her throat, choking her. A person hid in the bushes in her backyard, waiting. For what? For her to go upstairs to bed? So he could break into her house?

Her hands shook as she let the curtain fall into place. She was frozen to the spot, afraid to move in case the watcher saw her. Would he leave? Or would he storm the house?

Think! she commanded herself. Do something. Don't just stand here. Finally she dropped to the floor and crept, on her hands and knees, back into the kitchen. Grabbing the phone, she slid back into her chair, out of sight of the windows. Her hands shook as she dialed the number of the sheriff's office.

"Sheriff's office." The deep, reassuring voice of Devlin McAllister came on the line.

"There's someone outside my house," she whispered. The

words seemed to catch in the back of her throat, and she was afraid to raise her voice.

"Who is this?" Dev said sharply.

"Becca Johnson." She swallowed hard. "Someone is hiding in the bushes in my backyard."

"I'll be right there." Dev didn't even hesitate. "I'm not going to use my siren, so you won't hear me coming, but sit tight. I'm on my way."

The dial tone buzzed in her ear as she replaced the phone. Sit tight. She had to clamp her lips together to hold in the bubble of hysterical laughter. What did Dev think she was going to do, run outside to confront the prowler?

She sat frozen in her chair for what seemed like forever, straining to hear the slightest noise from outside. But she heard nothing but the wind, sighing around the corners of her house and rustling the leaves of her bushes.

Or was the rustling the sound of her prowler coming closer? She gripped the edge of the table, praying for Dev McAllister to hurry. Suddenly she thought of Grady, and how he'd appeared at the front door of her clinic when a prowler had been there. She longed for him to ring her doorbell right now.

A sharp rapping at the back door made her jump out of her seat. "It's Dev, Doc," he said.

Sliding out of the chair, she opened the back door with fumbling hands. "Thank goodness you're here. Did you find him?"

Dev shook his head with disgust. "Not a sign of him. But he could have run into any of your neighbors' yards when he heard me coming and be a half mile away by now. Do you think you could show me where you saw him?"

She nodded, but hesitated before walking out the door. "What if he's just waiting for us to leave the house? Cassie's asleep upstairs."

"Ben," Dev called, and one of his deputies stepped out of

the shadows in the yard. "Ben Jackson here'll keep an eye on the back door for me."

The deputy faded into the shadows, and Becca looked around nervously as he seemed to disappear. Dev saw her and smiled. "Ben's real good at this, Doc. No one'll see him until he wants to be seen. Believe me. And no one'll get into your house."

Reassured, Becca led the way into the backyard. Her house had always been her refuge, the place where she and Cassie were a family, the place where nothing in the world could touch them. Now it had been violated, and she looked at the tall bushes and rows of flowers in a different way. Now the garden she loved had become a place where an intruder could hide.

"It'll be fine in the morning," Dev said gently. "It'll be just a garden again."

"How did you know what I was thinking?"

"Everyone feels that way after something like this happens."

"I don't know if it'll ever be the same."

"It will. It just might take a little time." He stopped in the middle of the yard. "Where did you see him?"

Becca thought for a minute, mentally reviewing what she'd seen from her dining-room window. Then she stepped over to a dense mesquite plant. "He was behind this bush."

Dev nodded, then pulled out his flashlight. He crouched next to the bush for what seemed like a long time, looking but not touching anything. Finally he stood up. When he turned to face her, there was a grim look on his face.

"There was someone here, all right." He shined the flashlight at the base of the mesquite, and Becca could see what looked like shoe prints. "We might be able to get a good print from one of these, but they're pretty trampled. You go on back in the house. Ben will take your statement while I look around out here."

He escorted her to the door, and when Ben glided out of

the shadows, Dev took him aside and murmured instructions to him. Becca walked into the kitchen, feeling numb. Who had been outside her house tonight, and why was he there?

A half hour later, she'd answered all the questions Ben had and leaned back in her chair, drained and even more tired. Dev rapped on the door, then walked in and sat down across from her.

"Who might want to hurt you, Doc?" he asked without preamble.

Fear clawed at her again, and she looked at him numbly. "I have no idea, Sheriff."

"I heard Sy Ames has been giving you a hard time."

"Stella must have been talking," she said after a moment.

Dev lifted his shoulders slightly. "You know how it is in Cameron. Everyone talks. I make it my business to listen."

"Sy was a client," she said carefully. "We had an unpleasant confrontation at the clinic a couple of weeks ago, but as far as I know, he's gone. No one's seen him, and he has no place to live in Cameron."

"Does he have a legitimate beef against you?"

"No, he doesn't. Sy just doesn't want to take no for an answer."

Dev looked at her with knowing eyes. "I take it the no had nothing to do with your services in a professional capacity."

Becca squirmed, uncomfortable with discussing her personal business with anyone, even the sheriff. "No, it didn't. He wanted me to go out with him."

"It's all right, Doc," Dev said gently. "I don't gossip."

"I know." Becca looked down at her hands, clenched together in her lap.

"Anyone else?"

When she didn't answer, Dev shifted closer. "You told me you and Farrell had grown up together. Any unfinished business there?"

She wanted to laugh and cry at the same time. "Grady wasn't the prowler, Sheriff. I'm certain of that."

Dev studied her for a moment, then nodded. "All right. Anyone else?"

What should she do? Should she mention Ron? What if she was wrong? He'd have even more reason to hate her.

What if she was right?

"There is one person who works for Grady," she said slowly. "I've met him before, and he doesn't seem to like me. But I have no idea why he would be prowling around my house or my clinic."

"That's my job to find out," Dev said. "What's his name?"

She hesitated, then said, "If you go telling him that I accused him of prowling around my house, he's not going to like it. And I have to deal with him when I go out to the ranch."

Dev leaned back in his chair and smiled at her. "Give me a little credit, Doc. When I question him, he won't know who made the complaint or what he's supposed to have done. Believe me, he won't connect you with it. Unless he's the guilty party." The smile disappeared. "Then he'll have plenty to worry about."

He closed his notebook after she gave him Ron's name, then stood up. "I'll have the deputies drive by every half hour or so tonight," he said. "Try to get some sleep. I doubt if your prowler will be back tonight. We probably scared him into the next county."

She doubted it. The person she'd spotted in the bushes had been too furtive, too good at blending in. He had known what he was doing. He might not be back tonight, but he hadn't been scared off.

Becca carefully locked the screen door, and she was shutting the wooden door when she heard the sheriff speak.

"What are you doing here?" he said, and Becca heard the suspicion in his voice.

"I was driving by and saw the sheriff's cars. I wanted to

make sure Becca was all right.'' It was Grady's voice, and Becca had to stop herself from running out the door to him.

But as she listened, the silence was heavy with a suspicion Becca could hear even from inside the house. Finally Dev said, ''You seem to make a habit of showing up just when Doc Johnson has had a prowler. I find that interesting, Farrell.''

''Is that what happened? Another prowler?'' Becca heard the concern in Grady's voice. ''Is she all right?''

''She's fine.'' Dev shuffled his feet. ''You want to tell me where you've been for the last hour?''

''I was having dinner at the restaurant in town, Heaven on Seventh.''

''I'll check with Janie about that.''

''Who the hell is Janie?''

Becca heard the slap of Dev's notebook as he shut it. ''She's the owner of Heaven. She'll have noticed you. If you were there.''

''I was there.''

''Don't worry, I'll check.'' As the sheriff strolled down the driveway, Becca heard him say to his deputy, ''Ben, make sure all units know to roll past the doc's house every half hour or so.'' Becca realized that he'd made sure he said it loud enough so Grady could hear him, and she relaxed. She knew Grady wasn't the prowler, but she was glad Dev was taking the situation seriously enough to suspect him.

Becca thought Cameron was fortunate to have Dev as sheriff. He'd grown up in Cameron, but had spent time in the military, then had come back home to run against the old sheriff and won the job. Underneath his easygoing exterior was an intensity she found unsettling, but she intuitively knew he was good at his job.

''Becca?'' Grady stood at the screen door, and she opened it to admit him. ''Are you all right?''

She resisted the impulse to throw herself into his arms. ''I'm fine. Just a little shaken up.''

"What happened?"

She repeated the story she'd told Dev and his deputy, glancing into the yard as she spoke. The shadows were just as dark, but there was no one hiding in them. The prowler was gone for the night, and slowly she began to relax.

"Who the hell could it be?"

"I have no idea. The sheriff asked me if it could be Sy Ames."

Grady's mouth tightened. "I'll kill the bastard if he's threatening you."

Something inside her warmed at Grady's instinctive words. "Sy is long gone," she said. "No one's seen him around since the day he was at my clinic. Where would he stay? He doesn't have a house here anymore."

"You don't know him," Grady warned.

"I know him as well as you do."

"I doubt that. But if Sy's really gone, who else could be harassing you?"

"I gave them another name," she said slowly. She didn't want to tell him about Ron, but Dev was sure to question the ranch manager. Grady would find out sooner or later.

"Who's that?"

"Ron Perkins."

Grady's face darkened. "Ron! Why would you think he's responsible?"

"You haven't noticed the way he looks at me when I'm at the Flying W," she said quietly. "He doesn't like me. In fact, I think he hates me."

"That's ridiculous. Why would he care about you one way or another?"

She couldn't tell him that, at least not yet. "He's the only new person in town," she countered.

"Besides me." Grady's mouth was a grim slash of anger on his face.

"I told Dev that you weren't the prowler. I never thought it was you, not even for a minute. Do you think I would have let you into the clinic that night if I had even a smidgen of suspicion that it was you at my back door?''

Grady's face softened a little. ''Thank you, Becca. But I don't know why you've focused on Ron. I'll ask him what's going on in the morning.''

''No!'' Becca heard the panic in her voice and tried to steady herself. ''Don't say a word to him. Dev already promised me that if he questioned Ron, he wouldn't tell Ron who was involved. Maybe Ron has an alibi and we won't have to worry about it at all.''

''I've known Ron for almost twelve years. I trust him completely. He isn't the kind of man who would prowl around a woman's house or her place of business. That wouldn't make any sense to me at all.''

''I hope you're right.'' She turned around vaguely and waved at the stove. ''Would you like a cup of tea, or some coffee?''

Grady studied her, then shook his head. ''You look completely beat. Why don't you just go up to bed? I only stopped because I saw the sheriff's cars and wanted to make sure you were all right.''

''Thank you for that, Grady.'' She paused, then turned to face him. ''I'm glad you're here. It makes me feel safer.''

He reached out and trailed a finger down her cheek, then let his hand drop. ''Want me to sleep on the couch tonight?''

Her face heating from his touch, for one horrifying minute she was tempted to tell him yes. But she pictured Cassie discovering him there in the morning and shook her head. ''Thanks, but we'll be fine. You heard that the sheriff is going to have the deputies patrol the neighborhood tonight. And now that my prowler has been scared away by the police, I doubt if he'll be back.''

''Are you sure?''

''Positive,'' she said firmly. ''You have responsibilities at the ranch. You're needed there.''

''Are you going to be able to sleep?'' he asked quietly.

"I'm exhausted." She chose her words carefully. "I was tired before I saw the prowler."

"But are you going to be able to sleep?"

In spite of herself, a weary smile crept across her face. "You raise the meaning of persistence to a whole new level, Grady. You know that, don't you?"

He didn't bother to answer. Rummaging through her cupboards, he found her herbal tea and pulled out the container. He flipped through it until he found the packet he wanted. "Let's get some of this into you. That should help you sleep."

To her surprise, he'd chosen chamomile, which always relaxed her. "How did you know that type of tea would help me sleep?"

"I've used plenty of this stuff in my time," he said as he heated water.

"Don't let the other cowboys know you drink herbal tea," she teased.

His hands stilled on the teakettle. "There was a time when I had trouble sleeping. This helped."

"When was that, Grady?" she asked in a soft voice.

"A long time ago." His voice said the subject was closed. He stood by the stove, his back to her, as he waited for the kettle to whistle. As soon as it boiled, he poured the water over the tea bag and slid the cup in front of her.

He hesitated, then sat in the chair across from her. Looking around the kitchen, he said, "I like your house."

It was a clear sign that the subject of when he'd needed tea to sleep was closed. She forced herself to nod lightly. "I like it, too. I wanted a place of my own. And it's nice to have a yard for Cassie, and a place for a garden."

That reminded her of what had been in her garden earlier that night, and her hand tightened on her mug. Grady slid his hand over hers. "I'll keep an eye on Ron, if that would make you feel better. Keep track of his comings and goings."

She studied him. "But you don't think it's necessary."

"No, I don't. But I'll do it if it makes you feel better."

Slowly she shook her head. "Don't bother. You can't watch him twenty-four hours a day, and it'll just strain your relationship. But thanks for offering."

She sipped her tea and sat in the silence of the kitchen, grateful for his company. Gradually she felt herself relaxing, and was surprised to realize that she could fall asleep.

"Your tea seems to have done the trick," she said. "Thanks for suggesting it. I think I can actually fall asleep." For a treacherous minute she thought about how things might have been different, if it weren't for that wretched lie nine years ago. She and Grady might be going up to bed together, tucking their children into bed together.

"I'm glad it helped," he said, standing up. "I'll see you Saturday."

Saturday. With everything that had happened tonight, she had forgotten they had a date in a few days. She had forgotten what she'd planned to tell him.

"I'll see you then," she agreed.

"Mommy, who is that man?" The voice came from the kitchen door, and slowly she turned around to see Cassie standing in the doorway, clutching her blanket and staring at Grady.

And Grady staring back at her.

Chapter 9

Grady stared at the child, taking in her dark hair hanging in messy braids and her intense blue eyes. She looked familiar, as if he'd seen her before, but he knew that was impossible.

She waited, watching him carefully. Forcing himself to smile, he said, "I'm Grady Farrell, a friend of your mom's."

From behind him Becca said, "Mr. Farrell owns the Flying W, honey. But he's leaving and you need to go back to bed." Her voice was ragged, and Grady wondered why.

The child's face lit from the inside. "That's where Pete lives."

"Pete?" Grady turned to look at Becca.

Her face was sheet white. "A paint pony Cassie saw when she was out there with me. Tucker was training him in a corral, and Cassie took a fancy to him."

Grady turned back to the child. "You like horses?" he asked softly.

She nodded vigorously. "When I get older, I'm going to get a job at my mom's clinic. I'll earn enough money so that I can get my own horse. Then I can be in the rodeo."

"Cassie, that's enough," Becca said sharply behind him. "Go on back to bed."

The child turned obediently to go. But before she did, she looked at Grady one more time and gave him a huge grin. "I like your horses, Mr. Farrell." Then she scampered up the stairs and disappeared.

Again Grady was struck with the feeling that he'd seen this child before. As he turned around to face Becca again, he saw the shock in her eyes and the trembling hands she tried to hide.

"I'm sorry," she managed to say. "Normally she sleeps like the dead. All the noise tonight must have disturbed her."

"Why are you sorry? She didn't bother me."

"You were just leaving, and she interrupted."

"It's not a big deal," he said, wondering why she was so upset. He thought of Cassie again, of the huge grin on her face, and suddenly remembered where he had seen that face before. It was a picture of him with his mother when he was eight or nine. Cassie could have been the child in that picture.

It was as if someone had kicked him in the chest and driven all the breath out of his body. Shock held him immobile, but his head reeled as if he had fallen into a huge chasm and was tumbling head over heels.

And the answer to his question was staring back at him from Becca's white, numb face.

"She's mine, isn't she?" he whispered.

Slowly Becca nodded, her lips trembling and her eyes wide and dark. "Yes."

It stabbed into him then, twisting in his heart, the pain that had haunted him for nine long years. "Why, Becca? Why didn't you tell me? Why did you tell me to get lost when you knew you were pregnant with my child?"

"I didn't know," she whispered. "That last time I talked to you on the phone, I had no idea I was pregnant."

"There wasn't someone else, was there?"

She shook her head. "It was a lie, Grady, a stupid, foolish lie."

"Why?" he asked again.

"I wanted you to come home." Her fingers gripped the sides of her jeans, pleating the fabric with her fingers. "I thought if I told you there was someone else, you would come running home to me."

"Why didn't you just ask me to come home?"

"I'd asked before. Would it have done any good to ask again?"

He opened his mouth to tell her of course he would have come home, then closed it again. He remembered too many times when Becca had asked him to come home and he'd brushed her off, telling her about the important stop in the rodeo circuit that was coming up soon. But he thought again of the child sleeping upstairs, and dismissed his guilt. Becca had much more to answer for than he did.

"When is her birthday?" The words came out with a rush of pain. He didn't even know how old his own daughter was.

"She's just turned eight," Becca said in a low voice. "Her birthday was May 15th."

"Why didn't you tell me?" he asked again, his voice harsh. "Didn't you think I had a right to know?"

"I tried to tell you," she answered, and suddenly her voice was weary. "I called everywhere. I even went to a couple of rodeos. No one knew where you were or where I could find you."

"You didn't try very hard," he retorted. "I wasn't hiding. The rodeo schedule is pretty easy to find."

"I didn't have a lot of money," she said, her voice so low he could barely hear her. "I did the best I could."

He squashed the guilt that swept over him. It didn't matter what her life had been like nine years ago, he told himself. She'd had plenty of time to tell him since he came to Cameron. "What about the last couple of weeks? Why didn't you tell me then?"

At that she looked up at him, her eyes fierce. "Now I have Cassie to consider. I had to make sure I was doing the right thing by telling you. No matter what happens, she's not going to get hurt."

"Are you saying you think I would hurt my own child?" he asked, incredulous.

"Not intentionally. But I didn't know how you would react to learning you were a father. I know you don't want to be tied down. I know you want to travel light. Being a father means that you're tied down. And once you have a child, there's no such thing as traveling light."

"I take my responsibilities seriously, Becca. I always have."

"I know that, but she's not going to be someone's 'responsibility.' She will never feel like she has to apologize for being alive," she answered fiercely. "That's why I didn't tell you right away. I wanted to get to know you a little, to judge how you would react to the news."

It felt as if a giant hand reached into his chest and ripped out his heart. "Is that why you kissed me, Becca? Is that why we almost made love, more than once? Was that a test of some sort?"

"What happened between us has nothing to do with Cassie." She moistened her lips and looked away. "If I had been thinking of Cassie, it never would have happened."

"Just when were you planning on telling me?" he asked, taking a step closer to her.

She swallowed but didn't back up. "I'm sure that you won't believe me, but I was planning on telling you Saturday."

"Right. We'd be sitting at dinner in Heaven on Seventh and you'd say, casually, 'By the way, Grady, you know my daughter, Cassie? She's your daughter, too.' I'm not sure I buy that."

"I wasn't planning on telling you in a crowded restaurant."

Her voice sounded weary. "I thought we could go and park somewhere out of town, where no one would see or hear us."

"Were you going to soften me up with a little sex first?" He watched her flinch at his crude words and rushed on before his anger could dissipate. "Because if we parked off the road somewhere, that's exactly what would happen and you damn well know it."

"This hasn't been easy for me, Grady," she said, and he didn't want to hear the pain in her voice. "But I had to do what was best for Cassie. This isn't just about you and me. There's an innocent child involved, and I have to think of her first. Yes, you had a right to know. But I couldn't find you when I was pregnant with Cassie, and now she's old enough to understand what's going on. Nothing or no one on earth could persuade me to do anything that would hurt her. And that includes you."

He stood watching her. The shocked look had disappeared from her face, leaving her looking tired and vulnerable. And still fiercely protective of her child.

Their child.

Something moved inside him, a tenderness he wasn't ready to acknowledge. He pushed it away without a second thought.

"So where do we go from here?" he asked.

Becca shrugged her shoulders slightly and looked away from him. "I have no idea. I guess it depends on what you want. How do you feel about being a father?"

"How the hell should I know? It's not like I've had a long time to get used to the idea."

"Take all the time you need. We're not going anywhere."

"What do you want, Becca?"

"Every child deserves a father," she said, her voice low. "And every father deserves a chance to know his children." She looked up at him, her eyes flashing. "But if you decide you want to be part of her life, you're making a commitment for the rest of her life. I won't have you getting close to her, then deciding that you don't want to stick around. I won't let her be hurt like that.''

"So it's all or nothing?"

"It's your choice, Grady. Cassie is your daughter. If you want to get to know her, I won't stand in your way. I owe you that much, at least. But you'd better think about it before you decide. Being a parent isn't an easy job."

"I don't know jack about being a father."

She actually smiled. "No one does at the beginning. It's a learn-on-the-job proposition."

Suddenly the emotions swirling around inside him were too complicated, too painful to face. He stood up straight. "I've got some thinking to do. I'll talk to you in a few days."

She moved away from the door. "I'm sorry," she said quietly. "Sorry that it had to happen like this. But I'm glad you finally know."

He paused to look at her. He saw Becca's face, the face he had dreamed about for years, but suddenly it belonged to a stranger. The Becca he knew never lied. The Becca he knew wouldn't keep a secret like this from him. The Becca he knew had disappeared sometime in the past nine years, and he was afraid she was never coming back.

"Goodbye, Becca." The words twisted inside him, dropping like stones into his soul.

The door clicked shut behind him, and he felt her gaze on his shoulders. He knew that if he turned around she'd be watching him.

He gave a bitter laugh in the cool night air. He'd always thought he knew all there was to know about Becca. He'd been able to read her mind, predict what she would do. Obviously he'd been fooling himself for a long time.

He climbed into his truck, but he didn't start the engine. Instead, he stared at the house in front of him, the house where his daughter lay sleeping.

His daughter. Jesus, he didn't know anything about being

a father. He didn't even know if he could learn. He sure couldn't depend on what his own father had taught him.

A sudden thought chilled him. Maybe being a father was a genetic thing. Maybe he was doomed to fail at it, just as his father had failed. Maybe it would be best for Becca and Cassie if he just started driving tonight, and didn't stop. He didn't need the Flying W. He didn't need anyone or anything. He'd survived on his own for years, and he could do it again.

Starting the engine with a flick of his wrist, he backed out of Becca's driveway into the quiet street. Staring blindly in front of him, seeing nothing but the wide, impish grin of his daughter and Becca's white, shaken face, he passed the last house in town and stepped on the accelerator.

Becca sat in the kitchen, staring at nothing, long after the sound of Grady's truck had faded into the quiet of the night. *He knew.* The thought drummed in her head. Grady had seen Cassie, and now at least he knew the truth.

Relief swept over her, making her feel like she'd finally exhaled after holding her breath for far too long a time. All the worrying, all the speculating about what Grady would do, was over. He knew, and the next move was up to him.

With that thought a hint of panic rose in her mind. What would Grady do? What would he want? The part of her that had felt such relief just moments ago now slowly hardened and froze. Cassie was no longer hers alone. It wasn't just the two of them, secure in their own little world. Cassie had a father now, even if she didn't know it, and everything was going to change.

Becca rose from the table and bumped the edge, her motions jerky. The cup of chamomile tea that had cooled in front of her fell over, spilling its contents onto the surface of the table. Pausing to mechanically wipe it up, Becca turned out the lights on the first floor and walked up the stairs to Cassie's room.

Cassie. She slept in a beam of moonlight, the soft, pearly

light glinting off her dark hair. Her heart expanding at the sight, Becca sat on the edge of the bed and stroked her daughter's silky smooth braids.

"Do you think Mr. Farrell would let me ride one of his horses, Mommy?" Cassie's sleep-drugged voice was barely above a whisper in the dark room.

Becca closed her eyes, trying to block out the innocence in her daughter's words, trying to block out the shock she'd seen in Grady's eyes when he'd realized the truth. Trying to will away the pain she was afraid Cassie would suffer. "Mr. Farrell runs a big ranch, honey," she said softly and carefully. "I don't know if he has any horses that would be right for a little girl like you."

Cassie was two-thirds asleep, but her mouth curled into a smile. "Pete would be right for me. Don't you think so, Mommy?"

"Pete seemed like a fine horse," she agreed, her heart breaking. She knew if she could see Cassie's eyes, they would be full of longing, a longing she wouldn't be able to satisfy. Cassie's father owned the horse that Cassie had fallen in love with. It was another bitter irony in a situation that was already too painful.

"When I have enough money, I can buy Pete from Mr. Farrell." Cassie's words were slurred with sleep, but Becca heard the determination in her daughter's voice. She sounded just like Grady when he wouldn't take no for an answer. A wave of pain crashed over Becca again, then she pulled the blanket up to Cassie's chin.

"We'll see, honey," she murmured in a low voice. "We'll see."

The mother's mantra, she thought as she watched Cassie sleep. In this case, though, it was true. There were a lot of things they were going to have to see about. And the first one was what Cassie's father intended to do.

Becca longed to gather her daughter into her arms, to hold her safe and protect her from anything that could hurt her.

But she couldn't shield out everything, she knew. She couldn't prevent the sharp teeth of life from nipping at Cassie, taking tiny bites here and there. She couldn't wrap her in cotton and cushion every blow. It would be impossible, and unfair to Cassie, to boot.

Smoothing her hand down Cassie's silky soft hair, Becca watched her sleep for a moment more, then quietly stood and walked out of the room. She stopped at the door and looked back at her daughter sleeping. Her daughter and Grady's. And now he knew.

She wasn't sure what was going to happen. Grady had been shocked and angry, and he'd had a right to be. But at least he knew the truth. For the first time since she'd learned she was pregnant, the weight of her lie eased, just a little. Grady knew he was Cassie's father.

The ringing of the telephone pulled her out of a deep sleep. As she reached for the receiver, she remembered that it was Saturday. Three days since Grady had discovered the truth about Cassie. Three days, and still she hadn't heard a word from Grady.

It was her Saturday off, too, she remembered as she heard Stella's voice in her ear.

"Sorry to bother you, Dr. Johnson, but there's an emergency at the Flying W, and I thought you would want to know."

Becca struggled to shake off the haze of sleep. "What kind of an emergency?"

"Tucker said one of the cows was down, and someone needed to come right out."

She sat up in bed, pushing her hair out of her eyes. "Can someone else handle it?"

There was a delicate pause on the other end of the line. "Well," Stella finally said, "Dr. O'Connor's out at the Mc-Allister ranch at the other end of the county, taking care of a horse with colic. And Dr. Pickett has a full waiting room here and he's working on a dog that's been hit by a car. But I'm sure one of them could make time to get out to the Flying W."

"Never mind, Stella. I'll take care of it. Tell them I'll be there as soon as I can."

She hung up the phone as she swung out of bed. As she headed for the bathroom, she ran a mental inventory of the drugs she had in her truck. Fortunately she'd replenished her supply just the other day, so she should have whatever she'd need.

As she hurried down the stairs a few minutes later, she called out to Cassie, "Honey, have you had breakfast? We need to get you over to Laura's because I have an emergency call."

Cassie appeared in the doorway, her face a study in disappointment. "We were going to take a picnic and go for a hike today, Mom. Remember?"

"We'll still take our hike. We'll just get started a little later."

Suddenly Cassie beamed at her. "I can't go over to Laura's today. She was going to Cedar City."

"Are you sure?" Becca asked, her stomach clenching with anxiety.

Cassie nodded vigorously. "She told me all about it. Jenny and Todd were real excited, too."

"Maybe you could stay with Amy."

Cassie shook her head. "She and her mom went somewhere real early. I saw them leave."

Becca sank down onto the stairs. "Then what are we going to do?"

"I could come with you," Cassie said hopefully. "I'll be real good and stay in the truck."

Becca pulled her daughter over to her. "You're always good when you come with me, honey. I know you'll behave. But I might be there for a while. I don't know what's wrong with the sick cow." And she didn't want Cassie anywhere near the Flying W right now. She hadn't heard a word from Grady since she'd told him about Cassie.

"Please, Mommy?"

She didn't have a choice. She could have asked another neighbor, but it would involve explanations and talk that would take too much time. A cow that couldn't stand was a serious situation, and she couldn't afford to waste a minute. She'd have to take Cassie with her.

"Okay, Cass, you'll have to come with me. Let's go get in the truck."

Cassie was practically wriggling with excitement as they sped toward the Flying W. "What ranch are we going to?" she asked, her eyes shining.

"The Flying W."

"Really? Hooray!" she shouted. She bounced as high as the seat belt allowed her to move. "Maybe I can see Pete!" she exclaimed. "Do you think he'll be there?"

"I don't know, honey. He's probably somewhere on the ranch, but it's a big ranch. You may not see him."

"I'll see him." She sounded supremely confident.

Becca hoped she wouldn't be disappointed, but she couldn't afford to think about whether Pete would be around. The driveway of the Flying W was just ahead, and as she slowed down she began to review in her mind what could cause a cow to go down. As she braked the truck outside the ranch house, she saw Tucker pacing in front of the barn.

He hurried toward the truck. "Thank God you're here, Doc. I have no idea what's wrong, and that cow's been down for too long already. She's in the barn there." He jerked his head behind him.

"Cassie, I'll be right back."

"It's too hot for her to stay in the truck, Doc. You go take care of the cow. I'll make sure Cassie stays out of trouble."

Becca hesitated for a moment, but she knew Tucker was right. It *was* too hot for Cassie to stay in the car. "Pay attention to Mr. Tucker, Cass. He'll take care of you."

Grabbing her bag, she ran into the barn. As her eyes adjusted to the dim light, she heard Grady's voice crooning softly. Following the sound, she came to a stop in front of a large stall. Grady was inside, crouched in front of a Hereford cow that was lying on her chest, her head twisted to one side. She was staring at the wall, her eyes dazed and dull looking. Although Becca didn't make a sound, Grady turned and looked up at her.

"Hello, Becca." His voice was without inflection.

With a huge effort she forced herself to concentrate only on the cow lying on the floor. There would be plenty of time later to think about Grady. "Hello, Grady. What happened?"

She thought she saw a look of relief on Grady's face before he turned to the cow, and she gripped the handle of her bag more tightly. So he was afraid that she wasn't going to be able to separate her personal and professional lives? she thought grimly. He didn't realize that she'd had plenty of practice at that, starting back when she was in school and found out she was pregnant with Cassie.

Stepping into the stall, she pulled the door closed behind her and dropped to her knees next to the cow. She was so close to Grady that his body heat seemed to shimmer around her. Fingers of warmth caressed her cheek, her back, her chest. Ignoring her body's instant reaction, she reached for the cow's neck to check her pulse and said again, "What happened, Grady?"

He shot her an uncertain look, then shrugged. "Hell if I know. She was acting a little funny out in the pasture, so one of the hands brought her and her calf into the barn last night. We found her this way this morning."

"When did she drop her calf?" Becca asked as she took the cow's temperature.

"A couple of months ago, I would guess by looking at the calf. Before I owned the place, anyway."

"Do you know how old she is?"

"I looked her records up this morning. She's eleven. Had

a calf regularly for the past nine years, never had any problems. And the records don't say, so I assume her last delivery was normal, without any complications.''

Becca rocked back on her heels, looking at the cow, trying to move farther away from Grady. "I'm not certain, but I suspect she has milk fever.''

"How can that be? She had her calf a long time ago. If they're going to get milk fever, doesn't it usually happen right away?''

"Usually, but it can happen anytime. She's the right age, and her physical symptoms match. I could do blood work and check her calcium levels, but I'd rather give her an injection of calcium. It'll take too long to get the blood work back.''

Grady stared at her for a long moment, then stood up. "You're the doctor.''

His voice was still impossible to read, but she didn't care. Right now the cow on the floor in front of her had to be her only concern. She refused to let herself speculate on what Grady was thinking about. And she absolutely refused to pay attention to her nerves, which were smoldering with Grady's closeness.

Grabbing a vial of calcium solution, she pulled it into a syringe then began injecting it into the cow's vein. Her hand started to cramp as she pushed the plunger in as slowly as she could, but she blocked out the pain and watched the animal closely.

Grady hovered near the cow, one hand on the animal's head to steady her. As Becca injected the calcium solution, she watched the almost automatic way his hand stroked the cow's head. His long fingers moved in a slow, circular motion, and she shivered as she remembered the way his hand had felt on her skin. She forced herself to look away, to concentrate on her patient, but Grady was still too close. Her body wouldn't let her block that out of her mind.

Before Becca had emptied the syringe, the cow began to thrash on the floor. As she eased the needle out of the animal's vein, the cow gave one big heave and struggled to her feet. She stood there swaying, the dazed look slowly fading from her eyes. After a few minutes she shook her head, bellowed once, then ambled unsteadily over to the feed trough.

Grady rocked back on his heels. "Jesus H. Christ," he muttered, staring at the cow. "That cow was down for more than twelve hours. How the hell did you manage that?"

Becca watched the cow as she snuffled around in the feed trough, unable to repress the surge of triumph at the sight. Smiling, she sat back in the straw of the stall and watched her patient.

"I love treating animals that have milk fever," she said, her smile turning into a grin. "It always makes me look so good."

"It makes you look like a genius," he said bluntly, still staring at the cow. "Is that what always happens?"

"Most of the time, unless they're in a coma already. Once they get the calcium they need, their muscles begin working again immediately." She grinned again. "And vets love the drama of seeing the animal suddenly go back to normal. It always impresses the owner."

"It impressed the hell out of me." He stared at the animal, as if he couldn't believe what he saw. "Is she going to be okay now?"

Her smile fading, Becca stood up and brushed the straw off her jeans. "I hope so, but you're going to have to watch her closely to make sure she doesn't relapse. I'll come out again late today and give her another injection. And if she starts acting funny again, call right away. We'll get some calcium into her before she goes down."

Slowly Grady turned and looked at her. She realized it was the first time since she'd arrived at the ranch, that he'd really looked at her. She felt his gaze flicker over her uncombed hair, down to the loose T-shirt and old, faded jeans she'd thrown on.

"You look like you just rolled out of bed."

His voice was low and intimate in the barn, his words conjuring up remembered passion. She felt her skin warming at his words. Turning away so he wouldn't see how his words affected her, she began to replace her instruments in her bag as she answered.

"I did. Today was my day off, but my partners were both tied up and Stella knew your cow couldn't wait. So she called me at home."

"I'm sorry," he said after a moment. "I apologize for disturbing you."

His words were formal and stilted, and she whirled around to face him. His face was shuttered, and she couldn't read his thoughts.

"Don't be. I would have been very upset if Stella hadn't called me. I love my job, and part of it is handling emergencies like this." She picked up her bag and slid past him out of the stall, ignoring the way her skin tingled. "Cassie and I will just get started on our plans a little later."

"Did you leave her at home?" he asked, and his words quivered with a sudden tension.

Slowly she shook her head. "My regular baby-sitter is out of town, and my neighbor was gone. I had to bring her with me."

His face tightened, and his gaze slid past her to the door of the barn.

"Tucker is watching her," Becca said quietly. "It was too hot for her to wait in the truck. If that makes you uncomfortable, why don't you stay here for a few minutes while I find her and leave?"

His eyes lingered on the door of the barn for a moment, then he looked at her. She still couldn't read the expression on his face. "Does she know?"

Becca shook her head. "She has no idea who her father is. And I certainly wouldn't tell her without talking to you about it."

His face softened for a moment, then he clamped his mouth

together in a thin line. "I'm not going to hide in the barn," he said flatly. "Let's go see what my daughter has been up to."

As Becca raced to follow Grady, she wondered frantically what he intended to do. He wouldn't tell Cassie that he was her father, would he? Please God, she prayed, don't let him spring it on her like that.

He was already far ahead of her. Gripping her heavy bag, she struggled to catch up to him before he could say anything to Cassie.

Chapter 10

Grady stepped out into the sunlight, squinting against the brightness of the summer day. Becca's truck stood empty, so her daughter was somewhere on the ranch.

His daughter, too, he reminded himself. The surge of emotion that had propelled him out of the barn faded, replaced by the uncertainty, fear and confusion that had overwhelmed him for the past few days. Did he want to meet this child right now? Or should he just turn around and walk the other way?

As he wavered, he heard joyous, high-pitched laughter coming from his left. Almost against his will, he walked slowly around the corner of the barn. He stopped dead in his tracks when he saw the child on the horse in the corral in front of him.

He stared, fascinated, as Cassie clung to the reins of a paint pony as Tucker led the horse around the corral. He recognized the horse as Pete, a young gelding that Tucker had been training. And he remembered that Cassie had asked him about Pete when he'd seen her the other night.

He heard rather than saw Becca come up beside him. For some reason he couldn't tear his gaze away from the child perched on the horse in the corral. But when Becca drew in a shocked breath, he turned to look at her.

Her face was white and her eyes huge as she stared at her daughter on the horse. And Grady knew that in moments she was going to yell at Tucker to get Cassie off the horse.

"What's the matter?" he asked to forestall her.

"She's never been on a horse before," Becca answered, her gaze glued on her daughter. "I don't want her to get hurt."

"Tucker won't let her get hurt. He taught all his own kids to ride when they were much younger than Cassie."

"But..."

Becca bit her lip, and he wondered why she was so upset. "What's the matter, Becca?" he asked. "Don't all kids around here learn how to ride a horse before they're Cassie's age?"

"If they live on a ranch, they do." Her voice was sharp. "But we live in town, and we don't have anywhere to keep a horse."

"Tucker's not giving her the horse," he answered, wondering why she was so agitated. "He's just letting her sit on him."

Becca didn't reply, and Grady watched her stare at her daughter and Pete. He didn't understand her obvious unhappiness. "She loves it," he argued. "Can't you see how much she's enjoying it?"

"I know." Becca's voice was almost too low to hear. "That's what I'm worried about."

"What do you mean?"

She didn't say anything for a long time, then she sighed. "All Cassie has ever wanted was a horse. And to be in the rodeo." She glanced over at him, then looked back toward her daughter. "We didn't have much money for a long time, so getting her a horse was out of the question. Now we could probably afford a horse, but I didn't want to encourage Cassie to think about the rodeo."

He'd tried to shield his heart, but her comment still stung. "Afraid she'd turn out like her old man?" he asked, his voice sharp.

Becca didn't look at him. "Yes," she said quietly. "That's exactly what I was afraid of. Cassie is so much like you that sometimes she scares me. She's just as single-minded, just as determined as you always were. I didn't want her focusing on a horse and the rodeo before she'd had a chance to try other things, to develop other interests."

"I don't think I turned out to be a complete failure, even though I did focus on just one thing." His voice was tight to hide his pain.

She turned to look at him then. "That's not what I meant at all, Grady. The boy I fell in love with wasn't a failure in anything. But you had blinders on when it came to your rodeo career. I think it made you miss a lot of wonderful other things in life. I don't want that to happen to Cassie."

"Yeah, I did miss a lot. Like the first eight years of my daughter's life," he said bitterly. He watched Cassie reach out and pat Pete's neck, then sit up and grin again, and suddenly his heart ached for all he'd missed. "But you can't force children into a mold you want them to fit. You have to let them be their own person."

She continued to watch him instead of her daughter, and he began to squirm inside at her knowing gaze. "Is that why you were so obsessed with the rodeo, Grady?" she said quietly. "Because your father was so insistent that you forget about it and work the ranch?"

"That's ancient history," he snapped, turning his attention back to Cassie. "I joined the rodeo circuit because I was good at it."

"And if Cassie turns out to be good at it, she'll have her chance, too. I just want her to know that she has other choices."

"You're going to end up doing the same thing my father did to me." He stared at Cassie, not seeing her but seeing a much younger version of himself, clinging just as desperately to the back of a horse. "If you keep her from riding, it will become the one thing she has to do. It will become so important to her that she'll be willing to sacrifice everything to do it."

He could almost feel Becca pale beside him. "I'm not like your father at all," she said, her voice low.

"Of course you're not." He glanced down at her and saw the hurt in her eyes and immediately regretted his words. "I didn't mean that you were. But you're making a mistake if you try to prevent her from riding and keep her away from horses."

"You've talked to her one time and now you're an expert on what's best for her?" she asked, her sharp tone unsuccessful at hiding the hurt beneath her words.

"I don't know anything about my daughter," he answered, trying to keep the pain out of his own voice. "But I do know myself. It's one of the few things I'm an expert on. And I know how I reacted when my father tried to keep me away from the rodeo. Give her a chance to let horses be a part of her life, and they won't become the obsession of her life."

Without waiting for an answer, he strode up to the corral fence and leaned against it, watching the child and the horse. She sat in the saddle with a natural ease, and already had picked up how to use the reins. For a moment pride filled him as he watched the child in front of him. Then his mouth tightened. She was his daughter, but he was a stranger to her. He was merely the owner of this ranch, someone she'd seen once in her mother's kitchen.

And Becca was trying to erase all traces of him in his daughter. He hadn't thought he could feel more pain, but his heart proved him wrong. Becca didn't want Cassie to be interested in horses or the rodeo because that would make her too much like him. As he leaned against the fence and watched the child delight in the horse, something inside him rose up in rebellion. Before he realized what he was doing, he was across the fence and striding up to Tucker and Cassie.

"Hi, boss." Tucker sounded nervous. "Cassie here wanted to see Pete, and I didn't think it would hurt anything for her to take a little ride on him."

"It doesn't hurt a thing." He reached out and scratched the horse's nose as he took the lead rope from Tucker. "I've got a few minutes free, and I know you have a lot you wanted to get done today," he said. "Why don't you let me take over the lesson?"

Tucker watched him for a moment, then a knowing look filled his face. "Sure, boss. You go right ahead." He winked at Grady. "Doesn't hurt if the little gal's mom sees how good you are with kids, right?" he whispered.

"It's nothing like that," Grady said, too sharply.

"If you say so." Tucker walked off, whistling, a huge grin on his face. Out of the corner of his eye, Grady could see that he'd stopped next to Becca to talk. He forced his gaze away as he turned to the child on the horse.

"Tucker had some errands he had to do," Grady said to her, wondering how he was supposed to address her.

Immediately disappointment filled her face. "That means I have to go, right?"

He shook his head, moved by her willingness to get off the horse in spite of her obvious yearning to keep riding. "I told Tucker I'd take his place. That is, if you don't mind."

She shook her head and sent her braids flying around her face. "I'd like it if you taught me." She hesitated, then said shyly, "Is it true that you were a big rodeo star?"

"Did your mom tell you that?"

She shook her head again. "No, my friend Sally told me. She heard her mom and dad talking about you, and she knows I want to be in the rodeo, so she told me. Were you?"

He hesitated, then decided he had to tell her the truth. "Yeah, I was a rodeo man."

"What did you do?" Her voice was breathless.

"I was a bull rider and a roper."

"Did you win lots of medals?"

"I won my share."

"Could I see them sometime?" she begged.

Grady stole a glance over at Becca. She stood talking with Tucker, but she was watching him and Cassie. "That depends on your mom. We probably need to ask her."

"She'll say yes," Cassie answered with confidence.

"How can you be sure?" In spite of himself, Grady was fascinated.

"'Cause she always tells me that if I want something, and it's not unreasonable and not bad for me, she'll try to get it for me."

"What's unreasonable?" he couldn't stop himself from asking.

Her eyes clouded. "A horse. We can't afford one, and even if we could we don't have a place to keep it." Becca and her daughter had clearly had that conversation more than once.

"And what's bad for you?"

She grinned at him, and her cheeks dimpled. Just like his, he realized with a pang. "Too much candy. Staying up late. And too much TV."

"Maybe you're right," he said gravely. "Seeing my rodeo medals doesn't seem to fall into the category of unreasonable or bad for you. But we still have to ask your mom."

"Okay." She squirmed in the saddle. "But we don't have to ask her now, do we?" She sounded worried.

Suddenly Grady grinned at her, enjoying her enthusiasm, relishing her eagerness. "Naw, not right now. We're in the middle of a riding lesson. That's more important than a bunch of rodeo medals."

Cassie grinned back at him, then sat up straighter in the saddle. "I want to go faster now. Can you show me how to go faster?"

* * *

Becca stood next to the fence and watched her daughter ride around the corral on the paint pony. Grady held the lead rope as he told Cassie what to do. He was amazingly patient, never once raising his voice or scolding Cassie when she did something wrong. But she rarely did anything wrong. Even Becca could see how quickly Cassie was learning.

And how much she loved riding the horse.

Becca didn't want to think about what Grady had said. Surely she hadn't been so mean-spirited that she'd forbidden Cassie riding lessons because it would remind her of Grady. She was merely trying to protect her daughter, not stop her from doing something she craved. She wanted Cassie to have a well-balanced life. She hadn't let Cassie learn to ride because they *had* been short on money for a long time. She'd had too many school loans to pay back to even think about luxuries such as a horse or riding lessons.

But all her protests seemed weak and useless, and her heart knew the truth. The real reason she'd been reluctant to allow Cassie to learn how to ride had more to do with Grady than with anything else. And now she was ashamed of herself, ashamed that she'd forbidden her daughter this pleasure because it reminded her of Grady. She'd arrange for Cassie to take riding lessons as soon as possible.

After what seemed like a very long time, Grady stepped closer to the horse and gently lifted Cassie out of the saddle. Becca thought his hands lingered for an extra moment on the child's waist as he deposited her on the ground, then he stepped quickly away from her. Becca couldn't hear what he said to Cassie, but the girl nodded her head, a grin splitting her face.

As she scampered under the fence and back to her mother, Grady wrapped the horse's reins around the top rail and followed her more slowly. Cassie dashed up to her mother, breathless with excitement.

"Did you see me riding Pete, Mom? Did you?"

"I sure did. You looked like you were having fun." Becca smoothed a few wisps of hair away from her daughter's face.

"The most fun ever," Cassie said fervently. "And Mr. Farrell said I can ride on Pete again the next time I come out here with you. When are you coming back? Can I come with you? Please?"

Grady had reached them, and he stood a few steps behind Cassie as he listened to their conversation, his face impassive.

"I think that's something I need to discuss with Mr. Farrell," Becca said gently to her daughter. "Why don't you hop into the truck, sweetheart?"

Cassie turned to Grady. "Thank you very much, Mr. Farrell," she said earnestly. "Thank you for letting me ride Pete, and for giving me a lesson." Then she turned and ran to the truck.

Becca didn't speak for a moment, and neither did Grady. Finally he said, "She has a gift, Becca. Don't forbid her to use it."

"I know." She couldn't look at him. "I saw how she looked when she was riding that horse. I saw how well she did." She hesitated, then added in a low voice, "And I saw the joy on her face. I'll make sure she gets riding lessons."

"Bring her out here. Tucker and I will teach her how to ride."

Becca's gaze flew to Grady's face. "I couldn't take your time like that."

His face flickered with an emotion she couldn't identify, then he looked away. "She's my daughter," he said, his voice flat. "I wasn't allowed to give her anything for eight years. Let me give her this."

"So you've made a decision? You intend to be a part of her life?"

His gaze wandered to the truck, where Cassie sat staring at Pete in the corral. "I'm not sure if that would be a good thing," he finally said. "You're right to be cautious. Maybe I wouldn't be good for her. Maybe she's better off without knowing who I am. She's done fine without me for the last eight years.''

Her heart ached for him. "Grady, I don't think that's true at all. I think you would be a wonderful father.''

"Based on what?" His gaze skewered her. "My experiences with my own father? I learned a hell of a lot from him, but I'm not sure you'd want me to pass those lessons on to Cassie.''

"Based on the kind of person you are. Your father has nothing to do with it.''

"The hell he doesn't. I have no idea how to be a father, Becca. None at all. And I'm not sure I'm willing to take the chance on screwing up with Cassie.'' His face softened. "She seems like a great kid. You've done a good job with her.''

Becca's throat swelled at the words of praise. "Thank you, Grady. And thank you for offering to give her riding lessons.'' She hesitated. "I think Cassie would love that. And I guess it's a good way for the two of you to get to know each other.''

He nodded once. "Fine. We'll figure out a schedule.''

Becca watched him as his gaze lingered on the truck, feeling the distance that yawned between them. It was far more than the few feet that stood between them. Grady was still angry at her, and he had every right to be. Would he ever be able to put that anger aside? And even if he did, was the relationship they'd been slowly rebuilding now hopelessly smashed?

She studied the red dust that swirled beneath her feet, unwilling to let him see the regret she knew was reflected in her eyes. It was her own fault, she told herself, and she could blame no one but herself.

"I'll be back this afternoon to take another look at the cow,'' she finally said, trying to sound businesslike.

"Fine. I'll make sure someone keeps an eye on her during the day.''

Becca shifted the bag in her hand, knowing she should

leave, and afraid to actually get in her truck and drive away. She didn't want this anger to lie between them, to define their relationship from now on. Her treacherous body reminded her of what Grady had tasted like, what he had felt like, and her pulse quickened as she watched him.

"Are you going to compete in the Fourth of July rodeo in town next week?" she asked suddenly.

He turned to look at her, his face hardening into an unreadable mask. "No. My rodeo days are a thing of the past."

Beneath the hardness in his eyes was a glimpse of anguish. "I never asked why you stopped competing in the rodeo," she asked in a soft voice.

For a long time she didn't think he was going to answer her. Finally he looked away and said, "There was an accident. I had no choice."

"I'm sorry, Grady. That must have been painful."

At that he looked at her. "You have no idea what it was like." His eyes were chips of hard, glittering blue glass, and his face was absolutely expressionless.

She held her breath while she considered her request. Then, in a rush, she said, "Would you like to go and watch with Cassie and I? The Fourth of July rodeo is really our annual town party. Just about everyone from town and the surrounding ranches takes the day off to be there."

She could see his refusal on his face, could almost see him forming the words in his mind. Then his gaze wandered over to the truck and Cassie. Compressing his lips, he nodded once. "All right. I'll go with you."

With one more glance at Cassie and the truck, he turned and walked away. Becca watched him leave, his long legs striding quickly over the dusty ground. He didn't look back, and she waited until he disappeared around the corner of the barn before she picked up her bag and moved to the truck.

All the way back to town she listened to Cassie chatter about the riding lesson and Pete, the perfect horse. She had done the right thing, she realized, by telling Grady that he could give Cassie lessons. She had waited far too long to allow her daughter to do something she clearly loved.

As she drove toward home, another question haunted her. By waiting so long to tell Grady about Cassie, had she destroyed any hope of mending the rift between them?

The morning of the rodeo dawned clear and hot. Cassie was out of bed hours earlier than usual. As Becca fixed her breakfast, she wondered if Grady was really going to go to the rodeo with them. She hadn't heard a word from Grady since the day they'd been at the ranch to take care of the cow with milk fever. When she'd returned later that afternoon to check the cow again, only Tucker was waiting for her. And she hadn't been called out to the Flying W since then.

Her heart ached for the fragile, tenuous relationship that had started to build between her and Grady, now smashed and in too many pieces to be easily put back together. Humpty Dumpty had nothing on them, she thought sadly. If only she had told Grady about Cassie the first time she saw him out at the Flying W. If only Ron Perkins had told her where to find Grady when she'd been pregnant with Cassie. If only she'd been able to find Grady herself. If only, if only...

She had learned long ago to put the "if only's" behind her, she reminded herself. It didn't do any good to dream about what might have been. Scooping the slices of French toast off the griddle, she turned and pasted a bright smile on her face. "Breakfast, Cassie," she called.

Cassie came bounding into the kitchen and slid into her chair. "Are we going to eat at the rodeo?" she asked as she poured syrup on her plate.

"Probably." Becca slid a piece of French toast onto her own plate and sat down at the table. "But I'm not sure when we'll eat, so finish your breakfast."

Cassie grinned at her, cheeks full of syrupy toast. "Mr. Farrell used to be in the rodeo, you know. Is he going to ride bulls today?"

"No. He doesn't compete in rodeos anymore."

The child's face fell, then she brightened. "I bet he'd show me how he used to ride bulls if I asked him."

"You can't do that, Cassie," Becca answered sharply, then took a deep breath. "He has reasons for why he stopped riding in rodeos," she said more gently. "You don't want to make him feel uncomfortable by asking him about his reasons."

"Maybe he'll be at the rodeo today, just watching. He could tell me what the riders were doing."

"I'm sure he'd do that, if he was at the rodeo." She pressed her lips together, unsure of what to say to Cassie. If Grady had changed his mind, she didn't want her daughter to be upset. On the other hand, if he did show up, she didn't want Cassie to seem too surprised. Grady would know she hadn't told Cassie, and he would know she'd been afraid he wouldn't keep his word.

Somewhere in this ugly mix of hurt, regret and anger, she had to take the first step toward trust. Taking a deep breath, she said, "Grady is going to take us to the rodeo today. So you can ask him all the questions you want."

Cassie's face lit up and she bounced up and down in the chair. "Yes!" she yelled, waving her fork in the air. "That will be awesome, Mom!"

Becca was glad that at least Cassie thought so. She wasn't so sure, herself. From his reaction at the ranch the other day, she knew that he hadn't given up the rodeo willingly. And she suspected that going back as a spectator today would be hard for him. She hoped he wasn't regretting his promise. Or even worse, regretting that he'd agreed to spend the time with her and Cassie.

As she watched Cassie wolf down the rest of her French toast, she thought again of what might have been. A picture of Grady sitting at the table with them, eating breakfast together like a family, filled her mind. He'd turn to her and they'd share a parent's secret smile at Cassie's enthusiasm for the rodeo. Then they'd walk, hand in hand, to the fairgrounds a few blocks away.

Becca forcibly pushed the mental image away. That wasn't reality and wasn't likely to be. Right now she'd settle for Grady giving up some of his anger at her. Right now, she admitted, she'd settle for a single smile from him.

Pushing away from the table, she said briskly, "Go upstairs and get your clothes on, Cass. We want to be ready when Grady gets here."

"When is he coming?" her daughter asked, leaping up from her chair.

"Not for a while, I'm sure. The gates to the fairgrounds don't even open until ten o'clock."

"Okay." Cassie turned and dashed up the stairs. Becca knew she'd be dressed and ready to go in record time today.

Shortly before ten o'clock she heard Grady's truck pull into the driveway. Her heart started a slow thudding that she told herself was nerves. When his footsteps echoed on the wooden stairs of the front porch, she fluttered her hands over her sundress, smoothing out imaginary wrinkles, then hurried to the door.

"Good morning, Grady," she said, holding the door open for him to enter.

He looked around, and she realized that he'd never been in this part of her house. She tried to imagine what the living-room furniture, just this side of shabby, and the slightly faded rug covering the wooden living-room floor would look like through his eyes. Then she raised her chin a notch. She wouldn't apologize for the fact that she didn't have a lot of money.

His gaze met hers, and she saw an awareness in them that made her uncomfortable. Finally he said softly, "I like your house, Becca. It's very welcoming."

"Thank you," she murmured. "Come in while we wait for Cassie to get ready."

"I am ready," her daughter yelled as she came flying down the stairs. "Hi, Mr. Farrell," she said, breathless. "I'm ready to go."

Becca saw Grady's gaze linger on the child, and she thought his eyes softened, just a little. "Well, then, let's get in the truck and go to the rodeo."

Becca knew that only she would have seen the pain, deep in his eyes, as he spoke. Wanting to reach out to him, to ease his pain somehow, she touched his arm.

When he turned to stare at her, she almost snatched her hand away. But deep in Grady's eyes she saw a flicker of something that wasn't pain, something that made fire race through her veins and made her heart crash against her chest.

They stood staring at each other for what felt like hours. "Let's go," Cassie said from behind her, and Becca jerked her hand away from him. Grady turned to the child.

"Hop in my truck, cowgirl."

"Wait," Becca said. "The fairgrounds are only a few blocks away, and parking is usually a nightmare. Why don't we leave your truck here and walk over?"

Grady shrugged. "Fine with me. Lead the way."

As they walked down the street, joining in the stream of people heading to the fairgrounds, Becca looked over at Grady, walking on the other side of Cassie. If she tried, she could almost imagine that they were a family, heading over to the rodeo on a holiday like most of the other families in Cameron. Almost.

But Grady's rigid face and the stiff way he held himself as they got closer to the fairgrounds reminded her that they were no family. And as she caught the curious glances of her friends and neighbors from town, and the knowing smiles some of them flashed her as she walked with Grady, she began to wonder if her idea had been a horrible mistake.

Instead of being a pleasant day together, giving Grady a chance to get to know his daughter, was this outing to the rodeo going to be nothing more than a cause of pain for Grady and a source of gossip for Cameron?

Chapter 11

The scent of the rodeo wrapped itself around Grady's heart as they got closer and closer to the fairgrounds. The nervous excitement of the competitors, and the snorting, ground-pawing anticipation of the animals swirled around him like a living thing. He hadn't been near a rodeo since he'd gotten hurt five years ago, but that didn't stop him from reacting. His pulse tripped and sped up, and his fingers itched to curl around a rope.

"We're almost there!"

The child walking between him and Becca interrupted his thoughts as she skipped once and looked up at her mother. "Are we going to be on time? We're not going to miss anything, are we?"

Becca shot him an apologetic look, then said, "We're not going to miss a thing, honey. The rodeo events don't start for a while yet."

God, why had he agreed to this? He didn't want to be anywhere near a rodeo. And he especially didn't want to be near one with Becca. She knew him too well, was able to read him too easily. He had seen sympathy in her eyes back at her house, and rather than making him angry, as almost everyone else's sympathy had done, it had touched him. He knew how she felt about the rodeo, how she'd hated it and blamed it for separating them. And yet she was sorry he had lost that part of his life.

He didn't want to let that thought linger in his mind. He was angry at her for what she'd done, he reminded himself, and he didn't want to relinquish that anger. He was deathly afraid of what he would find had taken its place.

He looked down at Cassie, dressed in blue shorts and a red shirt. "What do you want to do today?" he asked her.

"I want to see everything in the rodeo," she answered promptly, and Grady kicked himself for asking. But he couldn't very well take the words back now.

"Have you ever seen a rodeo before?"

"We went last year and the year before, but we didn't see the rodeo. Mom let me go on the rides," she explained, her voice full of awe at the unexpected pleasure.

Grady glanced at Becca, who met his gaze and lifted her chin. "I gave her a choice," she said.

"And what child could pass up carnival rides?" he said in a mocking voice. Clearly she hadn't wanted to take Cassie to the rodeo, and had bribed her with the rides.

Becca didn't look away from him. "I had no idea who would be in the rodeo," she said softly. "It wasn't a chance I was willing to take."

He tried to summon his anger again, but one look at her face stopped it cold. Almost unwillingly he imagined what it would have been like for her if he'd been in the rodeo, seeing him appear in front of her with his child sitting next to her. Grudgingly he admitted to himself that she had a good reason for avoiding the rodeo.

Turning to Cassie, trying to escape from the moment of understanding, he said, "Do you want to go on the rides again this year?"

She shook her head and sent her braids flying around her face. "This year I want to see the rodeo. And my mom said we can stay for all of it. Right, Mom?"

"We can stay as long as you like." Becca glanced over at him. "But Mr. Farrell might have to leave early. He has a ranch to take care of."

Her words reached inside him, igniting a small flame that warmed him. Becca knew he would have a hard time at the rodeo, and she was telling him she understood. "Those cows will have to manage on their own today," he said lightly. "I'm staying at the rodeo until the last fireworks are finished."

"Can we stay for the fireworks, too, Mommy? Can we?"

"We'll see," Becca answered.

Before Cassie could press her mother for an answer, they'd reached the ring set up for the rodeo. Several riders circled the arena, and Cassie ran over to watch.

"I'll understand if you can't stay," Becca said in a low voice as they followed Cassie more slowly.

He looked at her for a moment, then let his gaze wander over the rodeo arena. It was all excruciatingly, achingly familiar, from the worn bleachers set up on one side of the ring to the chutes lined up on the other side. "Would you?" he asked, unable to hide the pain in his voice.

"I've lost things in my life, too."

He didn't want to think about the grief beneath her words. "Name one."

"I lost you, Grady."

At that he turned to face her. "That was your choice, Becca."

"I didn't say it wasn't my fault. I accept the responsibility for what I did. That doesn't mean it didn't hurt."

He was saved from a reply by Cassie. "What are they doing now, Mr. Farrell?"

He glanced at the riders circling the ring. "They're just warming up their horses. Those are some of the barrel racers and some of the calf ropers. They want to keep their horses loose and ready to work.''

By the time he turned back to Becca, she'd had a chance to gather her composure. Now she smiled at Cassie and reached out her hand. ''C'mon, Cass, let's get some cotton candy, then we can find our seats before the rodeo begins.''

As the child walked toward a vendor with her mother, Grady trailed behind them, trying to push Becca's words out of his mind. He didn't want to think about Becca, missing him, alone and afraid, pregnant. He wouldn't let his mind linger on that picture. He wanted to focus on right now, on how she'd kept the truth from him for so long.

But as he watched her bend over her daughter, her blond hair blending with Cassie's dark braids, he was afraid that his anger was draining away. All it left behind was a terrible emptiness, as if there were nothing but a black void where his heart used to be.

An hour later they were settled in the bleachers, Cassie's sticky, cotton-candy-covered fingers holding tightly to a program. She leaned forward between him and her mother, staring intently at the barrels that were being placed in the ring.

''What are they doing now?''

Questions had tumbled out of her mouth, one after another, ever since they'd sat down. But instead of becoming irritated with the constant stream of questions, Grady enjoyed watching her eyes shine, seeing her bounce up and down in her seat. Cassie was loving the rodeo; there was no doubt about that. His daughter, he thought, remembering his own first rodeo. There was something very satisfying about sharing this with her.

''What are they doing, Mr. Farrell?'' she asked again, a hint of impatience in her voice.

He tore his gaze away from her face and focused on the ring in front of him. ''They're getting ready for the barrel racers. They'll all come in and parade around the ring, then they'll take turns racing their horses around the barrels. The one who gets the fastest time is the winner.''

"Is it dangerous?"

He smiled as he looked down at her. Cassie's eyes were riveted on the spectacle in front of her. "Not like bull riding and bronc riding. But a barrel racer has to train herself and her horse very hard, and it's more difficult than it looks. Sometimes they fall off, or bump into a barrel. Then they can get hurt.''

Cassie continued to stare at the racers, until she pointed to a woman on a huge black horse. "I bet she's going to win."

Becca leaned forward. "Why do you say that, honey?"

"She looks like she's trying very hard."

"She's not even racing yet."

"I still think she's going to win," Cassie replied stubbornly.

Grady felt Becca glance over at him. He was staring at the intense woman on the black horse. "I think you're right, Cass," he said slowly. Turning to meet Becca's eyes, he asked, "Do you know that woman?"

Becca nodded. "That's Shea McAllister. She's the sheriff's sister. Shea runs their ranch. You haven't met her yet because the ranch is on the other side of town from yours." She looked over at the woman, now on the other side of the ring. "I don't think Shea ever does anything at less than full speed. Or less than complete intensity. I would certainly never bet against her. But as far as I know, Cassie's never met her."

Grady's gaze lingered on the child sitting next to him. "Why do you think she's trying very hard, Cassie?"

Cassie's eyes never left the woman on the black horse. "She's the only one who isn't goofing around."

Cassie was right. While the other riders talked to each other and fiddled with their reins, the woman on the black horse vibrated with intensity. And she had the look of a fierce competitor.

Grady looked down at the child sitting next to him, and

his heart fluttered once in his chest. "Cassie, I have a feeling that in a few years, you're going to look just like that woman when you're riding a horse. And I bet if you're in a race, you'll win it, too."

Cassie looked up at him, her face glowing. "Really?" she whispered.

"Really. When can you come out to the ranch for your next riding lesson?"

"Whenever my mom says I can."

Grady looked over at Becca, and surprised a look of profound sadness in her eyes. "Becca?" he asked.

He watched her force her lips into a stiff smile. "We'll talk later," she said. Motioning to the ring, she added, "The barrel racing is going to start."

"Cassie, would you like to go down a few rows to the rail, so you can get a better look?" he asked.

Cassie nodded and jumped up, but before she ran down the steps she turned to her mother. "Is that okay, Mom?"

"Just stay in front of me so I can see you," Becca said.

When Cassie had settled herself at the railing, he asked Becca, "Did you change your mind about the riding lessons?"

"Of course not. Why would you think so?"

"You didn't look too happy when we were talking about that barrel racer."

She looked away for a moment, then sat up straight and looked at him. "I can introduce you to Shea later, if you'd like."

"Why would I want to be introduced to her?" he asked, confused.

Becca didn't blink. "Because she's the kind of woman you'd get along with. She's very much like you."

Insight struck Grady like a flash of lightning. "You're jealous!" he exclaimed, joy leaping inside him before he could stop it.

"A person can't be jealous when there's nothing she's protecting,'' she snapped back at him. ''I know I've destroyed any chances we might have had. And you seemed interested in Shea.''

''I wasn't saying I wanted a relationship with the woman. I was interested in her only because of what Cassie said. If Shea McAllister is as much like me as you're saying, we'd probably kill each other within days of getting involved.'' He sat back and watched her face turn red, enjoying the rare moment. Since he'd been in Cameron, he'd rarely seen Becca lose her composure. Except for the times she'd been in his arms.

The taste of her mouth and the feel of her hands swept over him, taunting him, reminding him that he'd been completely unsuccessful at forgetting about Becca. No matter how hard he'd tried, this past week he hadn't been able to convince his body that he hated her.

''I'm sorry if I misunderstood,'' Becca muttered, then turned away to watch the first barrel racer.

He leaned over. ''I had no idea you cared so much,'' he whispered, and watched as hot color flooded up over her chest and onto her neck. ''I'm glad you wore that dress,'' he added. ''I had forgotten how you blush all over.''

''Stop it,'' she whispered. ''What if Cassie heard you?''

''What would be wrong with that? Haven't you gone out on dates before?''

She didn't answer, and her rigid back and refusal to look at him were his answer. ''My God, Becca, are you saying you've never dated?''

''I'm not saying anything.''

''But you haven't, have you?''

Finally she turned to him. ''While I was in school, I was too exhausted by my class work, my job and taking care of Cassie to even think about dating. And once I was out of school, I was working too hard to pay all my debts and then buy into the practice to have time to date. Don't make this into something significant, Grady. You have no idea what my life's been like.''

He didn't, and suddenly he wanted to change that. ''Maybe you can tell me sometime,'' he said.

She turned and looked at him, studying his face and his eyes. Slowly she nodded, the frosty glare fading from her eyes. ''Sometime I will.''

She turned to look for Cassie just as the child came bounding up the stairs. ''Look, Mr. Farrell, it's the woman on the black horse's turn. Will you watch her with me?''

Grady patted the seat next to him, grasping the opportunity to focus his attention away from Becca. His mind swirled with emotions he wasn't sure he was ready to acknowledge. Just because he and Becca had managed to talk without anger didn't mean that all their problems were solved, he reminded himself. There was too much between them to allow for an easy, happy ending. And somehow that thought made him more unhappy than ever.

Pushing it out of his mind, he turned to the child next to him. ''Okay, Cassie, she's ready to go,'' he said, watching the ring in front of him. ''Let's see how long it takes her to race around the barrels.''

They watched Shea McAllister fly through the course as she clung to her horse. When she raced past the finish line, he glanced at the clock and saw that her time was the fastest so far. ''She's in first place,'' he told Cassie, and watched as the child nodded with satisfaction.

''She was fast,'' Cassie said.

''Let's see if anyone can beat her,'' he answered.

No one could, and Cassie stood up and cheered as the woman rode into the ring as the winner. Then she turned to him, her face glowing. ''I want to do that,'' she said.

''That's up to your mother,'' he replied. ''But I'll teach you how to ride a horse.''

The child turned to Becca. ''Can I race the barrels, Mom? Can I?''

"You can't be a barrel racer until you're older, and first you have to learn to ride, anyway. Why don't we take it one step at a time?"

Grady looked for the disapproval he expected to see in Becca's eyes, but all he saw was a weary resignation. He turned to Cassie. "Your mom's right, cowgirl. One thing at a time. Let's teach you to ride a horse before we start talking barrel racing."

Cassie nodded her head vigorously. "Okay. But do you think Pete would make a good barrel-racing horse?"

Grady looked over and found Becca smiling in spite of herself, and he found his mouth curling up in a reluctant answering smile. Becca had been telling him nothing less than the truth when she said that Cassie's determination and single-mindedness were his traits. He thought about similar conversations he'd had with his father, but his smile faded as he remembered the outcome of those talks.

"Pete's too young to think about training him as a barrel racer, Cassie. He needs to learn the basics first." But someday he would be perfect for barrel racing, Grady knew, picturing the paint pony in his mind.

Cassie nodded, satisfied with the answer, and turned back to watch the rodeo in front of her. His gaze lingered on her for a moment, this small replica of himself, and a profound sadness swept over him. Would he be around to see her debut as a barrel racer? Did he want to commit himself to a role in her life?

His heart answered yes, but his mind shied away from the question. He wasn't going to be any good as a father. He didn't know the first thing about the subject. And did Becca want him around as part of Cassie's life? She had done a great job so far without him. Anyone could see that. As he watched his daughter, a bleak coldness filled his chest. Cassie would be better off without him. He had no doubts that he'd do nothing but screw up her life.

* * *

Shadows lengthened in front of them as morning turned to afternoon. Becca sneaked a glance at the man walking on the other side of Cassie. Grady had stayed with them all day, and even watched all of the rodeo events with them. She had watched his mouth tighten and his body tense as the bull riders had competed, one after the other, but he'd answered Cassie's questions patiently and never given the child a hint of the pain she knew he'd been suffering.

Her heart had ached for him. She couldn't possibly guess how difficult it had been to sit and watch the rodeo, knowing that he wouldn't be competing in one ever again. She knew Grady well enough to understand that his passion for the rodeo hadn't dimmed. Instead, she guessed, he'd buried it so deeply that he could pretend it didn't exist.

Except when he was forced to sit through several hours of rodeo events.

She never should have asked him to accompany them to the fair, she told herself for the hundredth time. She, of all people, should have known how painful it would be for him.

"Mom," Cassie's voice interrupted her thoughts, "can I be a mutton buster next year?"

"I think maybe you're too big for mutton busting," she said, ruffling her daughter's bangs. She thought about the event for young children and smiled. The little ones rode on sheep, trying to hold on for eight seconds just like the adults on the broncs and the bulls. It definitely got the title of cutest of all the rodeo events.

"Then I'll ride the calves," Cassie said, as if the issue was settled. Older children had ridden calves in an event similar to the mutton busting.

"Next year is a long way off," Grady said mildly. "There's a lot of time left before the next rodeo here in Cameron."

"I'll have lots of time to practice, then."

Becca tried to hide a smile as she watched Grady try to deal with this younger version of himself.

"I thought you wanted to learn to ride a horse," he said, raising his eyebrows at Cassie.

"I do," she answered fervently.

"Maybe we should concentrate on one thing at a time."

Cassie appeared to consider this for a while, then she nodded. "After I learn to ride Pete, then I'll learn to ride the calves."

Becca almost laughed as she watched Cassie run up to Laura and her children. "Welcome to Parenting 101. Cassie makes it a real challenge to stay one step ahead of her."

Grady shook his head. "Was I really like that?"

"You were worse," Becca answered lightly.

She watched Cassie chattering with Laura, then Cassie came racing back to her. "Can I go on the Ferris wheel with Jenny and Todd? Laura doesn't want them to go alone, and she said I could watch them." Her voice was filled with pride.

"Sure, honey." Becca reached for her wallet for money, but Grady handed her some bills first.

"Why don't you all have an ice-cream cone after the Ferris wheel?" he said.

Becca's first, instinctive reaction was to tell him no, tell him that she could afford to pay for her daughter's entertainment. But she closed her mouth slowly as Cassie nodded, her eyes glowing, and raced away to join Laura and her children.

Grady turned to look at her, a challenge in his eyes. "Aren't you going to chew me out for giving her the money?"

"I thought about it," she admitted. "But I guess I have to get used to sharing her."

Grady's mouth twisted into a scowl. "I haven't said anything about being a regular part of her life."

"You're going to give her riding lessons," she reminded him. "I would imagine that would happen on a fairly regular basis."

"Damn it, Becca, that's not what I meant and you know

it. I'm still not sure I want her to know that I'm her father. I don't know if there's anything good I can give her."

"You can give her a father," she said, watching him carefully. "That's far more important than riding lessons and money for ice-cream cones."

"You know what the issues are," he muttered. "I need time to think them through."

"Fine. You can have all the time you need."

She stepped away from him and took a deep breath, trying to steady herself. In spite of the warnings she'd been giving herself all day, she was still far too aware of Grady Farrell. Her body hummed whenever she got too close to him. And her hands ached to reach out and pull him even closer.

She was sorry she'd agreed that Cassie could ride the Ferris wheel, then have ice cream with Laura and her children. That left her alone with Grady for too long. And as the day deepened into night, the darkness would feel too intimate, too private, even with the crowds of people around.

Grady touched her arm lightly, sending ripples of awareness jolting through her. "Who are those people with your friend Laura?"

"They just arrived in Cameron. I ran into them the other night." After Becca had rechecked the cow that had been sick, she and Cassie had gone to dinner at the town restaurant. Devlin had introduced her to the couple, but Becca hadn't needed an introduction. She remembered Damien Kane.

Becca watched as the tall, dark-haired man and the slender woman with the chestnut hair stopped in front of Laura Weston. The two little girls with them, obviously twins, clung to the woman's hands. "That's Damien Kane. And the woman's name is Abby. I think the girls are her nieces."

The woman bent over and spoke to Cassie, and Becca watched as Cassie's face lit up. "Abby obviously likes children."

Grady watched the group, his eyes narrowed. "Weren't

you telling me about them? Didn't you tell me Devlin said there was some problem with them?''

Becca glanced over at him. ''He didn't spell it out, but I got the impression that something was wrong.'' She hesitated, then added, ''It must be serious, to bring Damien back here. I never thought I'd see him in Cameron again, after what happened to his family. And I never imagined he'd spend time with children again, either.''

''What happened to his family?''

Before Becca could answer, Laura and Damien and Abby and the five children turned and headed toward the Ferris wheel. One of the twins took Cassie's hand, and Cassie smiled happily down at her.

Grady said gruffly, ''Cassie's good with those little kids.''

''Yes, she is.'' Becca smiled at the group at the same moment that Abby turned around. The other woman gave her a hesitant smile and a small wave, and Becca waved back.

''They look like they're going to be busy for a while. Are you going to hover here until they're finished?'' Grady turned to face her and her pulse skittered.

''Of course not.'' She swallowed hard. Hovering close to the carnival ride, surrounded by crowds of people, was exactly what she wanted to do. But she would never admit that to Grady. It would tell him too much about how she felt. The last thing she wanted him to know was how his presence affected her.

''Then why don't we walk around? You haven't had much chance to see the fair. You've been too busy doing what Cassie wanted to do.''

''Is there something wrong with that?''

''Not a thing,'' he answered easily. ''But since she's going to be busy for a while, you might as well relax and enjoy yourself.''

Relaxing was the last thing she'd be able to do with Grady standing so close to her, but she nodded stiffly and let him lead her away. But before long she realized that Grady's idea of seeing the fair and hers were very different.

As they walked past the deserted bleachers set up for the rodeo and headed behind the darkened ring to the chutes, Becca slowed. "What are we doing here? I don't think there's much to see back there in the dark."

"I wanted to talk to you, and I thought it would be best if it was someplace where we couldn't be overheard."

"What did you want to discuss that couldn't wait?" She turned to face him. Shadows from the boards that made up the rodeo ring hid his face, and she moved closer so she could see his eyes.

He went still, and she felt the sudden tension that swept over him. "What's the matter?" she asked.

Slowly he reached out and curled his hands around her shoulders. For a moment he didn't move, and she wasn't sure if he was trying to push her away or urge her closer. Finally, with a groan, he pulled her into his arms and crushed her mouth beneath his.

Her heart leaped in her chest, and her first, instinctive response was to fold herself closer and give herself up to his embrace. She melted against him, molding her body to his and opening her mouth to murmur his name. Her eyes fluttered closed, and everything but Grady ceased to exist. She was lost in the taste of him, the feel of him, the magic of being in his arms once again.

He groaned and shifted so that she stood between his legs, every inch of their bodies touching. The thin material of her sundress was no barrier to the heat that pulsed from Grady. And when he wrapped his leg around hers, the coarse denim of his jeans rubbing against her bare leg sent exquisite showers of sensation coursing through her.

"I swore I wouldn't do this again," he muttered against her mouth as his lips lingered on hers. "I want to have a rational discussion with you."

"What do you want to discuss?" Tentatively she ran her

tongue along his lower lip, savoring the heady male taste of him.

She felt his hands tremble as they tightened on her back. "The situation." His voice sounded ragged and unsteady as he kissed his way to her ear.

"What about the situation?" She shuddered when he tugged gently on her earlobe. Without thinking, she pressed herself against him, crushing her breasts against his chest.

"We need to discuss it." He trailed kisses down her neck, leaving a trail of fire behind. When he smoothed his tongue along the hollow above her collarbone, she arched against him.

"I know." She barely recognized her voice, breathy and trembling. Then Grady captured her mouth again, and she found it impossible to think at all.

Need crashed through her, obliterating everything but Grady from her mind. His arms tightened around her, and he slid one of his hands lower to cup her hip. Desire throbbed and hummed in her abdomen and pounded through her veins.

Grady groaned into her mouth and moved suddenly, and she felt something hard pressing into her back. One small part of her brain recognized the boards of the rodeo ring, and suddenly she was aware of her surroundings. Cassie, the rodeo, the crowds of people only steps away flooded into her mind, and she unwrapped her arms from Grady's back and tried to lean away from him.

She opened her eyes to look up at Grady, and when she saw the passion and raw need on his face, she wanted to crawl back into his arms. But he wouldn't thank her if someone found them back here and gossip spread like wildfire through Cameron, so she said gently, "Grady, stop."

He opened his eyes to stare down at her. As she watched him gather his composure, suddenly two hands came between them and thrust them roughly apart. Grady reeled away, off balance, and she looked up in shock to see Sy Ames standing in front of her.

Chapter 12

"What are you doing?" she cried, edging closer to Grady.

Sy planted himself between them, flexing his hands into fists and staring from one of them to the other. "I heard you telling him to stop."

When he turned to gaze at Grady, his eyes were full of wild hatred.

"Were you watching us?" she asked Sy sharply as she moved to stand next to Grady.

Grady stepped in front of her before Sy could answer. "What the hell are you doing here, Ames?"

"This is a public fair," he sneered. "I have as much right to be here as you do."

"You have no right to harass Dr. Johnson," Grady answered, his voice cold and hard. "I suggest you get lost."

"I wasn't the one bothering her." Sy took a step closer, and Becca could feel Grady tense. "It looked to me like you were doing the harassing."

"What was going on between us is none of your goddamn business. Now get out of here."

Sy turned to Becca. "Stay away from Farrell, Rebecca. He's nothing but trouble."

Becca saw the hatred and hot anger flare in Sy's eyes again. Grady set her gently aside and took another step toward Sy. The other man stumbled backward, then with one more look of hatred he turned and ran, melting into the shadows.

"Everything all right back here?" a male voice called.

Ben Jackson, one of the sheriff's deputies, stepped out of the shadows. Becca wanted to crawl into a hole, but Grady put a hand on her arm.

"It is now," Grady said.

"That was Sy Ames, wasn't it?" Jackson said.

Ben was reserved and difficult to read, and no one in town knew him well. But Becca had enormous respect for him. She'd always thought him the most intelligent and observant of Devlin's deputies.

"Yes," Becca said. "I didn't know he was still around, but he's gone now."

Ben watched her for a moment, then slowly nodded. "I'll keep my eyes open."

Becca's fear eased. She knew that Ben would be watching for Sy, and if he found him, Sy would have some explaining to do. The thought cheered her, and she smiled at the deputy. "Thanks, Ben. I appreciate you taking the time to check on us."

"My pleasure."

Out of the corner of her eye, Becca saw a figure hurrying away to their left. Before the woman disappeared around a corner, Becca realized it was Janie Murphy, the owner of the town's diner. Ben clearly saw her, too. For just an instant he tensed, then he deliberately relaxed. Touching his hat, Ben said, "Stay away from these dark areas back here. They invite trouble."

He glanced back in the direction Janie had gone, almost as if he couldn't help himself, then turned and deliberately walked in the opposite direction. Becca watched until he disappeared, too, then turned to Grady.

"Maybe Ben is right," she said in a low voice. "These dark areas back here do invite trouble."

She didn't mean trouble with Sy, and she knew Grady understood. He nodded once. "It's time to find Cassie," he said, and despite the casual words, his low voice caressed her in the intimacy of the darkness. "The fireworks are going to start any minute."

So they weren't going to talk about what had flared between them just moments ago. It was probably just as well, she told herself. After all, what could be said? They had serious problems to solve, but they were acting like hormone-driven teenagers. Maybe it was best if they both pretended that the kiss in the dark had never happened.

They found Cassie finishing an ice-cream cone with Laura and her children and Damien, Abby and the twins. As Becca introduced Grady and they chatted with Abby and Damien, she couldn't help notice the way Damien's gaze swept the crowd almost continuously. Becca stirred uneasily. Was something truly wrong in her beloved town? After Damien, Abby and the twins said their goodbyes and left, she wondered what had put the haunted look in Abby Markham's eyes.

By the time they made their way to the field behind the fairgrounds, the first fireworks were shooting up into the night sky. Color exploded against the dark canvas above them, eliciting oohs and ahhs from the crowd.

Cassie leaned against her side, and Becca could feel the weariness in her daughter's slumping body. As soon as the streamers from the last rocket had faded away, Becca touched Grady's arm.

"We need to get started for home. Cassie's ready to crash."

They walked with the crowds toward the street, and soon they were alone on the corner near Becca's house. When they stepped up onto the porch, Grady looked over at Becca, a question in his eyes.

"Come on in while I get Cassie to bed," Becca said, holding the door open.

He watched her for a moment, then nodded. Stepping into the house, he said, "Take your time."

As they started up the stairs, Cassie turned to Grady and gave him a sleepy smile. "Thank you for 'splaining the rodeo to me, Mr. Farrell. I had fun."

"I'm glad," Grady answered, then he hesitated. "Sleep well," he finally said, his voice gruff.

Grady paced across the tiny living room as the sounds of a child preparing for bed drifted down the stairs. He wouldn't let himself think about those sounds, or what was happening at the top of the stairs. Bedtime rituals were none of his concern.

In order to distract himself, he looked around the room. The bright floral print on the couch and two chairs was slightly faded, as if it had been rubbed away by too many trousers and skirts. The rug on the floor showed similar signs of wear, and the curtains on the windows were simple and clearly homemade. Childish drawings in frames hung on the walls, and as he wandered over to look at them he realized that each one had been signed by Cassie and carefully dated by Becca.

His heart gave an odd little jump at the sign of Becca's devotion to her daughter. Every time Cassie saw these pictures, she would see how much her mother loved her. Staring at a picture that he decided must be a horse, he didn't realize Becca had walked into the room until he felt her beside him.

"She was five when she drew that. It was what her future horse was going to look like."

"I wondered if it was a horse."

Becca smiled. "She's never going to be an artist, but she likes seeing her pictures on the wall. And so do I."

He searched for the right words. "You're a good mother, Becca."

"I try to be."

He heard the weariness in her voice and longed to pull her into his arms and comfort her. Stepping away, he said, "I guess I should go."

But before he could escape, she said, "Why does Sy Ames hate you so much?"

"What do you mean?"

"I saw his face tonight. I saw the look he gave you. He hates you, Grady. How come?"

Grady shrugged. "Because I got the ranch from him, I guess."

Becca watched him, her eyes shrewd. "There's more to the story than that, Grady."

Sighing, he turned and sat down on her couch. "Yeah, there's more to it than that. I should have known I couldn't hide it from you."

"What is it?"

For a moment he considered not telling her the whole story. But remembering Sy's face that evening, he knew he couldn't withhold any information from her. It was likely that Sy was the person harassing her. "Remember that poker game I told you about?" he finally said. "The one where Sy bet more than he could cover?"

"I remember."

"He was cheating. One of the other players caught him red-handed. He was forced to forfeit the hand, and I won. So not only did I get his ranch, I witnessed his humiliation. Sy won't ever forget that."

"I thought he'd left Cameron."

"I think he's the one who's been stalking you." Grady stood up and paced around the room, anger coursing through him at the thought.

"Sy is a bully who's always backed down when someone

confronts him. Besides, he seems to be angry at you, not me,'' she argued. ''How does that translate into stalking me?''

''Use your head, Becca. By now most of the town probably knows that we grew up in the same town. Maybe he thinks that by attacking you he's hurting me.''

''That might be true if we were dating. But we're not, and no one in town knows about Cassie.''

''Are you sure?''

''I haven't told a soul. Laura probably suspects, but no one besides my parents knows who her father is.''

''Anyone with eyes in their head could see that there's history between us.''

''Sy has never seen us together before tonight. So how could he see that?''

He sighed. ''I don't know. But he's my choice for stalker.''

''There are other people who are possibilities, you know.'' She looked down at the floor, as if she'd just discovered something immensely interesting in the cracks between the boards.

''I still think you're crazy to suspect Ron Perkins.''

''Then we're going to have to agree to disagree.'' She stood up. ''This is a pointless discussion right now, Grady. It's not going to solve anything. Ben Jackson will tell the sheriff about seeing Sy, and they'll keep their eyes open for him. I'm too tired to worry about it.''

Grady stood up, too. ''I can take a polite hint, Becca. Thanks for going to the rodeo with me.''

Her face softened. ''Thank you for taking us.'' She hesitated. ''It meant the world to Cassie. I haven't been real understanding about her love of the rodeo, but I'm glad you can share that with her.''

''There aren't likely to be any more rodeos in Cameron for a long time,'' he said, unable to suppress the pang of longing. ''One day hardly makes for a permanent bond.''

''You're going to teach her how to ride a horse. That's a

far stronger bond than watching the occasional rodeo together.''

He scowled. ''She'll probably hate me before we're finished. I intend to make sure she learns properly.''

She smiled at him. ''She's not going to hate you, Grady.
Can't you see she already thinks you're wonderful?''

''Just because I could once ride a bull without falling off.
That's a far cry from being a father.'' His words came out
sounding more vehement than he intended.

''Give it some time.'' She tried to smile, but Grady could
see the effort it took.

''I'll call you about the riding lessons,'' he muttered.

''Fine.'' She walked with him to the front door. Even after
the long day, her elusive fragrance curled around him as she
moved. It tugged at something inside him, something that
wanted to reach out and pull her close, to hold her tightly.

''Good night,'' he said, his voice too gruff.

She looked up at him, and he saw painful understanding in
her eyes. ''Good night, Grady. And thanks again for today.''

Did she understand that today might be as much as he
could ever give Cassie? He suspected she did. The pain in
her eyes was too real, too raw. He didn't want to walk away
like this. He didn't want to think about her locking the door
behind him, the sadness still in her eyes.

''Don't, Becca,'' he said, smoothing one hand over her
face. His fingers tingled with the contact. ''Don't look like
that. Things will work out.''

''Will they, Grady?'' She didn't take her gaze off his, and
she didn't move away from his touch. ''I thought things
would work out nine years ago, but they didn't. I stopped
hoping for miracles a long time ago. Now I try to tell myself
that everything happens for a reason.''

''Like my showing up in Cameron?''

''Whatever happens, you at least know that Cassie is your
daughter. I should have told you long ago and I accept the

responsibility for that. But now the ball is in your court. What happens next is up to you.''

And she was afraid he was going to fumble the pass. Hell, so was he. "Good night, Becca."

"Good night." The door closed behind him with a quiet, final click.

Grady stood in front of the porch for a long moment, listening to the sounds of Becca closing up her house for the night. Windows slid down and the locks clicked into place. Then the lights winked out, and seconds later a light went on in a second-floor room. Her bedroom.

He spun around and fled, taking refuge in his truck. He'd enjoyed the day far too much, he thought grimly. Turning the key with a vicious crank, he backed out of Becca's driveway and waited until he was at the end of her block before gunning the engine. If he wasn't careful, he'd start thinking about Cassie far too often, and that wouldn't be fair to her. She deserved far more than a washed-out rodeo bum for a father. Especially a rodeo bum who had no idea how to *be* a father.

But as he drove down the dark road to the Flying W, he found his thoughts straying repeatedly to the rodeo. Instead of lingering on the pain he'd felt, however, what he remembered was the joy on Cassie's face.

When Becca picked up the cellular phone in her truck a few days later and heard Stella telling her she had a call at the Flying W ranch, she couldn't stop the hum of anticipation that raced through her veins. She hadn't seen Grady or talked to him since the night of the rodeo, but she knew that everyone at the Flying W was busy branding and castrating calves. It was the season in Cameron when the calves born in the spring were identified as part of the herd and most of the ranches in the area took turns helping each other out. From the grapevine she'd heard that the past couple of days had been the Flying W's turn.

Stella told her only that a calf was sick. Becca finished the paperwork from her last ranch visit, then stuffed the folder into the plastic file case she kept with her and pulled out the folder for the Flying W, laying it on the seat next to her as she headed for the ranch.

When she arrived at the Flying W, she first saw several dusty pickup trucks parked in the driveway. As she swung out of her truck, no one came to greet her, so she wandered toward the corral behind the barn.

A swirling, bawling group of young calves stirred up the dust as they huddled together, waiting for their turn to go through the chute. Several cowboys circled them on horseback, keeping them together, while another fed them through a chute one at a time. At the other end of the chute they were castrated if they were males, then branded and finally released back into the pasture to be reunited with their anxious, calling mothers.

It looked like a scene of total confusion, with the dust, the bawling, milling animals and the cowboys swarming around the corral. Instead, it was a tightly choreographed production, efficient and well organized. Becca rested her elbows on the fence and waited for a break in the action.

Tucker noticed her first. She saw him call over to Grady, who was wrestling with a struggling calf. Grady glanced over at her, then nodded to Tucker. When he let the calf go after branding him, he called to someone else to take his place, then hurried over to her.

"Thanks for coming out right away," he said, wiping the sweat and dust off his face with his arm. The dust left a dark red smear behind on his forehead, but his eyes gleamed with satisfaction as he looked back at the corral behind him. Becca tried not to let her gaze linger on his face. She wondered if he even realized how much he was enjoying what he was doing.

"It wasn't a problem," she answered easily. "I wasn't far away and my next call wasn't expecting me for a while, anyway."

"We've got a calf that's limping on one rear leg. He's not using it at all, and I was afraid he might have broken it. Some of the calves struggle more than others."

"Let's go take a look."

Becca picked up her bag and followed Grady into the relative peace of the barn. She could still hear the cries of the calves, but the animals in the barn didn't seem to notice. Grady led her to a large stall at the end of the barn closest to the pasture. Through the open door she saw an Angus cow hovering anxiously near the fence. The calf stood at the door of the stall, balancing on three legs. He held the other leg off the ground.

Slipping into the stall, she laid her hand on the calf's head, then slowly worked her way down his body. She didn't want to startle him, and she needed to see how he would react to her touch. A lot of calves were born on the range, and the branding ordeal was their first human contact.

The calf shied away, but she was able to trap him between her body and the wall of the stall. Once she had him pinned, he stood docilely while she ran her hand down his leg, probing the swollen hock area.

After a few minutes she stood up. "There's nothing broken there, but he does have a nasty sprain. I'm going to wrap it and give him some anti-inflammatory drugs, and he should be fine after a few days. But I'd keep him and his mother in the barn until the leg is healed. You don't want to take the chance of having him step in a hole and hurting it more. If he twisted it again, he could cause some real damage."

Grady nodded. "Thanks, Becca. Ron thought it was just a sprain, but I wanted to be sure." He hesitated. "I don't think he wanted to bother you about something this small. I didn't think about it before I called, but I hope we didn't disrupt your schedule too much."

"Not at all." She'd just bet Ron didn't want her at the ranch. The more time she spent with Grady, the greater the chance Ron's actions nine years ago would be revealed. And she was darn sure Ron Perkins didn't want that to happen.

Grady glanced out toward the pasture, where another batch of calves had been released to find their mothers. "Go ahead and get back to work," she said, interpreting his look. "I'm only going to write down what I did here. There's no reason for you to have to stay."

He turned to look at her. "I'm actually enjoying this, Becca," he said. She smiled at the surprise in his voice.

"I'm glad," she said simply. Grady would have to make his own peace with his past and his loss of the rodeo. But enjoying the work he was doing was a first step.

"I never thought I would, you know. I only agreed to buy this ranch from Sy because I didn't have anything better to do, and I was getting tired of drifting. I figured that I'd stick around until I got bored, then sell it and move on to something else."

"We all change," she said, watching him.

"Those are the last words I thought I'd ever say," Grady admitted, looking out at the pasture. "I never wanted to be tied down to anything, let alone a piece of land. I saw what my father was like, and I swore I would never be anything like him."

"You're not like your father," she said gently. "You never have been."

When he turned to look at her again, his eyes were bleak. "I'm more like him than you know. The apple doesn't fall far from the tree, after all."

Becca longed to wrap her arms around him, to offer him comfort, to assure him that he wasn't anything like his cold, demanding, loveless father. But she didn't. After that kiss at the rodeo the other night, she'd vowed to stay as far away from Grady as she could. She didn't want to cloud the issues between them with a passion she knew she couldn't resist. And she didn't want to substitute desire for a solution to those problems.

So instead of stepping closer to Grady, instead of comforting him, she took a step backward. "Everyone has to find their own way. You'll find yours, Grady."

"We'll see." He stared out at the pasture for a while, then turned to face her. "Go ahead and get your paperwork done. I'll talk to you later. We still have to set up a schedule for Cassie's riding lessons."

"I figured you'd want to wait at least until the branding is finished."

"It would be easier," he admitted. "But I know Cassie is anxious to get started."

She couldn't help the glow of pleasure that he'd been thinking about Cassie. But she didn't point it out to him. She wasn't sure he was ready to hear it. "Thanks for thinking of that, but she can wait a while longer."

"We should be done here in a couple of days. As soon as we are, I'll get Cassie out here."

"Thank you, Grady."

She watched as he hurried out the door and turned to go back to the corral. As she finished writing in her records, she listened to the animal sounds and relished the peace and quiet of the barn. Just as she closed her folder and stood up, a shadow fell across her.

"What are you doing here?"

She looked up to see Ron Perkins scowling down at her. Straightening her back, she lifted her chin and struggled to remain calm in the face of his angry stare.

"I was checking on this calf that sprained his leg. Grady called and asked me to come take a look at it."

"There was nothing wrong with that calf that a few days' rest wouldn't have cured."

"I agree with you, but Grady wanted to be sure. And it is his calf."

Ron's face darkened. "And I suppose you're hoping that pretty soon it'll be your calf, too?"

"What's that supposed to mean?"

"Everyone in town saw you together at the rodeo the other day. I'll bet you're just dying to get your hooks into him again," he sneered.

Becca curled her hands into the folder to stop them from trembling. "What are you implying?"

Ron stared at her with a cold expression on his face, but beneath the scorn she could see his fear. "Grady is too smart to fall for your tricks."

"And which tricks would those be?"

His eyes glittered with anger. "I won't let Grady be trapped into anything," he warned. "He's had too many tough breaks, and since he got hurt he hasn't been interested in anything until this ranch came along. I won't stand by and watch you destroy him."

"Destroying Grady is the last thing I would want to do, Ron." Becca softened her voice, because behind Ron's irrational anger, she could see that he truly cared about Grady. "And what do you mean, 'since he got hurt'?"

Ron immediately shuttered his face. "Never mind," he muttered. "Just stay away from Grady."

"What Grady and I do is none of your business," Becca retorted. She hesitated, then added, "And you'd better keep it that way."

"Are you threatening me?" he demanded.

"No more than you're threatening me." She watched in satisfaction as Ron was unable to hold her gaze. "Stay away from me, Ron. I'm not a nineteen-year-old child anymore, and I won't be bullied by you or anyone else."

She watched as the ranch manager spun around and headed out of the barn. Waiting until he was out of sight, she finally left the barn and climbed into her truck. As she stashed the records back in their box, she watched the activity at the corral.

Grady was in the middle of it, taking his turn wrestling with the calves and rounding them up. Ron was right about one thing, she thought, smiling as she watched him. Grady was enjoying this ranch, and there was nothing she would do to destroy that pleasure. He needed something to call his own, even if it was only a satisfying job.

Her smile faded as she thought about Ron. The ranch manager perceived her as a threat to Grady, and probably as a threat to his own job. Although she admired his loyalty to his friend, she was becoming more afraid he was the person stalking her. He must think that if he could frighten her into leaving town, both Grady and his job would be safe.

As she backed her truck away from the other trucks parked in the driveway, she wondered if she should go to the sheriff with her suspicions. After only a moment she decided against it. She'd already told Devlin that she suspected Ron, and what more did she have to add than one angry conversation? There was nothing concrete she could add.

But remembering the anger on Ron's face, she promised herself she'd be more vigilant. She wasn't sure Ron would actually try to hurt her, but she wasn't going to take any chances.

It was already dark that evening when she finally unlocked the door to her house and shooed Cassie inside. They had stayed at Laura's for dinner, and then Becca had talked to her friend while Cassie played with Jenny and Todd and some of the neighborhood kids. Becca hadn't had a chance to talk to Laura in a while, and the evening had crept away from them.

"Go on upstairs and take a bath, honey," she called to Cassie. "I'll be up in a few minutes to tuck you in."

"Okay, Mom."

Becca listened to her daughter clatter up the stairs and smiled. Cassie must be tired from playing outdoors with all the kids in Laura's neighborhood, or she wouldn't have given in so easily on the bath. She'd be asleep in under five minutes when her head finally hit the pillow.

Propping her briefcase on the floor, Becca dropped the pile

of mail on the table. A sheet of white on the counter caught her eye, and she walked over to see what it was.

"I know where you were this evening. You should have been home when I came to visit. Make sure you're here next time, or I'm going to be mad. You don't want to make me mad."

The note was unsigned. Backing slowly away from the counter, unable to take her eyes off the note, Becca swallowed to keep the bile from rising in her throat. Something dropped on the floor above her, and fear swept over her.

Cassie.

She raced for the stairs. "Oh, God, let her be safe. Please don't let there be anyone up there."

Chapter 13

"Cassie?" she called. "Honey, are you all right?"

"I'm fine, Mom," her daughter called, but her voice was muffled. Becca raced into her room.

Cassie was pulling her shirt over her head. There was no one else in the room, and Becca took a deep breath.

"What's wrong, Mom?"

"I heard something fall up here and wanted to make sure you were okay." Becca knew her voice was shaking.

Cassie rolled her eyes. "It was my boots, Mom. They always make a clunk when they fall on the floor. You know that."

It took every ounce of self-control that Becca possessed to force herself to smile. "I guess you're just getting stronger, then. Have you been taking extra vitamins behind my back?"

Cassie giggled, then ran toward the bathroom. Becca had to control her urge to yell at her to wait. Quickly checking Cassie's room and seeing for herself there were no intruders there, she followed her daughter into the bathroom. There was no place for anyone to hide in the tiny room, so she waited until Cassie was in the tub before hurrying out to check the other rooms on the second floor.

While Cassie was still taking her bath, she went down to the phone and called the sheriff's office. It seemed like only moments later when Devlin McAllister knocked on the door.

"Thank you for getting here so quickly, Sheriff," she said as she stepped aside for him to enter.

Devlin nodded as he raked the kitchen with his gaze. "What's going on, Doc?"

Becca pointed to the note on the counter. "That was lying there when Cassie and I got home tonight. It certainly wasn't there when I left the house this morning."

"Did you touch it?" he asked sharply.

She shook her head. "No. Cassie was upstairs. As soon as I saw it, I ran up there to make sure she was all right. Then I called you."

Devlin grabbed his hand radio and spoke a few terse words into it. Then he looked over at her. "I'm going to search the house, see if there's any other signs of an intruder. Then I want you to think about where you and Cassie could stay tonight."

She felt herself pale. "We have to leave?"

"I think you'd be stupid not to leave. Whoever left this note obviously knows how to get into your house. And there's an implied threat here. We'll drive by your house frequently to keep an eye on things, but we can't spare a deputy to sit in your kitchen all night. I'll feel better, and you'll be safer, if you're out of the house for a few days."

"I don't want to disrupt Cassie." She said the first thing that came to mind.

"What are your alternatives?" he asked.

"I don't know." Becca licked her lips and stared out the window. The backyard was dark, the bushes and flowers black shapes shrouded in mystery. She knew Devlin was right, but her mind felt frozen. Every time she glanced at the white sheet of paper on the counter, the fear rose up in her again. It robbed her of her ability to think clearly, to plan.

"I suppose I could go over to Laura's," she said finally.

Devlin shook his head. "I'm not sure that would be a good idea. Chances are your stalker knows that's where Cassie is during the day." He hesitated, then added, "Do you want to put Laura and her kids at risk, too?"

"Of course not!" she cried. "But I don't know where else to go."

"Why don't I call Grady Farrell?" Devlin watched her, his eyes impossible to read. "He probably has plenty of room out at the ranch. And you seem to be pretty certain that he's not the one stalking you."

"I can't do that." She stared at the sheriff, horrified by the idea. "I can't impose on him that way."

"You told me you grew up with him. Wouldn't he be willing to help you out?"

"That's not the point," she muttered. "And besides, I suspect that his ranch manager is the one stalking me. Why would I want to move closer to him?"

"He doesn't live in the house with Farrell, does he?"

"I don't think so."

"Have you mentioned your suspicions to Farrell?"

"Yes, I did."

"And what did he say?"

"He refuses to even consider the idea. He said he's known Ron for too long and knows he couldn't do anything like that."

"But you still suspect him?"

She nodded. Her stomach twisted into a knot as she remembered their conversation earlier in the day. "Ron and I had a nasty little run-in at the ranch today. He basically told me to stay away from Grady." She felt her face turning red. "He implied that I was after Grady, trying to trap him."

"Is that true?" Devlin's face was completely impassive as he waited for her to answer.

She looked past him out the window again, struggling to frame her reply. "Grady and I have a complicated past," she finally said. "And Ron knows some of it. I suppose I can understand why he would think that was true, but it's not. I'm not trying to trap Grady into anything." Sadness swept over her. "It's just the opposite, actually."

Devlin didn't say a word, but she could hear his pen scratching on the small notebook he carried. When he snapped the book closed, she looked over at him again.

"I don't want you to be alone. I'm not crazy about sending you to the ranch, but I can't think of a better alternative. There's always someone around on a ranch. Farrell knows you're concerned about Perkins, and I'm sure he'd keep an eye on him and keep him away from you. Why don't you call him?"

She wasn't sure if she could do that. "There must be some other place I can go."

He shrugged. "You can stay with one of your other friends in town, someone you don't know as well as Laura. Or you can go over to a motel in St. George, but it might make it a long commute for you to work every day. It's up to you."

She couldn't afford to stay in a motel, and she suspected that Devlin knew it. Just like he knew that she wouldn't impose on any of her other friends in Cameron, especially if it looked like she might be putting them in danger, too. After a few minutes she said grudgingly, "I guess I'll see if Grady will let us stay."

As Devlin watched her, his eyes softened. "You go check on Cassie. I'll give Farrell a call."

She wanted to tell the sheriff that she'd call herself, that she was capable of asking Grady for a favor, but she turned and headed up the stairs. Devlin apparently knew it would be hard for her to call Grady, and he was willing to do it for her. And right now she was too tired and too upset to be strong.

Cassie was asleep. She hadn't even bothered to pull the

quilt back, but was lying sprawled on top of it, clutching her favorite stuffed animal to her chest. Becca closed her eyes, thankful that at least the ugliness hadn't managed to touch her child yet. But it would soon, she reminded herself. She'd have to explain to Cassie why they were staying out at the ranch.

When she walked back into the kitchen, Ben Jackson was in the kitchen with Devlin and they were talking in low voices. They stopped as soon as she appeared in the door.

"Farrell's on his way," Devlin said. "Ben here is helping me look for evidence."

The letter was sealed in a plastic bag that sat on the kitchen table. Black dust covered the counters and the table, and there were black smears on the back door. "Fingerprint dust," Ben said, when he noticed her looking at it. "We'll have to get prints from you and Cassie, and everyone who's been in the house recently. When we eliminate your prints, we can see if there are any who don't belong here."

"It sounds like it'll take a while," Becca said, dismayed.

"It might. Or we might get lucky right away," Devlin said as he continued to search for fingerprints. "Either way, I think you'll be safe with Farrell."

Becca couldn't help herself. "I thought you suspected him."

Devlin turned to look at her. "You don't. And I checked him out. Thoroughly. I don't consider him a suspect."

She blew out a breath. But before she could answer, she heard the sound of a truck door slamming in the driveway. Moments later someone was pounding on the kitchen door.

"Becca?" Grady's voice came through clearly. "Are you all right?"

Ignoring the black dust that covered the doorknob, she threw open the door. "Grady," she said, but couldn't say another word when he grabbed her and crushed her against his chest. His heart galloped beneath her ear.

"God, Becca, are you all right? Are you hurt?" The pressure of his arms tightened as he spoke.

"I'm fine," she said, surprised to find her voice shaky. She burrowed more deeply into his arms. "There was just the note."

"How about Cassie? Is she all right?"

"She's sound asleep. She doesn't even know there's anything wrong."

His grip on her loosened, and he stepped back. His eyes were fierce and hard. "Get some things together. You and Cassie aren't staying here for another minute. I want you out at the ranch where I can keep an eye on you."

She deliberately looked away, as if she could stop herself from thinking about how safe she'd felt when he held her and longing for the comfort of his embrace again.

"Go get some things and leave, Doc," Devlin said quietly.

Without needing any further prodding, she turned and headed back up the stairs. "I'll just be a minute," she said, giving in.

Ten minutes later she was back downstairs, carrying suitcases for her and Cassie. Grady took them silently, then walked out to stash them in his truck. She turned to Devlin. "I guess you'll know where to find me," she said.

He nodded. "I'll talk to you tomorrow. Ben and I will make sure the house is locked before we leave." He hesitated, then added, "You'll be safe with Farrell while we catch this guy, Doc. He's all right."

That was high praise, coming from Devlin McAllister. Her eyes prickled with sudden tears, and she turned away as she heard Grady coming up the driveway. "I've got to get Cassie," she said, her voice thick as she fled up the stairs.

Easing her daughter into her arms, she grabbed a stuffed animal and then headed back toward the kitchen. Grady jumped forward. "Let me take her."

She shook her head. "She's fine. I'll carry her to the truck."

Cassie sighed and stirred in her arms as they stepped outside into the cool night air, but she didn't wake up. Sliding into the truck, Becca fastened her daughter's seat belt, then climbed into the truck next to her. Grady started the engine and backed out of her driveway. In moments her house was out of sight.

"I'm glad you had the sheriff call me," he said quietly.

"I didn't want to," she said, staring out the windshield at the dark road in front of them. "I thought it would be hard for you, having us living with you. And unfair. I don't want you to think I'm trying to corner you into a decision."

"This has nothing to do with us," he said roughly, and she heard the anger bubbling beneath his calm exterior. "This is for your safety, and Cassie's. Why would you even hesitate to call me?"

"What if it turns out that the stalker is Ron? Will you still be glad that I called?"

"Ron has nothing to do with this. I'm sure of it. But if he did, do you think I would take his side rather than protect you and Cassie? What kind of man do you think I am?"

Becca leaned back against the truck and closed her eyes. "I think you're a good man, Grady. An honorable one. Of course I trust you to protect us, no matter who the stalker is."

She sighed and turned to face him. "That's not why I didn't want to call you. There's too much baggage between us. How are you going to feel, having us in your house twenty-four hours a day? And it could be for a while. There's no guarantee that Devlin will catch this guy right away. You've been honest with me about not knowing how you feel about having a child. I don't want you to think that I'm trying to force your hand."

"I like Cassie," he said roughly. "It won't be a hardship, having her around."

She knew she should be grateful for that. It was a beginning, but his words curled around her heart like a fist. She wanted so much more for her daughter, and so much more for Grady. "We won't get in your way," she said carefully.

"Hell, you won't have a chance to get in my way. Did you think I was going to leave you alone to take care of yourselves? What good would staying in my house be if I wasn't there to keep an eye on things?"

"You can't be with us twenty-four hours a day," she protested, but her heart began pounding at the prospect of spending so much time with him.

"I know you have your job and you'll be gone most of the day. But once you're back on the ranch, you're stuck with me. You and Cassie both. Anyone who tries to get to either of you is going to have to go through me."

"Thank you, Grady," she said quietly, watching the lights of the Flying W get closer and closer. She turned to look at him over Cassie's dark head. "That makes me feel better. I'll feel safe with you."

For a moment his eyes met hers in the semidarkness of the cab of the truck. His gaze was steady, and she saw the promise in the depths of his eyes. "I won't let anyone hurt you or Cassie."

"I know."

And she did. Whatever Grady's faults, he would protect both of them with his life.

He stopped the truck at the front door of the house, sliding out to hurry around to her side of the truck. "Let me carry her upstairs, then I'll come back for your luggage."

She wanted to feel the weight of her daughter in her own arms, to reassure herself that Cassie was safe, but she nodded her head. Maybe Grady needed that reassurance himself, even though he might not be willing to admit it yet. So she followed behind him up the stairs of the ranch house, into a room tucked under the gables.

"Pull back the quilt," he whispered, and she angled over to the bed standing by the window.

Once Cassie was tucked into the bed, she stood watching

her daughter sleep while Grady hurried back down the stairs to bring in their luggage. How would Cassie feel about staying at the ranch for a while? She would love it, Becca admitted to herself. She would think she'd landed in heaven.

It felt too right to be in Grady's house, watching their daughter sleep, and Becca forced herself to remember all that still stood between her and Grady. She had to make sure that Cassie didn't get too attached to the ranch or to Grady. It wouldn't be fair to either of them.

Grady reappeared at the door, holding the two suitcases. "Why don't you stay in the room right across the hall from her? That way you'll be able to hear her if she wakes up."

She walked out of Cassie's room, into the light of the hall, and looked up at Grady. "Thank you," she said. "That's very thoughtful of you."

He dropped the suitcases on the floor and reached for her, folding her into his arms. "It'll be okay, Becca," he murmured into her hair. "I know this is hard for you, but they'll catch this guy and you can go back to your normal life."

The problem was, she didn't *want* to go back to her normal life. Her normal life was one that didn't include Grady. She told herself to let him go, to back away, but all she could do was hold on more tightly.

It was just the stress of the evening, she told herself. All the fear and worry. But she wound her arms around him and burrowed closer.

"Becca." Grady's breath moved through her hair like a caress. "God, Becca, I was so scared. My truck wouldn't go fast enough to get to you."

"I've never had a place that was just mine. I loved that house," she said, and felt tears overflow onto her face. "I felt so safe there. Now I'll never feel safe in my house again."

"Not for a while," he agreed, and he shifted her in his arms so she was looking up at him. "But they'll catch the bastard, and things will get better. No matter how bad things are, they always get better.''

She saw the pain, deep in his eyes, and knew he was speaking from personal experience. "I know." She drew in a deep, trembling breath and tried to control her tears. "I do know that. Thank you for understanding how I feel, Grady. And thank you for giving us a refuge.''

"There's nothing to thank me for." He looked down at her, and the pain faded from his eyes, replaced by a far different emotion. "This isn't the way I wanted it to happen, but I've thought about you here in my house, too often." He slowly bent down, until his lips hovered inches from hers. "Tell me to stop, Becca. Tell me that you don't want me to kiss you.''

It was exactly what she wanted, she realized, and she lifted herself up until her lips met his. He stilled for a moment, then took her mouth with a hunger that matched her own.

Would it always be like this between them? Would one touch kindle this fire that threatened to rage out of control? Would she always burn with this need for Grady?

She suspected that she would. Even during the past nine years she had yearned for him, at night lying in her lonely bed, in her restless dreams. They might not be able to resolve their differences, but right now it didn't matter. She and Grady were together, and they wanted each other. For now it would have to be enough.

"Mommy?"

Cassie's sleepy voice shocked her back to the present. For a moment she stood frozen in Grady's arms, then she tore herself away and raced into the room where Cassie slept.

"What it is, sweetheart?" She knelt by the bed and pushed her daughter's hair away from her face.

"There's something wrong with the bed," Cassie said petulantly. She hadn't yet opened her eyes. "It doesn't feel right.''

"That's because it's not your bed. We're not at home anymore, Cass. We're out at the Flying W Ranch."

She spoke softly, hoping to reassure her daughter, but her words brought Cassie wide-awake. "How did we get here?" she asked, looking around at the unfamiliar room.

"We had a little problem at our house," Becca said, praying that Cassie wouldn't ask for details tonight. "It'll take a few days to fix it. So Mr. Farrell said we could stay here. We carried you out to the car while you were sleeping."

Cassie looked out the window. Becca knew she could see nothing but the pasture, and maybe a few of Grady's head of cattle. But when Cassie looked back at her, her face was glowing.

"You mean I get to stay here, with Pete and all the other horses?"

Trust a child to put everything into perspective, she thought. Smiling at her daughter, smoothing her hair back, she said, "That's exactly what I mean. But you need to go back to sleep tonight, because it's very late. If you wake up again, I'll be in the room right across the hall."

"Okay." Cassie snuggled back under the sheet and quilt, and gave her a huge grin. "Can I go see Pete in the morning?"

"That's up to Mr. Farrell. But if it's all right with him, it's fine with me."

Cassie obediently closed her eyes, but her smile lingered, even after Becca could see that she'd fallen asleep again. She waited until her child's breathing was deep and even, then stepped back out into the hall.

She was surprised that Grady stood waiting for her. "Is she all right?" he asked. "Was she afraid about finding herself in a strange place?"

"Not once she realized what that place was," she answered, smiling at the memory. "The only thing she asked me about was Pete."

"Didn't she want to know why you were here?"

"I told her that there was something wrong with the house, and we might be here for a few days." She laid a hand on his arm, touched by his obvious concern for Cassie. "Kids are remarkably resilient. Right now Pete is more important to her than what's wrong with her house. And I'd like to keep it that way. I don't want her to know what's going on."

The worry faded from his eyes, slowly replaced by a faint smile. "And I know just how to make sure she doesn't think about it. We'll go visit Pete after breakfast in the morning, then she can help me feed and clean the horses' stalls. I'll keep her so busy that she won't have time to think about why she's not living at home."

Touched by his understanding of what Cassie needed, Becca skimmed her fingers along his cheek. "Thank you, Grady. That's exactly what will work. But I can't let you take a day away from your duties here on the ranch to baby-sit with Cassie. I'll take her to Laura's when I go to work, then bring her back with me tomorrow evening."

Grady captured her hand. "Are you sure you want to do that? We're done with the branding, so I can take a breather from the ranch. Hell, I pay Ron Perkins to manage the place for me. I can take a day off. And do you really want her at Laura's? We still don't know who your stalker is. I'd rather have her right here where I can keep an eye on her." He lifted their joined hands and ran a finger down her cheek. "You, too, for that matter."

"I have to work. I don't have a choice," she said, her face still tingling from the casual contact. "But if you're sure you don't mind, I will leave her here with you tomorrow. I don't think Cassie is this stalker's target, but I don't want to take a chance and put Laura or her kids in danger."

"You trust me to take care of her?" She thought he held his breath.

"Of course I do."

"I don't know anything about kids," he warned.

She grinned at him. "Then the two of you will probably

have a great time together. According to Cassie, I treat her like a baby most of the time.''

His hand tightened on hers, then he let her go. ''You're probably dead on your feet,'' he said roughly. ''Get to bed, Becca. I'll see you in the morning.''

He turned and headed down the hall. She watched until Grady disappeared, then turned and went into the bedroom he'd indicated. She'd seen the uncertainty in his eyes as he talked about taking care of Cassie, and the fear. But if she wasn't mistaken, she'd also seen joy. She'd also seen how quickly he'd tried to hide it.

As she lay in the huge bed, looking up at the ceiling, she wondered if Grady was ever going to be able to allow himself to get past the fear to the joy. If he wasn't, there would be no hope of a future for them.

Grady sat at the kitchen table the next morning, watching the dark sky slowly begin to lighten in the east. Days started early on a ranch, but even he wasn't usually awake at this time of day.

His bed had been a torture rack, knowing that Becca slept in a room down the hall. Finally sleep had become impossible, so he'd retreated to the kitchen to compose himself. What had he gotten himself into? he asked for the hundredth time. He'd volunteered to watch Cassie all day. What was he going to do with the kid?

He ignored the anticipation. He dismissed the small voice that kept whispering that he was going to have a great time with Cassie. All he wanted to focus on was the fear. He was afraid he would screw up. He was afraid that Cassie would get hurt. He was afraid that he would do something, everything wrong, somehow make her feel less than wonderful. And that was the last thing he wanted to do.

He was still worrying about it when Ron came into the house. His friend looked at him in surprise. ''What are you doing up so early?'' he asked.

"Couldn't sleep. We've got some guests," he said quietly. "Doc Johnson and her daughter. They had a break-in at their house, so they're staying here for a while."

Grady was surprised at the anger that flashed over Ron's face. "Why here? There must be other places they could stay."

"Because I wanted them here," he said mildly. "Do you have a problem with that?"

"We're busy here for the next few weeks. We don't have time to entertain guests."

"Doc Johnson won't even be around during the day. She'll be at work."

"And what about the kid?"

Grady was surprised at the angry tone of Ron's voice, surprised and faintly alarmed. "What about her?"

"Who's going to watch her? We can't have some kid wandering around the place by herself. God knows what she could get into."

"As it happens, I'm going to be watching her. So she won't get into anything." Grady knew his voice was too cold, but he was shocked at Ron's attitude. He thought he knew Ron Perkins. Clearly he didn't know him as well as he'd thought.

Ron apparently knew he'd gone too far. "Fine," he said as he backed out the door. He tried to smile. "I'll tell everyone not to bother you today."

Grady was still staring at the door when he heard footsteps on the stairs behind him. He turned around to see Cassie, completely dressed, standing on the bottom stair.

"My mom said I could go visit Pete this morning, if it's all right with you. Is it all right with you, Mr. Farrell?"

In spite of his warnings to himself to keep his distance, Grady could feel himself melting. "It's all right with me, Cassie."

The child started running for the door, and he just managed to snag her around her waist. "Whoa, there, wait a minute, cowgirl. On this ranch, we eat breakfast first."

Cassie turned around, and he could see the disappointment on her face. "Okay."

"What would you like?" he asked.

"Do you have Cinnamon Toast Cracklies?" she asked eagerly.

"Yeah, I can make you cinnamon toast."

She giggled. "Not cinnamon toast, silly. Cinnamon Toast Cracklies cereal."

What was Cinnamon Toast Cracklies cereal? "I don't think so. Is that what you usually eat for breakfast?"

She shook her head. "My mom says it's too sweet. But if you had some, I could probably have it."

Grady smothered a grin and stood up. "We don't have any of that. Why don't we take a look and see what else there is? I'll bet we'll find something you like."

Cassie slipped her hand into his and nodded. "Okay."

Grady stared down at their joined hands and felt his heart slipping away. And he reached out desperately to grab it back before it was too late.

Chapter 14

Grady sat on the porch of the house, his boots propped up on the railing, and listened to Cassie chatter away to his housekeeper. Mrs. Waters had fallen under Cassie's spell immediately, and right now they were baking cookies. Chocolate chip, if his nose wasn't mistaken.

He smiled to himself, wondering where the kid got her energy. She'd mucked out stalls with him, taken a riding lesson and generally dogged his footsteps all day. He was beat, and she was still going strong.

How did Becca keep up with her? He felt his smile fading as he thought about Cassie's mother. She had done a great job with the kid. Cassie was friendly, comfortable with adults and completely engaging. And every time he thought about the fact that she was his daughter, his stomach jolted with panic.

Becca had said he'd be a good father, but Becca didn't know him as well as she thought she did. He'd be a lousy father. Sure, it had been easy to spend time with Cassie today, but this had been one day. Anyone could manage one day out of a lifetime.

The door banged behind him, and Cassie appeared next to him with a plate and a huge smile. "Would you like some cookies, Mr. Farrell?"

"I'd love some cookies," he said, swinging his feet off the railing and sitting up on the swing. "Did you bake them yourself?"

He watched her struggle with herself, and she finally shook her head. "Mrs. Waters helped me. But I put in the nuts and the chocolate chips, and I took them off the metal things after they were cooked."

"That's the most important part," he assured her, biting into a cookie. "Now, that's the best cookie I've ever had."

"Really?" Her eyes lit up.

"Absolutely." And he realized it was the truth. "It must be your touch."

Cassie beamed at him, and he felt his heart twist a little inside him. "Mommy always says the same thing, but it's because she's my mom. You must be telling me the truth, because you hardly know me."

Grady felt his heart melt a little more, and tried desperately to resist it. "Are we going to save some for her?"

Cassie nodded vigorously. "My mom's always tired when she gets home from work. She says that a cookie is 'zactly what she needs to perk her up."

Grady saw a cloud of dust in the distance, and could just make out a truck turning into the entrance of the ranch. "Maybe this is your mother now," he said to her. He wasn't sure if he was happy or disappointed that his day with Cassie was almost over.

She leaned over the porch railing and stared at the truck. After a moment she turned to him and nodded. "That's her truck."

"Are you sure?"

"Yep. It's going fast, like her truck usually does."

Hiding a smile, Grady stood up as the truck got closer. "Why don't you run inside and get her some more of those cookies you made?"

Cassie raced through the door, and Grady walked out to the truck. He watched Becca slide stiffly off the seat and give the door an awkward shove to close it. As she walked toward him, his eyes narrowed.

"What's wrong?" he barked. "What happened?"

She stopped and stared at him. "What do you mean? Nothing's wrong."

"You're stiff. You're walking like you're sore. Did Sy find you again?"

"Of course not." She stopped in front of him, and her face softened. "I'm fine, Grady. One of my patients was a little rambunctious today, that's all. I was a little tired and wasn't paying attention like I should have been, so it was my own fault."

He grabbed her shoulders. "What was your own fault?"

She looked up at him, and he saw the pain and weariness in her eyes. "A horse tried to flatten me against the wall of his stall. I'm not hurt badly, just a little sore. I'll be fine tomorrow."

"Are you sure? Did you have the doctor take a look at it?"

She smiled then. "I don't need a doctor, Grady. This has happened before and it'll happen again. There's nothing wrong with me that a hot bath and a few aspirin won't cure."

Cassie exploded out of the house. "Mommy, I made cookies." She glanced at Grady and added, "Mrs. Waters helped me, and Mr. Farrell and I saved some for you. Do you want some?"

"I'd love a cookie, Cass." Reaching out, she hugged her daughter and reached for a cookie. As they walked toward the house, Cassie filled her mother in on what she had done that day. The name "Pete" played a prominent part in the conversation.

Cassie was still chattering when they reached the kitchen. "Cassie, why don't you let your mom take a bath and clean up before dinner?" he asked. "And maybe you could help me check on the horses one last time."

Cassie stopped and looked over at him. "Could I?" she asked eagerly.

"If it's okay with your mom."

"That's fine, honey." Becca smiled. "I do need a bath, so go ahead." She looked over at him. "Thanks, Grady."

"Nothing to thank me for," he said gruffly.

"I think there's plenty to thank you for," she replied, her voice quiet.

Cassie stood next to him, chattering, as he watched Becca move slowly up the stairs. When she had disappeared, he turned to the child. "Let's see what those horses have been up to, cowgirl."

By the time they returned to the house forty-five minutes later, Becca was in the kitchen, helping Mrs. Waters get dinner on the table. He scowled at her. "You were supposed to be taking it easy."

"I did. I had a bath and four aspirin. I feel much better."

She didn't seem to be as stiff, he grudgingly noted. And when Mrs. Waters told them all to sit down and eat, she slipped into her chair without any obvious soreness.

A few hours later Grady sat in the living room and listened to the sounds drifting down the stairs. He'd tried not to pay attention to the domestic activity after dinner, but the sounds of Becca getting Cassie ready for bed were hard to ignore completely. They ignited a yearning in him for things he'd long ago decided he didn't want or need. He was tempted to run from the house, to seek refuge with his horses, but he forced himself to stay. He had offered Becca hospitality, and by God she'd get hospitality.

Not that there was anything special about having Becca and Cassie living in his house. He was just being neighborly, doing what anyone would have done for them. He listened to

Becca walk out of Cassie's room, and he strained to hear what she said to Cassie. The door to Cassie's room squeaked as Becca eased it shut, and he held his breath, waiting to see what she'd do. He half expected her to go straight to her own room.

She'd had a long day, he told himself. And on top of the worry from the night before, she'd been flattened against a stall wall by some jerk of a horse. He held his breath as he listened for her footsteps. When they started down the stairs, Grady fought the anticipation that welled up inside him.

Becca smiled wearily as she walked into the living room. "Thanks again for taking care of Cassie today. You made a big impression on her."

"I think it was the horses that made the impression."

She smiled as she shook her head. "I heard 'Mr. Farrell' at least as much as I heard 'Pete,'" she said.

"She's a nice kid, Becca."

Her smile faded. "Yes, she is. And although I am sorry that you're forced to have us living here with you, I'm not sorry that you're getting a chance to get to know her."

He scowled. "Don't make too much out of this," he warned. "It doesn't mean anything."

"I know that." A deep sadness crossed her face, then she turned away to sit down at the other end of the couch. When she looked over at him, her face was composed.

"She doesn't need a rodeo bum in her life. I'm not good for anything but the rodeo, Becca."

She studied him, her head tilted to the side. "I don't know about that," she said. "It looks like you've done a pretty good job here at the ranch."

"I've only been here for a few weeks. I haven't gotten bored yet."

"Are you sure you will get bored?"

"Hell, Becca, I don't know. I bought the ranch because it was available, and because I didn't have anything better to do. That doesn't mean that I'm going to like what I'm doing, or even be here in a few years.''

"What happened, Grady? Why did you stop riding the rodeo circuit?''

Her voice was soft in the semidarkness, and he thought he heard genuine caring in her tone. He wanted to blow her off, to make a quick joke, but suddenly found that he couldn't. He wanted Becca to know what had happened.

"I got hurt. It was a freak accident," he said, staring at the cold fireplace and seeing the ring where it had happened. "Something that wouldn't happen again in a million years. But once was all it took.''

Becca slid down the couch, moving closer to him and taking his hand. "You don't have to tell me if you don't want to, Grady.''

He turned to look at her. "I want to tell you, Becca. No one else knows the whole story, but I want to tell you.''

She intertwined their fingers and pressed her palm to his. For a moment he allowed himself to imagine that he could feel her concern seeping through their connected hands. When he looked at her eyes, he saw that their soft gray depths were full of pain. For him, he realized, and he looked away before he could say or do something stupid.

"It had been a good year for me," he began, remembering the accolades, the applause that had followed him around the circuit. "I was way ahead of my closest competitor in points for the bull-riding championship. I had the devil's own luck when it came to the draws for my rides. I always got the right bull, the one that would give me the best ride. Maybe I was getting arrogant, or careless.''

The thought had haunted him for five years. Had he made a stupid mistake, one that had cost him his career? He didn't remember that he had, but he hadn't remembered a lot that had happened right around the accident. "I'd had a good ride, stayed on my eight seconds. But when I tried to jump off, my leg got caught in the rope that wrapped around the bull's belly.'' He turned to look at her. "I put that rope on the bull. To this day I don't remember whether I did something wrong or not. But my leg was caught, and by the time they got the bull under control, my leg was ruined. I spent a long time in the hospital, and longer trying to rehabilitate it, but finally I realized that I was through with the rodeo. I'd never be able to ride bulls again.''

"Oh, Grady, I'm so sorry.'' Her voice was barely more than a whisper in the quiet room. Her hand trembled in his.

He pushed away the urge to turn to her, to accept her comfort, staring instead at the wall on the other side of the room. "I drifted for a long time after that. I'd spent enough time working my father's ranch that I had no trouble getting a job as a ranch hand. And there was never anything I wanted, so I managed to save a lot of money. But nothing could take the place of the rodeo. I was empty inside, and there was nothing I cared about. Then I got into the poker game with Sy, and the rest is history.''

"You seem to be doing a good job with the Flying W.'' She squeezed his hand. "I think you'll be a wonderful rancher.''

He stood up at that and shoved his hands into his pockets. But he couldn't shake the feeling of her hand clinging to his. "That's the whole point, Becca. I'm not sure that I will. Sure, it's fine now. I'm enjoying myself and I feel like I'm doing something useful. But will I be happy with this ranch three years down the line? I fell into this job, like I fell into all the others, but I don't know if it's what I want to do, or what I'm settling for.''

"No one knows that about themselves when they start a job,'' she said. "All you can do is give it time.''

"But time is something I don't have, is it?'' he asked.

"What do you mean?''

"I have to make a decision about Cassie. Am I going to be a part of her life, or do you go on without me?''

"You don't have to own the Flying W ranch in order to

be a father to her. All you have to do is give her part of yourself.''

He sat back down beside her. ''She doesn't need a drifter for a father. She needs someone who can provide a stable life for her, someone who'll be there when she needs him.''

As Becca studied him, he could see the disappointment deep in her eyes. ''She doesn't need someone who's perfect, Grady. All she needs is someone who'll love her.''

''Tell me about her,'' he said abruptly. ''How did you manage to go to school and take care of a child at the same time? What did you do?''

Becca looked at Grady and saw the need to know about his daughter in his eyes. She looked down at her hands, gripped together in her lap. He hadn't been able to make any kind of a commitment to them. He hadn't been able to promise that he would be there for Cassie. But he wanted to know about her, and she owed him that, at least. He had shared a part of himself that she was very sure he always kept hidden. And, she realized, she wanted to share this with him.

Taking a deep breath, she bit her lip and looked over at the massive stone fireplace. She wasn't sure where to begin. She didn't want to hurt Grady or make him feel guilty, but he had a right to know what had happened.

''I found out I was pregnant about a week after the last time we talked on the phone. I was scared to death. I was supposed to leave for college later that week, and suddenly my world was turned upside down.''

Swallowing, she turned to look at him. ''I called your father, Grady. I didn't tell him why I needed to know, but I asked him where you were. He had no idea. No one else on the ranch did, either. So I told my parents I was pregnant.''

When she didn't say anything more, Grady took her hand. His touch was comforting, and she curled her fingers around his. ''They weren't too pleased, I'm sure.''

''That's an understatement.'' Thinking of their fight, the ugly things that had been said, could still make her cry.

"They gave me an ultimatum. I would have to have an abortion or give the baby up for adoption if I wanted them to continue to pay for my schooling.

"I refused, of course. I went back to school anyway, and managed to patch together enough scholarships, loans and jobs to pay my way. I'd always wanted to be a vet, and knowing I would have a child to support made me even more determined. By the time Cassie was born in May, I had been accepted to veterinary school. The next year, I lived in a boardinghouse. The woman who owned the house took care of Cassie while I went to school, and I did chores around the house to pay for that and for our room."

She looked down at their joined hands, remembering all the evenings when she'd been too tired to do anything more than play with Cassie. And she remembered the despair of the nights, sleep eluding her, wondering if going to vet school had been the right path to take.

"When I got out of vet school, I had a mountain of debt, but I also had a way to support myself and Cassie. We came here to Cameron because Laura was moving back here. She was getting married, and she watched Cassie for me while I worked. It was a good arrangement for both of us. And now that her husband has left her, she needs the money even more."

"I knew I'd heard of Cameron before. Laura was a friend of yours from college, wasn't she?"

"We were roommates our freshman year. So yes, you probably heard me talking about her." She looked back up at him and shrugged. "End of story. After the first year, my partners asked me if I wanted to buy into the practice. I did, even though it'll take me longer to pay off my college debts. So now I never have to worry that I'll be without a job. Cassie and I both like Cameron. We're here to stay."

"What about your parents?"

"What about them?"

"Did you ever patch things up with them?"

"Eventually. My mother couldn't resist the fact that she had a granddaughter. So after a few years, they came to see me. We go back to see them in Trinity every once in a while. But our lives are here in Cameron."

"I'm sorry, Becca," he said, softly, and his voice warmed her. "It sounds as though you've had a rough time of it."

"The past is the past," she said firmly. "We're happy now, and that's what matters. I did what I had to do, and I'm glad that everything worked out."

"I thought I knew you," he murmured, "but I guess I didn't know you at all. I've been carrying around a picture of you in my head for the past nine years that now seems completely wrong. But I think I like the strong, competent Becca better than the child I remember."

His words filled her with pleasure. "I had to grow up, Grady. I had no choice. And I had to be strong, because there was no one to count on but myself. It's amazing what you can do when you're doing it for your child."

"I tried to forget you. I refused to think about you, but my mind wouldn't let me forget. I dreamed about you every night. And after I was hurt, I imagined you talking to me. That got me through the worst of the surgeries, and the rehabilitation."

Her heart cried for the pain she knew he had endured. "I wish I could have been there for you, Grady." She touched his face, and he covered her hand with his. He felt warm and vital and alive, and she longed to move closer to him.

"Sometimes I dreamed that you were there. You'd be standing at the end of my bed, telling me to get off my lazy butt. I always seemed to do better in physical therapy the day after those dreams."

She smiled at him, seeing the vulnerability in his eyes. "And sometimes, when Cassie was small, I'd dream that you would walk in the door and sweep both of us up in your arms. Everything would be all right then, because you were there."

"We've both grown up, Becca, but I still dream about you. In my arms, in my bed." His gaze locked on hers, and her breath hitched in her throat.

Her heart tripped and sped up, and she couldn't look away. "I dream about you, too, Grady." Her voice was so low it was almost a whisper. "I always have."

"Becca…" He leaned forward and brushed his mouth over hers. The contact was brief, a mere sweep of his lips over hers. But she tasted his need, his yearning for her, and she was lost. She could resist the charming Grady, she could resist the smooth, handsome Grady, but she had no defenses against his vulnerability. He'd kept it hidden too long, buried it beneath layers of charm and cockiness. But now it was there, in his eyes, as he leaned back and looked at her.

If she said no, she knew he'd stand back and watch her walk up the stairs to her own bed. Alone. But she didn't want to say no. She needed him, every bit as much as he needed her. Maybe they would never have a happy ending. She was willing to take that chance. Because on this evening when they'd revealed parts of themselves that they'd always kept hidden, she wanted him, too.

"Grady." She touched his cheek, letting her hand linger, allowing her fingers to remember the faint roughness of his beard and trace the cleft in his cheek.

He stood and watched her, his blue eyes dark and hot. "Go upstairs, Becca. Now."

Slowly she shook her head. "I'm not going anywhere tonight, Grady. I'm not running away again. I've done all the running I intend to do in my life. From now on, I'm going to go after what I want."

"And what do you want tonight?"

She swallowed once, hard, then stepped over the edge of the cliff. "I want you, Grady. You're all I've ever wanted."

He stared at her for a long moment, then pulled her into his arms. "I can't promise you anything," he warned.

"I know." Her heart contracted, but she didn't move away

from him. She would just have to hope that everything would work out. This was what she had dreamed about for the past nine years, and yearned for since he'd come to Cameron. She had never stopped loving Grady, and she was finally willing to admit it. "I want you anyway."

Then his mouth was fused to hers, and there was no room for doubt, no room for regret. There was only Grady, and the desire that roared to life inside her.

She twined herself around him, and he threaded his fingers into her hair, holding her mouth against his. She tasted the desperate need burning away the edge of his control and felt herself respond to it. Her body quivered with desire, with the memory of the passion that had always flared between them with the slightest touch.

"I dreamed about your hair," he murmured against her mouth. "I dreamed of the way it used to wrap around us, holding us together. I used to wake up at night, hard and aching, the scent of your hair all around me."

"I cried when I had to cut it. I always thought of you when I brushed it."

He slid his fingers through her hair again, until he reached the back of her neck. When he brushed his hand along the sensitive skin there, she trembled in his arms.

"There won't be any interruptions tonight," he warned her. "If you want me to stop, tell me now."

"I don't want you to stop. I want to make love with you, Grady."

His hands tightened on her again, then without warning, he swept her up into his arms and moved toward the stairs. As they headed up into the darkness, she reached over and nibbled on his ear.

She felt the hitch in his breath as she gently sucked on his lobe. Then he walked into the bedroom next to hers and kicked the door shut behind them.

Grady eased her down onto the bed, then stood and watched her as he swiftly removed his clothes. His body was

hard and muscled, but she frowned when she saw the scars
that hadn't been there nine years earlier. A long, thin white
line traveled down his ribs and around to his back. A smaller,
circular scar stood out on his flat abdomen. And as he pulled
his jeans down his legs, she saw the scars around his knee.

White lines, some thick, some thin, zigzagged around his
left knee. Two of them trailed up his thigh, and one down
onto his calf. When she looked up at him, horrified, she found
him watching her with a grim expression on his face.

"Gruesome, aren't they?"

"They're awful, Grady." Bending down, she kissed the
largest scar, letting her mouth linger on the ravaged knee. "I
can't even begin to imagine how painful it must have been
for you."

He shuddered as her mouth moved higher than his knee.
"It doesn't hurt right now, believe me." He pulled off his
briefs, then reached down to bring her up to him. His erection
burned into her abdomen, even through her clothes.

When she reached up to unbutton her blouse, he gently
pushed her hand away. "Let me," he breathed.

As he peeled away her blouse, he trailed kisses down over
her collarbone to the edge of her lacy bra. When he reached
between them to unhook her bra, she felt his hand trembling
where it brushed against her.

Easing the bra down her arms, he tossed it onto the floor
as he stared at her. "You're more beautiful than I remembered," he said, reaching out to cup her breasts in his hands.

She moaned and moved closer, and he brushed his thumbs
over her nipples. When she gasped, he took her mouth again.

Suddenly neither of them could wait another moment. He
fumbled with the button on her jeans, and she tried to help
him push the button through the hole. She needed to feel him
inside her, to become one with Grady. The sound of the zipper echoed in the quiet room, and Grady shoved at the material of her jeans, pushing them to the floor. As she stepped

out of the restrictive denim, they fell onto the bed together, clinging tightly to each other.

He slid his hand between her thighs, touching her gently, and she arched up to meet him. He bent over her, kissing her again, and she wrapped her arms around him, trying to pull him closer. As she savored the dark, male taste of him, she heard him fumbling in the drawer beside the bed. Then the sound of a foil packet being ripped open resonated through the quiet bedroom, and he paused for a moment before he kissed her again.

When he moved between her thighs, she rose eagerly to meet him. As their bodies joined, she wrapped her arms and legs around him and held on tightly. She thought she heard him breathe "Becca, love," then the world exploded into dizzying sensation.

She floated for a long time, holding on to Grady, letting herself revel in the sensation of his weight pressing her into the bed. Finally he nuzzled her ear and murmured, "I promise we'll do better next time."

It took a massive effort to open her eyes and look at him. "I thought we did pretty well just now."

"I didn't love you nearly as thoroughly as I intended. I plan to spend a lot of time getting to know you again."

"Mmm," she murmured as he slid to the side and gathered her against him. "I like the sound of that."

"In fact, I think I'm going to begin right away." He propped himself up on one elbow next to her, and she opened her eyes to find him smiling down at her. It was a smile she hadn't seen in his eyes for a long time, tender and completely open. It was the way she remembered Grady smiling, long ago, when they were alone.

"Can I play this game, too?"

"I hope you will." Leaning forward to kiss her, he let his hand drift down her side and over her hip. When he reached her thigh, she couldn't stop the tiny flinch.

She felt him tense, then deliberately draw away from her. "What's wrong?"

She shook her head, trying to pull him closer again. "Nothing, really. My leg just hurts a little."

He moved so that he could see her thigh, and she closed her eyes. She knew what her thigh looked like. And it wasn't pretty.

"My God, Becca. Is this what happened today? Why didn't you tell me? Did I hurt you?"

She shifted over and fitted herself to him again, shielding her thigh from his view. "Did I act like you hurt me?"

But he wouldn't be distracted. "Why didn't you tell me to stop? My God, I was all over you like a rutting bull. I didn't even think about the fact that you were hurt."

"Neither did I, Grady." She took his face in her hands. "I didn't even notice until just now, so stop it. I'm not a delicate, shrinking violet that you have to worry about crushing. It's all right. I'm fine. And my leg will be back to normal in a couple of days."

"I'll be more careful," he promised, bending to kiss her again.

Desire bloomed in her again, stronger and more powerful than just moments ago, and she answered his kiss with one of her own. "I'd like to see you try," she told him.

Chapter 15

Sometime during the night, Becca forced herself to move away from Grady and climb out of his bed. He immediately rolled over and reached for her. "Becca?"

"I have to go back to my room," she whispered, bending over to kiss him one more time, not daring to linger. "Cassie might come looking for me."

At the mention of their daughter, she felt him stiffen. "I'd forgotten about her."

Becca couldn't stop the tiny spear of pain that lanced through her at his words. But then he rolled out of the other side of the bed and reached for his briefs. "I'm sorry, Becca. I shouldn't have rushed you up here, into my bed, without thinking about Cassie."

The pain dissipated, and warmth slowly spread through her. "It's okay, Grady. I did think about her. Cassie sleeps like the dead. She wasn't likely to wake up. But she does sometimes wander toward morning, and that's why I have to go."

She threw on her clothes and started to leave, but he came around the bed and took her into his arms once more. "I wish we could wake up together, but I understand.'' His kiss was tender and lingering, and when he finally lifted his head, she saw the desire rekindled in his eyes. ''You'd better go now, or I won't be responsible for what happens.''

''Good night, Grady.''

He kissed her again. ''I'm not going to tell you to sleep tight. I want you to think about me, sleeping here by myself.'' His mouth brushed hers once more, making her shiver. ''I'm beginning to hope that it takes the sheriff a little time to catch your stalker.''

She slipped out the door and paused to look into Cassie's room. Her daughter was sound asleep. It didn't look like she'd moved since she'd lain down in bed.

As she settled in her own bed, she thought about Grady's last words, and a chill swept away the memory of their passion. Rediscovering the magic they'd had together, intoxicated with her love for Grady, she'd forgotten the reason they were at the Flying W in the first place. Alone with Grady, with only the night and the darkness for company, it had been easy to pretend that there were no problems to solve, no barriers between them.

But their problems couldn't be ignored or forgotten. Rolling over on her side, she thought about the closeness she'd felt to Grady tonight, the sharing that had seemed to bind them together, even before they'd made love. But the shadows of their problems hovered over the memory, a dark presence that seemed to grow bigger as she watched.

Had they just created more problems by making love tonight? Had they made a huge mistake by allowing their bodies to promise what their hearts could not? Becca hoped not, but she was afraid they had made a terrible error in judgment.

After lying awake most of the night, Becca came downstairs late the next morning. Cassie was already in the kitchen, chattering to Mrs. Waters about what she wanted to do that day. When she heard her mother enter the room, Cassie turned around.

"Hi, Mom."

"Good morning, sweetheart. Did you have a good sleep?"

"Uh-huh. Mr. Farrell said we could have another riding lesson today. He's out checking on the cows. Someone came and told him there was a problem with some of the cows, but he said he'd be right back."

"Great," Becca managed to say. The housekeeper handed her a cup of coffee, and she said fervently, "Thank you, Mrs. Waters." The older woman headed up the stairs, and Becca took a gulp of the hot, strong brew and sat down at the table.

"I'm going to help Mr. Farrell with the horses again today. He said after we clean the stalls, we could exercise some of them. That means letting them out into a pasture. But Pete gets to stay in the barn, 'cause we need him for my lesson later."

Becca smiled at Cassie and put her arm around her, drawing her close. "I'm glad you're having a good time here at the Flying W, sweetheart, but we're going to have to go home soon."

Cassie's smile disappeared. "I don't want to go home. I want to stay here and help Mr. Farrell and have riding lessons."

"Even if we stayed here, Mr. Farrell couldn't spend all day with you. He has to take care of the ranch and make sure everything is working."

"I could help him. I could keep him company."

Becca gave her daughter another hug. "I'm sure he likes having you with him, but sometimes adults have to do a job and they can't have children with them. Sometimes the job is dangerous, or just hard, and they have to concentrate on what they're doing. But you can still have riding lessons, honey. I'll bring you out here regularly, and Mr. Farrell will teach you how to ride a horse. We've already decided that."

Cassie's lower lip quivered, and she said, "I don't want to go home. I want to stay here."

Before Becca could say anything, she dashed out of the kitchen and up the stairs. Becca watched her go, then turned around to see Grady watching from the back door.

"What was that all about?"

"I told her we were going to have to go home, and she wants to stay here."

Grady scowled and threw himself into a chair. "She's a smart kid. I don't want either of you going anywhere."

"I appreciate your hospitality, Grady, but we need to go home." She looked down at her hands in her lap and tried to keep color from flooding her face. "After last night we can't stay."

"I thought last night was pretty wonderful."

At that she looked up at him. His face had softened, and she saw the memory of passion in his eyes. "It was wonderful," she said softly. "And that's why we need to leave. As wonderful as it was, it didn't solve any of our problems."

A spark of anger lit his eyes. "It sure as hell solved a few of mine," he said.

She flushed. "That's not what I meant and you know it. I can't think when you kiss me or touch me. And I need to be able to think about what we're going to do."

"You always did think too much, Becca."

"And you didn't ever think enough," she snapped back at him. "You always acted on impulse."

"Last night was impulsive, but it felt pretty damn good."

The anger drained away from her, and she was merely tired. "Last night I wanted to make love to you. Last night I needed you. I still need you, but I have to be able to think about what we're going to do. I can't let lust control me."

"So you want to run away?"

"Can you think of another solution?"

"You can stick around and we'll work it out."

"How much talking will get done if I stay here, Grady? Both of us know exactly what will happen."

"Maybe that's not such a bad thing, Becca."

Before he could say anything else, Ron Perkins called in to him. "You coming, Grady?"

"Yeah, Ron, hold on. Get the cattle into the corral, and I'll be right there." He closed his eyes. "I forgot when I walked in and saw Cassie running up the stairs. You can't leave now. We have a problem here."

She remembered that Cassie had said something about Grady checking the cows, and fear trickled up her spine. "What's wrong?"

"A bunch of the cattle in the near pasture ran into the barbed-wire fence during the night. A few of them are cut up pretty badly."

"How did that happen?"

His face darkened. "They were herded into that fence. There were too many of them with injuries for it to be an accident. Every once in a while we have a cow that gets tangled up in the fence, but never fifteen or twenty at a time."

"Was it an animal?" she asked, wondering if a coyote or some other wild animal had gotten into the pasture.

"Only a two-legged one," he answered grimly. "There was some mud on one side of the fence because we'd been irrigating. He left behind a set of footprints."

Fear and shame swept over her. "Did someone do this because I'm staying here?"

"I'd say it was because of me, and my connection to you. Sy hates me, and having you stay at the ranch would be poison to him."

"There's another possibility," she said, watching him to gauge his reaction.

Anger flushed across his face. "Don't tell me Ron did this. I refuse to believe it."

"You don't know everything there is to know about Ron," she began.

"I know damn close to it. Ron and I have been friends for years."

"I know. He was such a good friend of yours that when I came looking for you nine years ago, he wouldn't tell me where to find you." The words burst out, and she made no effort to stop them. It was past time Grady was told the truth. "I was pregnant at the time, clearly pregnant. He thought I was a rodeo groupie and told me to get lost. I tried to tell him who I was, but he wouldn't listen."

Shock filled Grady's eyes. "What?" he whispered.

"He hates me, Grady. He's been afraid I would tell you what happened, and that you'd fire him. I think he's hoping to scare me away from Cameron before I tell you what happened. He knows that Cassie is your daughter, because he saw me when I was pregnant with her. And he's afraid you'll blame him for not telling you." She held her breath, waiting for his reaction.

"My God. He's known all along?"

"He probably didn't put it together until he saw me again here on the ranch. But I'm sure at that point he knew he'd made a huge mistake."

He sat in front of her, looking stunned. After a long time he slowly shook his head. "It still doesn't make sense, Becca. Why would Ron be afraid I would fire him for a mistake he made nine years ago?"

"Maybe he wasn't thinking logically. I've heard through the grapevine that he's a gambler. Maybe he has a lot of debt and can't afford to lose his job."

He shook his head. "I still don't think it was Ron. My money's on Sy, and I'm going to call the sheriff and tell him to keep an eye out for him."

"That's probably a good idea, but no one in Cameron has seen Sy since the rodeo. Why would he take a chance on coming back, and especially coming here to the ranch? He has to know there are a lot of people on the ranch who know him."

"He also knows the ranch. If anyone would know how to sneak on and off the property without being seen, it would be Sy."

"Maybe the person who injured your cattle didn't have to sneak onto the ranch. Maybe he was already here."

Grady stood abruptly. "I'm going to talk to Ron. I have to admit, what you've told me puts him in another light. But I still don't think it was him. Ron's too straightforward to be a stalker."

He ran his hand through his hair and glanced in the direction of the corral. "In the meantime do you have what you need to sew up a bunch of the cattle? Some of the cuts from the barbed wire are pretty nasty."

"I should have everything I need in the truck. Let me check, then I'll call the clinic and let them know what I'm doing."

Becca pushed away from the table, slipping into her professional mode. Whatever had happened last night between her and Grady, whatever she was going to do about it today, would have to wait. She had patients to care for, and that was all she could afford to think about right now.

As Grady held the rope on the head of the last steer and watched Becca suturing him up, he wiped the sweat out of his eyes with his forearm and wondered how she managed. He'd seen her wince more than a few times that morning as one steer after another had bumped her bruised thigh. The sun blazed down on them from a clear sky, its heat baking the earth and turning the ranch into an oven. She'd taken a couple of water breaks, but otherwise she worked steadily, without missing a beat.

She had to be tired. Hell, he was beat. Neither of them had slept more than a couple of hours last night. But she showed no signs of fatigue, working just as carefully and diligently on this final patient as she had on the first steer.

His admiration for her skyrocketed at the same time as his

frustration with her stubbornness escalated. She still intended to leave today and move back into her own house.

Finally she stepped back and reached for the syringe full of antibiotic. Injecting it into the steer's rump, she watched as Ron led the animal into the barn, leaving her alone with Grady.

"I'll check on all of them later today." She picked up the instruments she'd used and dropped them into a pan of disinfectant, then straightened up. "Do you want me to take Cassie to Laura's? You probably have a lot of work to catch up on."

"No. I want her here with me, where I can keep an eye on her. The stalking is escalating, Becca. You realize that, don't you?"

She nodded wearily. "Yes, I know. And I would feel better if she was with you today. But you must have a lot to do. You can't spend the day with Cassie."

"I can be creative. She can ride with me in the truck." He shrugged. "We'll figure out a system."

"I'll probably be late getting back here tonight. I still have to see all of my appointments, and I'm getting a late start."

"Are your other clients going to be angry that you're late?"

She managed to smile at him. "They all know about emergencies. And they know that when the emergency is at their ranch, I'll take care of them while everyone else waits. No one will give me a hard time."

"Stay here tonight."

She hesitated. "I don't know, Grady. I think it would be better if we left."

"If you're running late, it could be dark before you get back to your house. I don't want you going home in the dark."

He could see that the idea didn't appeal to her, either. "I'll see what time I get back."

He stayed in the corral and watched as she stowed the dirty

instruments in the back of the truck, then picked up the phone to call in to the clinic. After a few minutes, she got in the truck and drove off with a wave of her hand.

Battling the odd feeling of loneliness, he vaulted over the fence and headed up to the house. Mrs. Waters had promised to keep Cassie entertained while her mother sutured the cattle, and he was sure the girl would be ready to go. Imagining the greeting she would give him when he asked her if she wanted her riding lesson now, he walked a little faster, then ran up the steps and into the house.

For the second night in a row, Grady listened to the bed-time ritual between Cassie and Becca. He ached to be in the bedroom with them, wondered what went on between mother and daughter before bed, but stayed firmly in the chair in the living room. There were some things it was better not to know.

Again he waited for Becca to come out of Cassie's room, and wondered if she would come down the stairs. He bet that she would. Becca didn't lack courage. She wouldn't run off and hide in the bedroom. She would come down and confront him.

He found himself holding his breath, waiting to hear her footsteps on the stairs. When she did start down the stairs, he hurriedly picked up a piece of the newspaper that he'd tossed to the floor earlier.

"I'm glad you decided to stay," he said as she entered the room. He casually folded the paper and laid it on the floor, as if he'd been reading it the whole time she was upstairs. "I think you're safer here."

"We're going back home tomorrow." She watched him steadily. "Unless you can give me a reason to stay."

He pretended not to understand. "I think you have a very good reason to stay. I don't think you should be alone in your house until this guy is caught."

"That's not what I meant, Grady, and I think you know

it.'' She sat down in a chair, facing him. "You've made quite an impression on Cassie.''

"She's a good kid.''

"She's a wonderful child. And she clearly adores you.''

"I'm the source of the horses.'' He tried to make it into a joke.

"It's more than the horses, Grady. It's you she loves. Oh, the horses are a nice side benefit, but she told me all about your day today, all the things you did together. She didn't understand, but I could read between the lines. She wasn't out of your sight all day, was she?''

"It worked out fine.'' He shrugged. "I didn't go out of my way.''

"I think you did,'' she said quietly. "And I know I promised not to push you, but you have to make a decision pretty soon. What's it going to be, Grady? Do you want to be a part of her life? Do you want to be a part of mine?''

"Why can't we let it go on this way for a while?'' he asked, scrambling for an answer. The last thing he wanted was to lose Becca again, or Cassie. But he couldn't bring himself to say the words. "Give it some time.''

"So you want an occasional roll in the hay? You want time with Cassie when it's convenient for you?''

He winced. "That's not what I said, Becca.''

"That's what you're implying.'' He saw the ripple of muscles in her throat when she swallowed twice, then she looked away. "A few days ago I might even have agreed with that. That might have been enough. But it's not anymore.''

When she looked back at him, he saw the moisture glazing her eyes. "I love you, Grady. And so does Cassie. Even though she doesn't know you're her father, she loves you. I can't settle for crumbs from you, and I won't let Cassie settle, either.''

"Becca, don't you see that you're asking for more than I can give?''

"How do you know you can't give it?" she challenged. "Have you ever tried before?"

"What if I screwed up somehow? What if you got hurt, or Cassie did? I would never forgive myself."

"That's what life is all about. It's about making mistakes, about getting up and trying again. Nobody said it would be perfect. No one said that a relationship didn't have any bumps. You work them out as you come to them."

"I just need a little time," he said, desperate to stop her from leaving.

"How much time, Grady?" she asked softly.

Slowly he shook his head. "I don't know. I don't know how long it'll take."

Becca shook her head. "That would be fine if we only had to think about the two of us. We could work things out as slowly as we wanted. But we have more to worry about than just you and I. Cassie needs to know the truth, and she needs to know what she can expect from you. She deserves more, and to tell you the truth, so do I."

She took a deep, trembling breath. "It has to be all-or-nothing, Grady. My heart won't settle for anything less."

"Are you going to tell Cassie the truth, then?" He held his breath as he waited for her answer.

"Do you want me to?"

Slowly he nodded. "Yeah, I want her to know."

"What else do you want me to tell her?"

That sounded a lot like a goodbye. "That she can come out here whenever she wants."

"Is that all?"

"What else do you want me to say, Becca?"

She rose from the chair. "Nothing, Grady. I guess there's nothing more to say." As she walked toward the stairs, she said, "We'll leave tomorrow morning. I don't want to wake Cassie up tonight."

He listened to the sound of her footsteps moving slowly up the stairs and wanted to call her back. He wanted to tell her that they would get married and live happily ever after. But he couldn't do it. Because he knew, for him, there would be no happily-ever-after. He'd never been happy in one place in his life, and he didn't know if he could be. And if he couldn't guarantee Becca and Cassie that he wouldn't hurt them, he would walk away from them and not look back.

But as he heard the door of her room closing, quietly and with a very final click, he wondered if he'd made a horrible mistake.

Becca looked around her kitchen the following evening and wondered when it had become such a lonely place to her. Had it been when she'd found the note three nights ago? Or had it been this evening, when she'd walked away from Grady and the ranch?

The sheriff had tried to clean up the mess he'd left, and she found herself smiling faintly at his efforts. Black powder still clung to some of the surfaces, and in spots he'd smeared it more than cleaned it up. But he'd tried, and she appreciated his thoughtfulness.

"This house is boring," Cassie declared, stomping down the stairs. "Why couldn't we stay at Mr. Farrell's house?"

"Because we couldn't," Becca told her, reaching out to put an arm around her shoulder. Cassie resisted stiffly, pulling away from her. "Sometimes there are adult reasons for doing things, reasons you can't understand yet."

"There was no reason not to stay with Mr. Farrell," Cassie insisted, her lip beginning to tremble.

Putting an arm around her daughter's shoulders, Becca led her into the living room. "Yes, honey, there was. And I think you're old enough now to know what that reason is."

Cassie looked at her, sudden interest in her eyes. "What is it?"

Becca swallowed once and drew her daughter down onto the couch. When she realized her hand was trembling, she tightened her hold on Cassie. How did a person tell a child something like this?

"I know you like Mr. Farrell, honey, and I'm glad that you do."

Cassie nodded vigorously. "He's awesome."

"Cassie, you've rarely asked me about your father. Do you think about him much?"

She nodded. "I thought you didn't talk about him because it made you sad."

"Have you ever wanted to know about him, about who he was?"

She nodded again. "I did, but I didn't want to make you more sad."

"That's very sweet of you," Becca managed to say, and gulped down the lump in her throat. "But I haven't been fair to you. I should have told you about him a long time ago, especially when you got interested in the rodeo. Your father used to be a rodeo star."

"Like Mr. Farrell?" She sat upright on the couch, her eyes shining.

"Yes." Becca felt the room dip around her, and forced herself to continue. "The fact is, Cassie, that Grady *is* your father."

For a moment her daughter simply stared at her, unbelieving. Then her mouth dropped open. "Mr. Farrell is my for-real, truly father?"

"Yes, he is."

As Cassie stared at her, a grin lit her from within. "That means we can live at his ranch forever. We don't have to stay at this stupid house anymore. And he can give me riding lessons whenever I want. And I can learn to be in the rodeo, just like him."

Becca brushed the hair away from her daughter's face and watched her shining eyes, feeling her own heart break a little more. "I'm afraid that it doesn't mean all those things, honey. You can see your father whenever you want to, but we can't live with him. We're going to stay in this house, and Grady will live on the ranch. He'll still give you riding lessons, and when you're a little older I'm sure he'll teach you how to be a barrel racer.''

But we won't be living together as a family, she whispered silently. We'll talk regularly and manage to be civil, but I'll shrivel up and die inside.

''Why not? Didn't he come here to Cameron because he knew we were here?''

Becca wished she could shield Cassie from the truth, let her go on believing in happy endings to her fairy tales, but she couldn't lie to her. ''No, honey, he didn't know we were here. It was a coincidence that he bought the Flying W Ranch.''

''But why can't we live on the ranch if he's my father?''

Becca saw Cassie's bewilderment, and the stirrings of her pain, and ached inside. ''Grown-ups can't always live together. It doesn't mean they don't love their children, or each other, but sometimes it hurts more to live together than to live apart.''

''Do you love Mr. Farrell?''

''Yes, I do.''

''Does he love us?''

''I know he loves you.'' At least that was the truth. At least she didn't have to lie to Cassie about that.

Cassie looked at her, pain filling her blue eyes, which were such a mirror image of her father's. ''What am I supposed to call him now?''

''Whatever you like. His name is 'Grady,' if you want to call him that.''

''If he's my father, shouldn't I call him 'Daddy'?''

''I think he'd like that,'' she whispered. ''Is that what you want to call him?''

Cassie nodded, then buried her head in her mother's arms. ''I want to live with him, Mommy. I don't want us to be here by ourselves.''

Me, too, Becca cried to herself. Me, too. Rocking Cassie in her arms, she murmured to her, "I know, honey. But we've been happy by ourselves so far, and we'll go on being happy. Now you just have someone else who loves you."

But it wasn't as easy as that, or as simple, and as she held Cassie in her arms, she wondered if either of them was going to be completely happy ever again.

Chapter 16

The next morning Becca asked one of her partners to take over the Flying W account. She sidestepped Pat's questions about why she was giving it up, brought him up-to-date on what she had done during the past few weeks and asked him to check on the cattle she had sutured the day before. As she watched Pat climb into his truck and leave, heading toward the ranch, she told herself she was making the right decision.

This was the best thing for both of them. She wasn't about to let her feelings for Grady drive her out of town and away from her practice, but she couldn't face seeing him on a regular basis. They'd run into each other in town, and they'd talk about Cassie, but she wouldn't have to feel her heart race and her hands tremble each time she visited the Flying W. She couldn't handle it.

She managed to keep herself busy all morning, then took off for ranch calls after lunch. By the time she picked Cassie up from Laura's house, she was thoroughly exhausted. Cassie was subdued, too.

"Did you have a good day with Laura?" Becca asked, watching her out of the corner of her eye.

Cassie nodded. "It was okay."

"What did you do?"

"We played rodeo." Her lip started to tremble. "Jenny is stupid. She said I was a liar when I told her that my father was a rodeo star. She said I was making it up."

"Jenny doesn't know, honey."

"I told her, Mom. I told her he was, but she wouldn't listen."

"I'll talk to Laura." She suspected her friend had already guessed the truth, but it was time Becca told her. Before long, everyone in Cameron would know about her and Grady. Holding the steering wheel more tightly, she said, "Laura will tell Jenny that you were telling the truth."

Slightly mollified, Cassie flopped back into her seat. "What are we doing tonight?"

"We're having dinner, then going to bed. Don't you think we've had enough excitement for one week?" she asked, trying to sound cheerful.

"No." Cassie's voice was sulky. "Having dinner and going to bed is stupid."

She was willing to lay odds that before Cassie fell asleep, her mother would be found to be stupid, too, Becca thought grimly. "Well, I guess we're going to be stupid tonight, then."

By the time Cassie was in bed, Becca was ready to crawl up the stairs and collapse in her own bed. But as tired as she was, she knew she'd lie awake, staring at the ceiling, unable to banish Grady's face from her mind. So instead, she headed for the kitchen and made herself a cup of tea, then pulled a stack of professional journals out of her magazine basket. They, at least, would give her something to think about besides Grady. And they were almost guaranteed to put her to sleep.

She hadn't read more than one article before she heard a truck pull into the driveway. At the sound of gravel crunching on the driveway she tensed, but she immediately realized that her stalker would never announce his presence that way. Pushing away from the table, she walked toward the front door just as the doorbell rung.

When she pushed aside the curtain window, she saw Grady scowling at her. Yanking open the door, she said, "What are you doing here?"

"I want to talk to you."

"Come in, then," she said, standing back.

When the door closed behind him, she said, "What do you want, Grady?"

"Why the hell did you send someone else out to the ranch today?" He glowered down at her, his eyes flashing blue sparks.

"Because I thought it would be best for both of us if someone else was your vet."

"Best how?"

She glanced at him in exasperation, then turned and walked into the living room. "Come on, Grady. Do you really want to see me as often as you will if I'm coming out to the ranch to take care of your animals? And I know I can't handle seeing you that often."

"I thought you were tougher than that. You've made your decision and put it behind you. So where's the problem?"

"Do you think it was an easy decision to make?" she cried, knowing he was goading her but unable to stop herself from reacting. "Do you think I wanted to walk away and not look back?"

"I don't think you know what you wanted. I sure as hell don't. But I don't want you to stop coming out to the ranch." His mouth softened, and some of the anger faded from his eyes. "You're a damn good vet, Becca. I don't want to jeopardize your job."

"You won't. I have plenty of other places to go, and Pat

didn't mind taking over for me. I just couldn't do it, Grady. I couldn't keep seeing you, every day, knowing what we could have had together and knowing that you're throwing it away.''

''You're the only one throwing it away,'' he said, and now the anger was completely gone, replaced by sorrow. ''I didn't say I wanted you to go. I just said I wanted a little time.''

''Time for what, Grady?'' she asked wearily. ''We've both had nine years to think about what we wanted. I know what I need, and what Cassie needs. And you're not able to give it to us.''

''Why can't you let things go on the way they have been, at least for a little while longer?''

''I've tried,'' she said. ''I can't do it.''

''What about Cassie?''

''I told her last night.''

She thought he paled a little beneath his tan. ''What did she say?''

Becca felt her mouth tremble and looked away from him. ''She wants to know why we can't all live together on the Flying W. I had a hard time explaining it to her.''

''Becca…''

She heard the pain in his voice, but refused to look up at him. If she did, she would be lost. She'd give in, give him what he wanted and lose her self-respect at the same time. She wanted him so badly, but she couldn't settle for what he thought he was able to give. And neither could Cassie.

''She'll adapt to it.'' She drew in a shuddering breath. ''Parents get divorced all the time. And if they care about their kids, they work together to make sure the kids know they're loved and cherished. You can see her whenever you want. We can even set up a schedule if you like.'' She turned away, unable to bear the thought.

Grady swung around to face her, swearing roughly, hating the image she projected. ''That's not what I want, and you know it. I don't want to be a goddamn weekend father.''

"Then what do you want?" She held her breath.

But before he could answer, he heard footsteps on the stairs. Becca ran into the hallway and found Cassie almost at the bottom of the stairs. "What's wrong, honey?" she said.

"I heard voices. Is Mr. Farrell here?"

"I sure am, Cassie." He stepped into the hall, feeling his heart swell at the sight of his daughter, her hair rumpled and her eyes sleepy.

Cassie looked over at him. "Is what my mother said really true?"

"I don't know what she said."

"She said that you're my father."

He nodded, watching the expression on the child's face, holding his breath for her reaction. "Yes, it's true. I'm your father."

A huge grin spread over her face as she hurled herself at him. He caught her just as she twined her arms around his waist and buried her head in his shirt. His embrace was awkward at first, but as her arms tightened around him, he found himself hugging her without restraint. A lump lodged itself in his throat, and he had to clear his throat twice before he could speak.

"Does this mean you're happy with the news?"

She lifted her face from his shirt. "Ever since we went to the rodeo, I've been pretending that you were my daddy," she said in a low voice. "I wished for it so hard that now it's real."

"I'm glad it's real, too, Cassie," he said. "I can't imagine a daughter who would be more wonderful than you." The truth was, he'd never thought about children at all before Becca had told him the news. But now he realized he was telling Cassie the truth.

"What should I call you?"

He glanced over at Becca, but her face was impassive. He didn't have a clue what she was thinking. When he looked back at Cassie, she was watching him expectantly.

His gut twisted into a knot. This was his first test. What should he say? "What do you want to call me?"

"Mom said I could call you 'Grady,' if I wanted to."

The depth of his disappointment shocked him. "Is that what you want to call me?"

Slowly she shook her head. "Can I call you 'Daddy'?" she whispered. It looked like she was holding her breath, waiting for his answer.

"I'd like that," he managed to say. His eyes filled with a suspicious moisture, and he blinked a few times. "I'd like that very much, Cassie."

"Good." She beamed at him, then turned to her mother. "When can I go out to my daddy's again?"

"We'll discuss it later, Cass," Becca said. "But you can go out to the ranch soon, all right?"

"Okay." Grinning again, she turned and headed back up the stairs. "Good night, Mom. Good night, Daddy."

He watched as Cassie disappeared up the stairs and around a corner, then turned to face Becca. "She seemed to accept it so easily."

"Children are very adaptable." She made an effort to smile. "And you heard what she said. Apparently she's been pretending that you were her father for a while. This all probably seemed very logical and right to her."

"Jesus." He ran his hand through his hair, his emotions still raw and too close to the surface. "I'm no good at this, Becca. This just proves what I've been saying all along. I had no idea what to say to her."

"What you said was just fine." A flicker of anger appeared on her face. "I told you before, Grady, that being a parent was a learn-on-the-job proposition. No one expects you to be perfect. No one expects you to know what to do in every situation. I don't know what to do in every situation, and I've been with her for eight years. All you can do is try. But you're not even willing to do that."

"What if I hurt her?" He knew his voice was desperate,

but he couldn't let go of that fear. What if he did to Cassie what his father did to him? He would never be able to forgive himself.

"You are going to hurt her, and so am I. Neither of us is perfect and we'll both make plenty of mistakes. Thinking that you can avoid those mistakes by not making a commitment to her and to me is just another mistake you're making."

Suddenly her face was unbearably weary. "We've had this conversation before, Grady, and it's obvious that you haven't changed your mind. We'll talk about Cassie later in the week, when we're both less tired and less emotional." She walked to the door, and when she opened it he saw her hand tremble. "Good night, Grady."

He hesitated for a long moment. He didn't want to leave, didn't want to throw away all that she was offering. But the specter of failure, of inflicting pain on these two people he loved, hovered above him. It sealed his mouth, pinned his arms to his side, and the moment when he could have gone to Becca, taken her into his arms, passed. He saw the moment that it was too late, the moment the acceptance and resignation seeped into her eyes.

Without looking at her again, he strode out the door. He heard it close behind him, heard the lock click into place with a very final sound. As he sat in his truck, he watched her extinguish the lights on the lower floor, one by one, until finally only one light glowed yellow from an upstairs window. He should drive away, he told himself. There was nothing here for him now. He'd made his choice, and he'd have to live with it.

But instead of driving away, he dropped his head into his hands. He'd thrown away his last chance for happiness, and he didn't know what to do next.

The next day Becca was numb. She dropped Cassie off at Laura's and went to work, but she was just going through the motions. Maybe letting Pat take over the calls at the Flying

W wasn't enough. Maybe she would have to leave town. How could she bear to be this close to Grady and not be a part of his life? But how could she leave now? Cassie deserved a chance to get to know her father, and Grady deserved time with his daughter.

The thoughts chased themselves through her mind as she smiled at her clients and tried to force herself to concentrate on their animals' health. By the time noon arrived, she was exhausted, physically and emotionally.

She'd just thrown herself into the chair in her office and was staring at the pile of records she needed to update when Stella stuck her head through the office door. "Sorry, Doc, but you've got one more client who'd like to see you."

Becca gave a silent groan as she stood up and headed for the closed door of the exam room. "Where's the record?" she asked when she didn't see the folder stuck in the basket on the door.

"He said you wouldn't need a record," Stella replied, then disappeared before Becca could ask her anything else.

Becca drew a deep breath and opened the door. She stopped in her tracks when she saw Ron Perkins standing in the room, holding his hat in his hand.

"'Morning, Doc," he said. She could almost swear he sounded nervous.

"Good morning, Ron," she said cautiously. "Is there a problem at the Flying W? Dr. O'Connor is taking care of you now."

"There's nothing wrong at the ranch. This is personal."

She braced herself as she closed the door behind her. "What can I do for you?"

"I came here to apologize to you. Grady and I had a talk a couple of nights ago. He asked me what happened nine years ago when you came looking for him, and I told him the truth." He hesitated, then looked away. "I told him I was afraid you'd get me fired when he found out about what I'd done. As soon as I saw you at the ranch, saw you were a vet and all and realized that Grady knew you, I knew I'd made a mistake. A big one.''

"What did Grady say?'' she managed to ask.

"He was royally pissed off. I don't think I've ever seen him that mad. But he said that he knew I was only trying to do what was right for him. There are a lot of women out there who'd do just about anything to get a rodeo star. Kind of like the groupies who follow the rock stars, I guess. Anyway, when you came looking for him, you were about the fourth woman that month who'd claimed to know him. I figured you were trying to pass off someone else's brat as his. I didn't think any more about it until I saw you here at the ranch. That's when I knew I'd made a mistake.''

"Thank you for telling him the truth,'' she said wearily, "but it doesn't matter anymore. It only matters if you're the one who's been stalking me.''

"No, ma'am, I have not.'' Ron shook his head vigorously. "I wouldn't do that.''

"That's what Grady said.'' She looked at the man standing in front of her, wondering if he was telling her the truth or was only covering his backside. "What did Grady do after you told him the truth?''

"He didn't fire me,'' Ron answered. "I can't repeat what he said in mixed company, but he finally told me that one mistake wasn't going to change all the good things I've done at the ranch.'' The man actually blushed. "I feel real bad, Doc, and I'm going to make it up to you somehow.''

"Thank you, Ron.'' As far as she could tell, the man was sincere. "I'm glad it's cleared up, and I'm glad Grady didn't fire you. I know you've been a good friend to him, and he's going to need you to stay and help him with the ranch. And thank you for trying to make it up to me. I think it's too late for Grady and me, but I appreciate the thought.''

"Don't you go thinking that, Doc. I have an idea, so you just be a little patient.'' He stuck his hat back on his head, looking more cheerful than when he'd come in. "And I hope that you start coming out to the ranch again. No offense to Doc O'Connor, but he doesn't have the same touch with the horses as you do.''

At that she managed a genuine smile. ''Thanks for the vote of confidence. Maybe after a while I can start coming out to the ranch again.''

That wouldn't happen for a long, long time. She'd have to get over Grady first.

He nodded once. ''I'll be seeing you around, Doc. I've got some planning to do.''

Ron disappeared out the front door of the clinic, and Stella popped her head around the corner of the exam room. ''What did that nice man from the Flying W want?'' she asked.

Becca shook her head. ''It was a personal thing, Stella. He and I haven't been getting along, and he wanted to straighten it out.''

''Well, wasn't that sweet of him?'' Stella beamed at her, then retreated. Becca wandered into her office, sat down at her desk and stared at the pile of records in front of her. The last thing she wanted to do right now was think about her job. But it was the only thing that would save her from thinking about Grady. So she picked up the first file in the stack and began reading it.

Three days later Becca hadn't heard a word from Grady or Ron. Pat had been out to the Flying W to check on the cattle she'd sutured, and although she hated herself for asking, she hadn't been able to resist questioning him about whether he'd seen Grady. He hadn't seen either Grady or Ron, although he gave her a strange look for asking. Telling herself that what Grady did wasn't her concern, she tried not to think about him at all. She didn't succeed.

It was close to dark by the time she finished at the office, but she hardly noticed. Cassie was staying overnight at one of her friend's houses, so Becca wasn't in a hurry to go home to an empty house. Sleepovers had lately become very pop-

ular among the eight-year-old set, and Cassie had been excited about her big plans. Finally, when she couldn't ignore
her growling stomach any longer, Becca pushed away from
her desk and headed home.

"I should have left some lights on," she muttered to herself as she pulled into the garage. The house stood dark in
front of her, and as she closed the garage door and headed
for the back porch, she felt a momentary twinge of fear.

But who could have known she would work so late tonight,
she thought? Feeling foolish, she fitted the key into the lock
of the porch door and pushed it open.

She was almost in the door when someone shoved her from
the back and she went flying into the kitchen, stumbling
against the table. The door slammed shut behind her, and she
whirled around.

Sy Ames stood in front of her. His face was twisted with
rage as he stared at her. "You wouldn't listen to me, would
you?" he growled.

"Listen to you about what?" She dared a glance around
the kitchen, but she'd been too careful to clean up their breakfast before they left that morning. There was nothing on the
counters or the table that could be used for a weapon.

"I told you to stay away from Farrell."

Her gaze snapped back to Sy. "I haven't been near him
for several days."

"That's not what I've heard. You were living out there
with him."

"Only because someone had broken into my house. That
was you, wasn't it, Sy?"

"You weren't supposed to go out to the ranch with him.
You were supposed to be there with me." Fury blazed from
his eyes.

"You don't own the ranch anymore, Sy. How could I be
there with you?" She began edging toward the drawer that
held the knives.

"That's Farrell's fault. He cheated me, you know. He

cheated in that poker game, but I had no choice but to let him win. All the others there were on his side."

"He paid you for the ranch, didn't he?"

It was the wrong thing to say. Sy's face grew livid. "He stole it from me. Gave me less than half of what it's worth. But he's had to put out more money since he took it from me. He's had to pay plenty for vet bills, hasn't he?" he sneered.

"That was you who gave Beau colic and drove the cattle into the fence?" she whispered, horrified.

"Yes, and I'll do a lot more before I'm finished. Because taking my ranch wasn't enough for Farrell. He had to have you, too. He stole you right from under my nose, goddamn him."

Becca's stomach began to roll. "You never had me, Sy. We were never involved."

"I was giving you time to get to know me. And then you took up with Farrell the minute he hit town."

"That's all over," Becca said desperately as she watched Sy work himself up into a frenzy. "Grady and I aren't seeing each other anymore. And I'm not even going out to the Flying W now. One of my partners is handling the ranch. So I won't see Grady at all."

Sy stared at her for a moment, then said flatly, "You're lying. I can see it in your eyes. You're still in love with that lying cheater Farrell." He pulled a gun out of his pocket. "Get away from that counter."

Becca pulled her hands away from the drawer and held them in front of her. Why hadn't she listened to Grady's fears about Sy, instead of dismissing him as harmless? And why hadn't she been more careful about coming home at night to a deserted house?

"What do you want, Sy?" she asked. "I've already told you that I'm not having anything to do with Grady. I'm not going out to the ranch anymore. What more can I do?"

"You're going to come with me. We'll have a good life together," he said, and there was a mad gleam in his eyes.

She refused to remind him that she had a child, that she couldn't go away with him. She didn't want him to remember Cassie. "I can't leave my job," she said, thinking quickly. Sy was obsessed with money. "How will I earn my living? And I can't leave my practice behind without getting my money out of it. What would we live on?"

"I got money from Farrell for my ranch. I still have most of it. You won't have to worry about money."

"But I can't just leave my clients without any explanations. And I can't leave my partners in the lurch. Give me a few days to get my business in order."

Sy's face turned an ugly shade of red. "Do you think I'm stupid? If I let you have a few days, you'll never go with me. It has to be now." He waved the gun at her, and she backed up a few more steps. "Let's go."

"Can't we talk about this first?" she asked, moving into the living room. In a quick scan of the room, she saw nothing she could use as a weapon.

"I've done all the talking I'm going to do. You didn't listen to me when you had the chance, when I still had the Flying W and you were coming out there every week, but you're going to listen me now."

Becca's legs banged up against an end table, stopping her progress into the room. She heard the lamp on the table wobbling as she stood staring at Sy. He moved closer, pointing the gun at her chest. "Let's go, Rebecca. We'll have plenty of time to talk after we get where we're going."

Reaching behind her blindly, she grabbed the lamp and threw it at Sy. It hit him on the side of the head, and he staggered backward, thrown off balance.

It was the only chance she would have. Lunging for him, she knocked the gun out of his hand. Then she picked up the lamp and hit him again, harder this time. He crumpled into a heap on the floor.

Sy lay motionless on the floor, but she was afraid to approach him, afraid he was trying to fool her. When he groaned and one hand twitched, she realized he was knocked out, but that he wouldn't be unconscious for long. Looking around frantically for something to tie him with, she finally pulled her belt out of her slacks and wrapped it around his hands.

That wasn't going to be enough. Running into the kitchen, she grabbed a dish towel and a roll of plastic wrap. She knotted the towel around his ankles, then wound the plastic wrap around his arms up to his shoulders before she tied it.

Keeping an eye on Sy, who was now moving his head, she ran to the telephone and managed to punch out the numbers for the sheriff's office. As she told the dispatcher what had happened, she heard the woman calling into her radio to Devlin, telling him to "get over to Doc Johnson's house, on the double." When she put down the phone, she saw that Sy was struggling against his bonds, and she hurried over to pick up the lamp.

"You'd better lie there quietly, or I'll hit you with this again." She saw the gun a few feet from Sy and kicked it under the couch. Then she lifted the lamp above his head, and his expletive-laced tirade stopped abruptly.

It felt like she stood there for hours, watching Sy's hate-filled eyes staring at her, but she knew it was really only minutes before Devlin was pounding on the door.

"Go to the back door," she yelled. "It's open."

Moments later Devlin and Ben Jackson burst into the kitchen, then hurried into the living room, guns drawn. They looked down at Sy on the floor, his arms completely covered with plastic wrap, and Devlin's lips began to twitch.

"That's a real original use of plastic wrap, Doc," he said. "Were you afraid he was going to spoil on you?"

"It worked, didn't it?" she retorted.

The smile disappeared from his face. "Yeah, it did. And thank God for that."

He pulled out a pair of handcuffs and snapped them on

Chapter 17

Her legs were suddenly shaking too badly to keep her standing, and Becca sank down onto the couch. "He was waiting for me when I got home from work," she said, her voice trembling. "As soon as I opened the back door, he pushed his way into the house."

"Where's Cassie?" Devlin asked.

"She's at a friend's house, thank God."

Devlin looked at her, then set his notebook down. "I'm going to make you some coffee," he said. "You look like you need something hot."

"Tea," she said, and struggled to get off the couch. "I'll get it."

"You sit still," the sheriff ordered. She heard him rummaging in her cabinets, and a moment later he turned on the water in the kitchen. Minutes later he handed her a steaming cup of tea, then picked up his notebook again.

It seemed like hours later when he shut his notebook and stood up. "You shouldn't be alone tonight, Doc," he said quietly.

"I'll be fine." Her lips felt stiff and cold. "Since I won't have to worry about my stalker, I'll sleep like a baby."

She felt his gray eyes studying her. "I doubt it," he finally said. "Can I call Grady?"

"No, please don't," she said too quickly, and closed her eyes.

Devlin's silence hung in the air between them for too long. Finally he said, "That's up to you. But I'd rather you had someone here with you. I'd stick around myself, but Cameron appears to be having a crime wave. Damien Kane needs my help."

"I'll call a friend if I decide I don't want to be alone," she answered, opening her eyes to see the worry on his face. She gave him a strained smile. "Thank you for worrying, Sheriff, but I'm fine now. I'm just tired. And it sounds like you have your hands full."

He gave her a doubtful look, but nodded. "I'll talk to you in the morning, then." He hesitated, as if he was going to say something else, then headed for the door. "I'll be on duty all night. Call me if you need me for anything."

"Thank you, Devlin." She gave him a genuine smile. "That's very thoughtful of you."

He nodded again and slipped out the door. Becca listened to the sound of his car fade into the distance, until finally she was alone in the silence. She sat on the couch for a while, still feeling numb, and stared at the lamp tumbled onto the floor. Slowly, aching with a deep chill, she stood up and replaced the lamp on the end table. After checking to make sure the doors were locked, she wandered from the living room into the kitchen. She was amazed that her house didn't look completely different after what had happened here tonight. But nothing had changed; nothing looked out of place.

Knowing she wouldn't be able to sleep, she curled up on the couch in the living room and turned on the television. A late-night show was playing, and the host and his guest were laughing together over an unknown joke. Staring at the screen, she tried to concentrate on the show, but her mind kept replaying the moments of terror with Sy in her house.

She almost didn't hear the knocking on the door. It was soft and tentative, as if her visitor was unsure of his welcome. Devlin must have forgotten to ask her something, she thought wearily. Turning off the television, she went to the door and looked out the window.

Grady stood on the porch, staring at her. Trying to ignore the way her pulse bounded at the sight of him, she pulled the door open.

"What are you doing here, Grady? Did Devlin call you?"

"Why would the sheriff have called me?" he asked, then his mouth hardened and his face tensed. "Did something happen tonight?"

Nodding, she stood aside for him to enter. "Come in. I thought that was why you were here."

He slammed the door behind himself and grabbed her upper arms. "What happened, Becca? Are you all right? Is Cassie?"

"Cassie isn't even here. She's staying the night at a friend's house. And I'm fine." She took a deep, shuddering breath, more glad than she wanted to admit that he was here. She didn't feel so alone, or so weary, anymore. "Come on in and I'll tell you what happened."

Neither of them sat down. She stood and watched Grady pace. "You were right. Sy was the stalker. He was waiting for me when I got home tonight, and he forced his way into the house. He had a gun, and he wanted me to go away with him."

Grady paled beneath his tan. "My God, what did you do?"

For the first time she was able to smile about what had happened. With Grady here she could feel good about what she'd done. "I hit him over the head with a lamp, then tied him up and called the sheriff. He's safely behind bars."

Without a word Grady folded her into his arms and held her tight. Closing her eyes, she drank in the scent of him, the feel of his arms around her and the sound of his heart beating against her cheek. She wanted to burrow in forever, to never let go of him.

"It's a good thing the sheriff has Sy in jail," Grady said quietly. "Because if he didn't, I'd hunt the bastard down and kill him with my bare hands." His hands shifted, then he held her away from him so she could see his face. "Why didn't you call me, Becca?"

"The sheriff wanted me to," she said, and held his gaze. "I couldn't bear the thought."

Bitterness filled his eyes. "You were held at gunpoint by a madman, but you couldn't force yourself to ask me for help?"

She ached for his pain, but she held her ground. "Every time I see you, my heart breaks all over again. I'm sorry, Grady, but that's the way it is."

He studied her for a moment, then dropped into a chair. "You didn't ask me what I was doing here tonight."

"I assumed that Devlin called you."

"And I told you he didn't."

"All right, then, what *are* you doing here?" she asked, refusing to let herself hope.

"You haven't been out to the ranch lately." His eyes were unreadable.

"Pat O'Connor has been seeing your animals. You know that."

"I thought maybe you'd changed your mind, especially after Ron talked to you."

"Did you put Ron up to that?" she demanded.

"I had no idea he planned to talk to you. But I'm glad he did."

"So am I," she said. "I'm glad we've cleared the air, but Ron was never the reason I stopped coming out to the ranch."

He studied her for a long time. Finally he said, "I know. I think I finally understand why you walked away and didn't look back."

Her heart started pounding, the sudden sound echoing in her ears and making her chest hurt. "What do you mean?"

"You walked away for the same reasons that I walked away from home all those years ago. And I did exactly what my father did, which was to let you go."

"How did you figure that out?" she whispered.

"Ron has been a busy guy. After he talked to you, he asked me for a couple of days off. You were right—he had a lot of gambling debts, so I figured that he was off taking care of business. He came back to the ranch yesterday, but he didn't come alone."

"Who was with him?" She held her breath, waiting for his answer.

"My father."

"What?" she gasped. She knew that Grady hadn't seen his father in at least nine years.

"Ron didn't know how to make things up to me, or how to make things right between us, but he figured that mending fences with my father was the first step."

"And did you?" She held her breath again.

"We have a lot of history, Becca, and there's a lot of pain between us. It's not going to be glossed over that easily. But we made a start. And I saw a couple of things real clearly."

"What was that?" She was afraid to move, afraid that what Grady was saying would disappear in a puff of smoke.

"The first one was that although I told myself I'm nothing like my father, I've been fooling myself. I'm so much like him that it's scary. He's a bitter, dried-up old man who has no one, and I won't let myself have anyone. He's pushed everyone away who wanted to be close to him, starting with my mother and continuing with me, and now I'm doing the same thing to you and Cassie."

"You're not bitter and dried up," she said, wanting to go to him but knowing that she couldn't. Not yet. "You're a very loving man."

"Give me a few years," he said. "I'll be just like him.

When I was a kid, all I saw was that he wasn't there for me, wasn't willing to hold out his hand to me to bridge the gap that was developing. I was too angry with him to even try to talk to him, to understand what he was doing, let alone to see his point of view.'' He gave her a bitter smile. ''What kid is willing to listen to his father?''

''You can be so much more than that,'' she said, willing him to believe her.

''That's the second thing I learned from him. That I have to be willing to take chances, to reach out for what I want. Because if I don't, I'm going to lose it all just as surely as he did. He wasn't willing to take that chance, and how did he end up? He's alone and lonely. That's what I claimed I wanted, but it isn't, not really. I told myself that I was afraid that I was going to hurt you, and Cassie, and I was. But deep down I was scared that you would leave. So I figured that I would just do it for you first. I couldn't get past my fear to admit what I really did want. I was afraid that if I asked for it, it would all disappear like smoke in the wind.''

''And what do you want, Grady?'' she whispered, her heart swelling.

''I want you, Becca. And I want Cassie. I want us to be a family, in every sense of the word. I want you to marry me. I'm slow to catch on and I know I'm nine years too late, but I love you, Becca. Teach me how to love you the way you love me. Help me be a good father to Cassie, and, if you're willing, to the brothers and sisters that Cassie might have.''

''I love you, too, Grady. I always have, and I know I always will.'' She stepped into his embrace, and he folded his arms around her. ''You're all I've ever wanted,'' she said.

''You could have fooled me,'' he said as he nuzzled her hair. ''The way you've been avoiding me this week, I figured you'd suddenly gotten smart and wised up about me.''

''I wised up about myself,'' she said, leaning back to trace the cleft in his cheek. ''I wanted you too badly, and I didn't want to beg. I didn't want to put you in that position. So I stayed away.''

"What did I ever do to deserve you?" he said, his voice humble.

"Where do you want me to start?" She smiled at him, her heart soaring, and traced his mouth with her finger. As she watched, his eyes blazed bright blue.

"How about right here?" He lowered his mouth to hers, and she melted into his kiss. It was a declaration of possession and a passionate vow. Desire leaped to life inside her, and she felt an answering tension in Grady. His hands shook as he cupped her face and tasted her mouth. When she opened her eyes and looked at him, he was staring at her, his eyes steady on hers.

"I'm not perfect, Becca," he warned. "I'm used to doing things my way, and I'm going to make mistakes."

"I'll make mistakes, too," she said, reaching up to kiss him. "We'll learn together."

He lowered his mouth to hers again, and suddenly both of them were frantic with need. Sliding his hands under her blouse, he unsnapped her bra and cupped her breasts in both hands. Catching her breath at his touch, she shuddered when he flicked his thumbs over her nipples. As she grew hot and began to throb with desire, she unsnapped his shirt and ran her hands over the hard planes of his chest. His hair curled beneath her fingers, and she leaned down to taste his hard male nipples.

Grady sucked in his breath, and the next moment he leaned back, his eyes hot and wild with passion. "Where's your bedroom?" he muttered.

"This way." She took his hand and led him up the stairs and into her room. He wrapped her in his arms and laid her down on the bed, and the next moment they were locked in each other's arms.

"I want to lie with you, like this, every night of my life," he murmured, his words punctuated by kisses. "I want to wake up with you every morning, to fall asleep with you in my arms every night.''

"Yes," she whispered, blazing with need for him. "I want to make love with you every night, to feel you beside me when I wake up during the night."

"I need you, Becca." He peeled away her clothes, and his, and she felt the desperation that fueled him. She felt it, too, the need to claim him, to make him her own.

"I want you, Grady. Now," she said, her nails scoring his back. His grip on her was almost painfully tight, but she reveled in it. As they came together, she wrapped her legs around him, pulling him deeper inside her, until she wasn't sure where she ended and he began.

She soared over the peak almost immediately, and he followed her. As he poured himself into her, he murmured her name, over and over. Becca held him tightly with her arms and her legs, loving the feel of his weight on top of her, wishing she never had to move again.

After a long time Grady shifted, pulling her against him, cradling her head against his chest. "Is Cassie really going to be gone all night?"

"I don't pick her up until tomorrow morning."

He nuzzled her hair. "So we can spend the night together?"

"Just you try to leave."

"I want to get married quickly," he said, stroking his hand down her side. "We can't send Cassie to a sleepover every night."

She felt tears gather in her eyes. "As quickly as we can manage it," she agreed.

She felt him tense and gather himself, and she leaned away to look at his face. "What's wrong?"

"How do you think Cassie is going to feel about us getting married?" he asked.

"You're kidding, right?" But she could see that he was serious. "She's going to be thrilled. You heard what she said the other night. How could you imagine that she wouldn't be happy about us getting married?''

"She'll be moving out of town, away from her friends. And on top of that, she's used to having you to herself. Now she's going to have to share you."

"But now she'll have a father, as well as a mother. I think she'll consider it a fair trade."

"Maybe I can sweeten the pot a little."

She propped herself on her elbows. "You mean you're going to bribe her?"

"I didn't say that." He tried to look wounded. "I'm going to use the incentive system to make her move a little easier."

"What are you planning, Grady?" she asked, loving the light in his eye. It had been a long time since she'd seen him so relaxed, so happy.

"I'm going to give her Pete."

"Oh, Grady, you don't have to do that. I'm sure Pete is a valuable horse." She felt her eyes fill with moisture again.

"Can you think of a better reason to give him to my daughter? In a few years he's going to be one hell of a barrel-racing horse. And I think Cassie's going to be one hell of a barrel racer. So they can learn together."

"And I can't think of a better person than my rodeo man to teach them." Her heart overflowed as she smiled at him.

"I thought my life was over when I couldn't perform in the rodeo any longer." He reached down and kissed her deeply. "But now I see that it had to happen before I could get on with the rest of my life."

"You're not going to miss the rodeo?"

"I'll always miss it. It was a part of my life for a long time, a part I loved. But the way I felt about the rodeo is a pale substitute for how I feel about you and Cassie. You make my life complete, Becca. If I had to give up the rodeo in order to find you again, it's a sacrifice I'd gladly make. The rodeo was all glory and accomplishment, but its charms were

only surface ones. What I feel for you is a part of my soul.
I love you, Becca.''

"And I love you, my rodeo man.''

* * * * *

Watch for Abby and Damien's story,
FOR THE CHILDREN, coming from
Silhouette Intimate Moments
in October.

MATERNITY LEAVE

Coming September 1998

Three delightful stories about the blessings
and surprises of "Labor" Day.

TABLOID BABY by Candace Camp

She was whisked to the hospital in the nick of time....

THE NINE-MONTH KNIGHT
by Cait London

A down-on-her-luck secretary is experiencing
odd little midnight cravings....

THE PATERNITY TEST by Sherryl Woods

The stick turned blue before her
biological clock struck twelve....

*These three special women are very pregnant...and very
single, although they won't be either for too much longer,
because baby—and Daddy—are on their way!*

Available at your favorite retail outlet.

INTIMATE MOMENTS®
™ Silhouette®

invites you to go West to

Cameron, Utah

Margaret Watson's exhilarating new miniseries.

RODEO MAN...IM #873, August 1998: When ex-rodeo star Grady Farrell set eyes on his childhood sweetheart again, he vowed to put the past behind them. And then he met her—*his*—daughter...and decided to dust off those cowboy boots and stay forever.

FOR THE CHILDREN...IM #886, October 1998: Embittered agent Damien Kane was responsible for protecting beautiful Abby Markham and her twin nieces. But it was Abby who saved him, as she showed him the redeeming power of home and family.

And look for more titles in 1999—
only in Silhouette Intimate Moments!

Available at your favorite retail outlet.

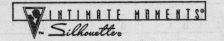

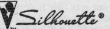

COMING NEXT MONTH

#877 LONE WOLF'S LADY—Beverly Barton
Way Out West

The last person dark and dangerous Luke McClendon ever wanted to see again was his former lover Deanna Atchley. With just a few careless words she had stolen five precious years of his life—and now she was at his doorstep, looking for salvation. Was this Luke's golden opportunity to seek revenge...or rediscover love?

#878 IF A MAN ANSWERS—Merline Lovelace

Molly Duncan was being hunted for what she'd heard! The love-shy lady had *intended* to call her supremely obnoxious, superbly masculine neighbor Sam Henderson to insist he quiet down, but instead of Sam's deep, sexy "hello," she heard gunshots. Could this spirited woman who'd accidentally dialed *M* for murder, redial *L* for love?

#879 A STRANGER IS WATCHING—Linda Randall Wisdom

Years ago, Jenna Wells had gotten too close to federal marshal Riley Cooper, and it had cost her everything—true love, career, even her identity. Now a dangerous stranger had pieced together her past... and was determined to destroy her future. Impenetrable Riley was once again her protector, but who was keeping watch over this loner's heart?

#880 GIRLS' NIGHT OUT—Elizabeth August
Men in Blue

Detective Adam Riley's investigation uncovered the rocky terrain of Susan Hallston's secret past. In fact, proving her innocence to this cynical cop would be about as effortless as climbing Mount Everest. But unearthing the truth could cause a monumental landslide of emotion...in granite-hearted Adam!

#881 MARY'S CHILD—Terese Ramin
Whose Child?

Gorgeous Hallie Thompson had agreed to be a surrogate mother for her best friend, Joe Martinez, and his wife. But that was before Joe's wife was killed, and before Hallie discovered that she was pregnant...with Joe's child. Now Hallie wanted to adopt the beautiful baby girl —but was she willing to take on a husband, as well?

#882 UNDERCOVER LOVER—Kylie Brant

John Sullivan was the one man Ellie Bennett trusted. He was her dearest friend—and now he was her lover. But what she *didn't* know about him was immense. Like his troubled past, his top-secret profession...and whether he could love her forever....